The

Stolen

Gods

The

Stolen

Gods

Jake Page

UNIVERSITY OF NEW MEXICO PRESS / ALBUQUERQUE

© 1993 by Jake Page
University of New Mexico Press paperback edition 2002
Published by arrangement with the author.
All rights reserved.
Originally published 1993 by Ballantine Books, ISBN 0-345-37928-4

LIBRARY OF CONGRESS CATALOGING-IN-PUBLICATION DATA:

Page, Jake
    The stolen gods / Jake Page—1st University of New Mexico Press pbk. ed.
        p.   cm.
    ISBN 0-8263-2860-1 (pbk. : alk. paper)
    1. Hopi Indians—Antiquities—Fiction. 2. Archaeological thefts—Fiction.
    3. New Mexico—Fiction. 4. Sculptors—Fiction. 5. Blind—Fiction. I. Title.

    PS3566.A333 S76 2002
    813'.54—dc21

                                                        2001052517

Thanks, Lew
and Renee
and especially Susanne

Author's Note

Among the Pueblo Indian tribes of the American Southwest, and perhaps most notably among the Hopi Indians of north-eastern Arizona, there are spirit beings who arrive in the village plazas in season and, in the course of a day or sometimes two days, create what one art historian has called the "most profound works of art in North America." These are the *kachinas*, beaked figures adorned with paint, evergreens, bells, and turtle shells, and through the day they sing in low, aeolian voices, and dance to the hypnotic rhythms of a drum and the wind gusts, siring small clouds of dust while, overhead, the larger white clouds set out across the landscape.

Not only do the Hopi provide the kachinas with a good place to perform, they feed these visitors with cornmeal, the food appropriate for spirits. And in turn the kachinas are enjoined to go forth to that lordly place where the rain spirits are commanded to bring moisture to the fields the Hopi have so loyally planted. This is not a supplication: it is a matter of reciprocity, and it has sustained both humans and spirits since times too ancient to know.

There is more, of course, to the Hopi view of the universe—

what we call their religion—than weather management, as important as that is to dwellers in such an arid and unforgiving part of the world; and much of it remains, appropriately, secret, known only to those who are inducted into certain priesthoods of which even many Hopi people know little. Or at least they will say little about them.

Each priesthood has its own role within the greater tribal intent of the Hopi, its own ceremonies, prayers, and sacred objects. These rites, never seen by others, are the philosophical core of the Hopi world. And among a small group of non-Hopi who have the hubris to call themselves *art* collectors, these secret and sacred, even immortal, objects command a high price. There is an archaic word for this trade: *simony*. It has always been a sin. In most countries today it is also a crime, and in the nation of which the Hopi are a part, a federal crime.

Over the years, many Hopi people have enriched my life and my family's lives in ways that one does not count. This tale is offered, in one sense, in the spirit of reciprocity to those people and will, I trust, be taken as such. They call it *paying back*.

It goes without saying that the events and characters in this work of fiction are utterly imaginary (with one exception whose permission I have to move from Flagstaff to Santa Fe in the thinnest of disguises). Any resemblance the rest of the characters herein may bear to real people, living or dead, is more than coincidental—it is miraculous. For example, once this novel was written, I happened to be in attendance at the Navajo Fair in Shiprock, New Mexico, and during the parade that preceded the fair, I saw among the mostly Navajo crowd a large man with an ample paunch, beefy arms, a close-cropped blond beard, and a black cowboy hat that seemed a size or two too small. I couldn't catch up with him—probably just as well—but I hope that he still walks in beauty.

The

Stolen

Gods

O n e

A lone candle guttered in a garish red glass, and its light glowed from Mo Bowdre's dark glasses.

"Now let me explain to you about that," Mo said, turning his big head toward the young woman sitting across from him in the restaurant's gloom. Mo smiled, big healthy teeth sharking through a dense, close-cropped blond beard.

"Of course, I've been asked that before." He emitted a staccato laugh as musical as a snare drum: "Hah—hah—hah—" The reporter lowered her eyes to her narrow notebook. "—hah. You see, it goes back to early man. Yeah, early man, running around, keeping out of the way of the predators, scared half to death of leopards and hyenas and all, scrounging out a living from leftovers, sniffing the air like dogs."

Mo leaned across the table, his forearms lying like pork roasts among the beer glasses and bottles.

He pursed his lips, then grinned and whispered, "Carrion. The sweet smell of flesh. Oh yes, a fine perfume on the breeze. Meat. *Meat!*" Mo's eyebrows, pink in the candlelight, danced above the rims of his opaque glasses. He put his thumb and forefinger together and sniffed loudly. "Just a vanishing trace of hyena scent . . . and the lush odor of blood and marrow."

The journalist felt nauseated.

"Come on, Mo," said the broad-shouldered woman with glistening black hair seated to Mo's right.

"That's how it was, Connie," Bowdre protested, turning to face her.

"How do you know? It was a long time ago."

"Because it makes sense that way, that's how I know," he said, and turned back to the reporter across the table. "You can check it out with the anthropologists down at the university. We had to use all our senses then." He made an outlandish clicking sound in his throat. "Uh-oh," he said, drawing back in mock fear. "What's that? Something's out there. Now what? See, *survival* depended on it, on reading the landscape with all the senses." He leaned back into the shadows.

"Our other senses have atrophied. Is that what you're saying, Mr. Bowdre?"

The massive head bobbed in assent.

"That's what I'm saying."

A white-haired woman appeared beside the table.

"Everything all right here, Mo?" she asked.

"Everything's fine, Emma."

"I just want you all to be happy," said Emma, and slipped away.

"She really does want everyone to be happy," Mo said. "Now let me explain. You take painting. Flat as a board. All of it—depth perception, perspective, kinetics—all that is an illusion. Your brain does it all for you, but that's just how we see the world itself—as flat, two dimensional. Our brains make up the third dimension—depth, volume. But the world *is* three-dimensional. And so is sculpture. It's real, it's in the round. With sculpture you got to be involved with more than your eyes. You got to feel it, maybe even hear your voice bounce off it—if you hear good enough. See what I mean? Are you married?"

The reporter smiled and nodded. "Yes, I am."

"Well, how do you suppose you could best make a clay model of your husband's—"

Connie's mouth opened with an audible protest, and Mo leaned farther out over his forearms.

"—well, of your husband? You could stand here and draw him, and stand there and draw him, and squint and squint and add up all the two-dimensional views and see if you got it right. But if you touch him, if you feel him, even smell him and—"

"Mo," interrupted his companion. "Mo, for—"

"Now, Connie, all I'm saying is the sense of touch is a better guide to the three-dimensional world than any of the other senses, including vision."

The reporter scribbled. "I see what you mean," she said, not looking up.

"These here," Mo went on, holding up his large hands, "these here are the most reliable guide to reality. I can't stand these finicky-assed gallery owners that won't let people touch the goddamn sculpture. That's what it's all about. Form. Texture. You can't *see* texture. You got to feel it, touch it. Well," he continued, now in a mock whine, "if everyone touches it, it'll wear away. Poor, poor gallery owner, watching his investment abraded. Hah—hah—hah. There aren't enough tourists coming here in the next five hundred years to wear away anything important from one of my pieces."

The reporter wrote on and then looked up at him. "I see what you mean," she said. "That's great, just what I need. Also, I've got to get some details on your life—uh, you know, so you were born . . . ?"

"Hah—hah—yes I was. Born a pig in the horse stable. Oh, you mean where, when, all that. Okay . . ."

An hour and a half later, and fifteen minutes after leaving the sculptor and his woman in the gloom of Tiny's on Cerillos Road, Samantha Burgess pulled up in her old Toyota at the curb before a wooden staircase that led up one flight to the balcony of her one-room apartment on the southern outskirts of town. Traffic hissed by about a quarter of a mile beyond. Rush hour on the Old Pecos Trail.

I've never met someone so full of shit, Samantha thought as she stomped up the staircase, keys in hand. Phony redneck, with his macho esthetics and all that crap about early man, for God's sake, I thought I was going to throw up. And that stone-faced half-breed duenna—Connie, Connie Barnes—"Oh, Mo, oh no, Mo"—doesn't she know any vowels but *O?*" Samantha let herself in. So why did I lie? She looked around at her home with dismay.

Samantha Burgess tossed her pocketbook onto the sofa bed, still unmade, and wondered why she was so angry. On the wall above the bed, a kachina loomed out of a desert landscape, bright reds, purples, and gold, a framed poster commemorating an opening a few years back of an exhibition by the Hopi artist Dan Namingha. Posters. All she could afford. Over the desk where her computer sat was a T. C. Cannon poster showing the artist's pregnant grandmother in a gold-flecked dress, striding pridefully along the desert holding an open umbrella over her head. Samantha thought yet again that she would never possess a real T. C. Cannon, a real Namingha, a real Bowdre. Or a real husband, probably. It was unfair. She looked in the mirror that hung near the Cannon. Plain face, mousy hair.

T. Moore Bowdre, she thought. An immense man, maybe six-four, with a big redneck belly. Hands like a what? Like steel-mill cauldrons, she thought. God, I'd love to have a

T. Moore Bowdre. Just a little one. She recalled in her mind's eye the towering, agonized coil of bronze torsos and limbs she had seen the day before at the foundry near Cerillos, some thirty miles out in the desert, a soaring tangle of equine life gleaming orange in the dying sun of the late afternoon. She had asked what it was called.

"I make these," Bowdre had said, sweating profusely in the sun. "I don't name 'em. Old Frazier down at the gallery, he names 'em. People need labels, I guess, before they can see anything. Dingbats." And Bowdre said no more, just climbed into the pickup, part Chevy and part junkyard, and sat there facing straight ahead until Connie, the broad-shouldered woman, part Hopi and part Anglo, started up the engine.

T. Moore Bowdre, the fabled blind sculptor. Earlier in the day she had asked him what the T stood for.

"Maternal pretension," he had replied. "Hah—hah—hah."

Connie Barnes's head rested on a pool of inky black hair which luxuriously covered the pillow. A light down comforter was drawn primly up to her collarbones—ingrained Hopi modesty—and she smiled, white teeth gleaming from her round, copper face, as she watched the big man shuck his jeans. He was seated on the bed, his back to her. In the hall, a clock rang eleven.

Connie laughed. "Such a big tail end you've got there. It's getting bigger."

"You got a big nail, you need a big hammer," he replied. "Besides, my rear end ain't so big. It's just that all you Indian women are flat-assed."

"What do you mean, *all* us Indian women? What would you know about it?"

Bowdre sat naked on the edge of the bed. "Do you suppose that reporter—what'sername, Burgess—you suppose that she's gonna get it straight?"

"I thought I was going to die," Connie laughed. "When you

gave her the spiel about early man and blood and marrow . . .
she turned green."

"That's no spiel, Connie. That's the latest archeological insight, playing right into my hands. You can check it out."

"Still, you freaked her out. I told you she was a vegetarian."

"Well damn, I forgot all about that. You mean one of those
people with transparent skin? Hah—hah. Goat cheese and
bark? Now I'm in trouble. Well, what difference does it make
what she says? Nobody reads that dumb little hotel handout of
a magazine except Texans, and they have trouble with English
anyway."

"Turn out the light, Mo. Get in bed."

"Yeah, okay, I'll get it." Bowdre stood up and crossed the
room. He flipped the switch and the room went dark. "Ah,"
he said. "The sweet smell of fresh bone marrow."

Samantha Burgess stared blankly at the screen. Nowhere in the
computer's innards was the lead sentence she sought. It was
eleven o'clock and she had implanted in the machine a few
disjointed paragraphs about Bowdre, but there was no sense,
no organizing principle, no lead. The man didn't make sense.
She pawed through her notebook again, irritation turning to
panic. The piece was due tomorrow. This was a bullshit assignment, peanuts, but it was a start. Like college again, she
thought. Okay, take it from the top. She flipped the pages.

T. Moore Bowdre. Born in 1946 in Lincoln County, New
Mexico, home of the Lincoln County wars and Billy the Kid.
Father owned a hardware store in Ruidoso. Grew up like any
bumpkin, hunting, fishing, screwing around with horses, guns,
cars, got a scholarship at the University of New Mexico. Grad-
uated sixth in his class, biology major, off to med school in
Austin, Texas, dropped out after a year and a half. Her notes
read: *Said I wouldn't make surgeon, told them to stick it.*

Jesus, Samantha suddenly thought. Bowdre. Wasn't that the
name of a guy in Billy the Kid's gang? Why didn't I think of

that? Descended from a bandit, still ripping people off? No, no, can't say . . . I'll call him tomorrow. No, I won't call him tomorrow. He's sick of me.

Okay, back to the notes.

Bummed out, bummed around. Wound up working in a molybdenum mine in Colorado, lost his eyesight in a mining accident. *One of those things, just stupid.* I.e., no comment.

That's 1973. In 1984, first show at the White Feather Gallery. What about those eleven years? The notes: *Just moved around, made a little trouble, tried out stuff. Nothing noteworthy. Job back home in Ruidoso, taxidermist's assistant. Better than working for a mortician.*

Then the grating laugh. Damn, Samantha thought. The guy's a windbag, full of phony redneck yarns and that stupid laugh, but he's a ghost, a vanishing act, a facade. Okay, forty-eight monumental bronzes in four years, one a month . . .

Samantha was blinded by the facts. She got up from the chair, stepped over to the unmade sofa bed and picked up her alarm clock. Eleven-ten. She set it for five o'clock and, fully clothed, lay down with a sigh. Tomorrow, she thought. Tomorrow.

Walter Meyers hung up the phone and looked at his watch: 11:05. An early riser by nature, Meyers was normally asleep in bed by this time, his stomach calmed by a measured teaspoon of Pepto-Bismol. He yawned. Late hours were the price of dealing some days with that lunatic in Singapore.

Small price to pay, he thought, and smiled primly to himself.

Outside his office, through the open door, the gallery was black, but the desk lamp dimly lit a feathered mask mounted on a pedestal in the middle of the long room beyond. It was a magnificent Zuni kachina mask, and the FBI had asked him about it, the busybodies. One man in a charcoal-gray suit, white shirt, and maroon tie—a blond—and the other a slob in a windbreaker, those ugly athletic shoes, and a bush of curly black hair, with a horrible New York accent. But Meyers had produced the papers, a file documenting his purchase of old Alvarez's estate when they auctioned it off. Perfectly legal, aboveboard. So off they had gone, Yin and Yang. That—the FBI visit—was after the old men from the Zuni reservation had come, in their purple and blue shirts and red headbands, moaning as always about how the mask was sacred, how it should go *home* to Zuni. In his practiced way, Meyers had told them that it was a Zuni, after all, who had presumably sold it to someone—years ago—who had sold it to Alvarez, a respected man, former lieutenant governor of the state, and all that. And yes, of course they could have it back. All they had to do was pay the price on the label. It had been $35,000 then. Now it was $45,000, sitting there mute in the gloom. Meyers smiled. Inflation, lovely inflation. Chicken feed compared to the deal he was sure was as good as clinched with Singapore. He looked lovingly out at the outline of the Zuni mask, one of the most beautiful he had ever seen in a lifetime of fondling such things. A pity that someone would soon enough come along and buy it. But Walter Meyers was a seller, not a collector. He had kept only a handful of artifacts over the years.

Meyers sighed and turned to face the computer, punching three keys in succession with a long, thin forefinger. The machine made its routine electronic check of the gallery's security system: OKAY. Meyers punched two more keys and the machine checked again: OKAY. The gallery owner stood up, pressed a hand against his irate abdomen, and turned to the door behind his desk, flicking a light switch on the wall. The desk lamp winked out and Meyers opened the door to the anteroom that connected his office to his small apartment. The anteroom was, of course, without light, and before Meyers could react, before he could step backward, he felt rather than saw motion, felt the air move. His brain flashed with a vermilion fire, and even as his nerve cells began to transmit pain, he was dead.

The sudden rag-doll corpse wobbled and sagged to the floor, and the last thing to hit the expensive Mexican tiles was its crushed skull.

T w o

A breeze hissed pleasantly in the evergreen trees outside the brown adobe wall that obscured from public view the spacious courtyard of Martha Elaine Forbush Oliver Benton Wilamette. Once divorced, once widowed, she was now married to the city's most prominent horseman, a self-made millionaire many times over (television stations in California). Martha Wilamette stood arms akimbo and smiling, admiring the twelve-foot-high bronze, an abstract, tormented shape at the base which resolved itself into a grizzly bear, rising halfway to a standing position, alert, alive. It was not her first T. Moore Bowdre, but it was her latest, and her favorite.

Hers was one of the largest private homes in the older part of town, several adobe buildings ranged around a large greensward with several theme gardens, one given over to cacti and desert wildflowers, another to her beloved irises, another devoted to all-white blossoms, some of them night bloomers, all bespeaking the moon. Martha Wilamette was one of the few newcomers to the town who had almost immediately become part of the inner core of its society. She was perfect, a person of the kind of unmistakable class that arises in places like Connecticut over the generations but is at home anywhere.

Martha Wilamette wore a simple light blue cotton dress, the same shade as the irises that rimmed the adobe wall to the south, and for the moment she was lost in the freshness of the air, the morning breeze, the scents, the swaying irises, and the magnificent bear—the beauty of it all.

"I love the sound the breeze makes," she said.

"I don't," said Mo Bowdre. He was standing like a tower, motionless beside her in jeans and a multicolored cotton shirt imported from Guatemala, and a black cowboy hat that looked about one size too small for his big head. "Wrong place."

"The trees?" asked Martha. "I'm talking about the sound of the wind in the trees."

"It's singing," said Bowdre. "I told you not to put it there. You got a prevailing wind from there, and it's always gonna set that bear to singing."

"I don't hear it singing, Mo," the woman said sweetly.

"I do."

"Well, what's the matter with it singing?"

"It's singing off-key, damn it, Martha. It's gotta be moved. Everytime I think of that bear from now on, I'll hear it singing a quarter tone off. It's got to be moved. Larry, that you? You've got to move this here sculpture."

Startled, Martha Wilamette turned to see her husband emerge from the shadowed patio onto the grass. Under his glowing horseman's tan, Larry Wilamette somehow looked blanched.

"What's the matter, Larry?" Martha asked with a hint of impatience.

"Walt Meyers was murdered last night. I just heard it on the radio."

"My God! How? What . . . ?"

"They found him this morning, skull was broken open, clubbed to death. The place was ransacked."

"Ransacked?"

"That's what they said. That's all they said."

"How horrible," said Martha. "How horrible. Poor Walt."

Mo Bowdre, still facing south toward the sculpture, made a sibilant sound, a low whistle. "A whole lot of people didn't admire Walt Meyers," he said. "A whole lot of people."

"I can't believe it," said the woman. "I was in his gallery just yesterday." She hugged herself and shivered at her proximity to an incomprehensible violence. "Fellana and I, we went by after lunch. Fellana found a Ganado Red she liked. They dickered over the price. Walt said he'd come down to eighty-five hundred, no lower, and she said she'd think it over. I guess that's one Navajo rug Fellana won't get. Oh, what am I saying? Walt is dead? Dear God."

"I told him he shouldn't live in that damn gallery," Mo said, evidently to himself, and he whistled tunelessly, his face expressionless behind the dark glasses, facing blindly south.

"What do you mean?" asked Martha. Her husband fidgeted in his horseman's costume.

"Well, let me explain it to you," said Bowdre. "See, Walt offended just about everyone from the Indians to the cops to all sorts of other people. Smug little crooked bastard."

"Mo, that's a terrible thing to say—"

"Martha," Bowdre said, his voice rising in pitch, "just because he's dead doesn't make him a better man. You know perfectly well he was as nasty as a centipede. Anyway, I told him. I told him last spring that what with crime going up in beautiful downtown Santa Fe, he could get killed one day by someone—anyone—who hated his guts, and it would look like a burglary on his gallery. Probably go unsolved like all the other burglaries around here, and no one'd know just who the guy was who rose up out of the legion of Meyers-haters and did it."

"Mo, you're contemptible."

"I told him it would be unfair to leave us all guessing."

"Mo!"

"He didn't think it was all that funny either. Well, I'll be off now. Think about it, Martha."

"How can I help thinking about it. It's just—"

"I mean moving that bear."

The blind man, erect with shoulders pulled back, turned and headed for the courtyard door.

"Never mind, Larry," he said. "I can find my way."

Santa Fe, or Holy Faith, is the oldest capital city in North America. It lies nestled against the southern edge of the Sangre de Cristo mountains (the Blood of Christ) at an altitude of some seven thousand feet, where the air begins to thin significantly and cool breezes generally prevail in the warmer months. At such an altitude, one finds both plants of the desert and those of the evergreen forest in a wondrous diversity. Santa Fe, on the other hand, is a city of almost unparalleled architectural uniformity: city ordinances ban any new structure that is not within the neo-pueblo style called adobe and faced with a rather narrow range of browns. Even the likes of Exxon and Chevron, whose iconography is otherwise sacrosanct, were forced to conform. Indeed, such is the unity of architectural style that a grouchy critic visiting from New York City's polyglot traditions had the chutzpah to call this city of holy faith "an adobe theme park."

But Santa Fe enjoys a considerable cultural as well as botanical diversity: chiefly Hispanic and Anglo, with some live Indians here and there, and much Indian symbolism, though virtually any cultural style can find a niche—and most have. Among the various social tribes that effectively define the city, however, and provide the world at large with what is called Santa Fe style, there are two overriding convictions.

One is that Santa Fe is as close to the original Eden as mankind has come since Adam and Eve were banished.

The second conviction is that, though the city has a population of some fifty thousand residents—and even more when the state legislature is in session, with its attendant lobbyists and toadies—and anywhere up to ten thousand tourists on a given day, it remains a small town, albeit a small town with a sophistication unrivaled anywhere west of the Seine and east of San Francisco Bay. Santa Feans who move in these circles rarely deign to drive the fifty miles south to the bland sprawl of Albuquerque for anything but the most urgent reasons—to use the airport, for example. There is a certain truth to the notion of Santa Fe as a small town. For example, news, as in most villages, often travels most effectively by word-of-mouth— passed from boutique to coffeehouse to gallery.

By ten o' clock the morning after Walter Meyers died in his tracks, even people without much interest in Santa Fe's art scene were abuzz. In a warehouse-like structure in the downtown area that had been remodeled to house two floors of indoor galleries, jewelry stores, and a coffee shop, three young people sat around a table drinking espresso. They were the poorly paid employees of an organization called CAN, Citizens Against Nuclear, which operated from a tiny office of stunning clutter located between two stores that happily competed with each other in the sale of clothes imported from South America.

"It's horrible," said a young woman with close-cropped black hair, a wide mouth with thin lips on a nearly colorless face, and an elaborate necklace of quartz crystals arrayed against a bony chest.

"So was he," said a red-haired man in jeans and a floppy cotton shirt. "Hey, Francis, did you hear?" he asked as a clean-cut man improbably dressed in a blue business suit approached. This was the director of CAN, once a computer salesman, then a hot-tub contractor who had founded CAN on a shoestring, soon discovering that he was a fund-raising demon in the fallow fields of Santa Fe (where concern about almost everything runs deep and earnest). He was now one of the leading antagonists of all nuclear works of any kind, with branches in San Francisco, Cambridge, Massachusetts, and Aspen, Colorado.

"Hear? Hear what?"

"Walt Meyers was murdered," said the young woman, fingering her crystals. "Last night. Clubbed to death. In his own place, you know?"

At that moment an artist walked by with his portfolio under his arm. A lanky man dressed in denim and turquoise that matched his eyes, he stopped a few feet away from the table.

"What?" he asked. "Who?"

"Walt Meyers," the red-haired man explained. "In his gallery, last night."

"A burglary, would be my guess," said the director of CAN sagaciously.

"Jesus H. Christ," intoned the blue-eyed artist. He looked blankly at the people hunched over their espressos. "Mother Earth strikes back." He looked skyward, then down again. "Know what I mean? She gets her vengeance one way or another." He turned and arrowed off toward a gallery that had just opened its doors for the morning.

"That guy is missing a few feedback loops," the director of CAN said. "Well, let's go to work. We've got a war to prosecute here, a world to save."

"He paints nice coyotes," the crystal woman said with a smirk.

Not far from the famed plaza of Santa Fe, Julian Baca eyed the curved hips of his assistant, Maria Sanchez, as she bent over to pull a file from the lower drawer of a gray filing cabinet in the New Mexico Office of Economic Development. Maria was all business. Julian Baca continued to watch his assistant's hips as she stood up and smoothed her skirt with one hand. Julian had met her husband, a big Anglo, a carpenter, a man who dwelled in anger and jealousy. In the flush of romance, Julian reflected, some men persuade themselves that the succulence of their wives' melon patch is exclusive property. Later, they perceive that all other men are invaders, poachers, at least in their minds, and for men like this such attentions are too much to contemplate, so they live in a state of uneasiness, even fury.

"Here is the file," said Maria, and returned to her desk. Julian Baca dropped his eyes to the label on the file: WALTER MEYERS GALLERY.

"You know, Maria, this is not good. Not good at all. This weekend the Japanese from Mitsubishi arrive to look over New Mexico again, and we will have this bloody business all over the newspapers."

Baca noticed the back of Maria's neck redden slightly.

"A terrible business," Baca resumed. "A man's life . . . boom! Gone. Just like that. What are we to think?"

Maria swiveled slowly in her chair and faced her superior. "It was my aunt—she cleans up the gallery every morning—it was my aunt who found him. I think we should pray for him." She swiveled back to face her desk.

"Maria, perhaps you should take the rest of the day off, to be with your aunt. The poor woman, did she . . . ?" But Baca thought better of snooping, and, sadly but appreciatively, he watched his assistant walk out of the office. He turned in his chair and punched the soft plastic buttons on the machine that doubled as phone and fax.

"Hey, beautiful," he said into the receiver. "This is Julian. I'd like to talk to the mayor. Yeah, his very self, the alcalde. But first, hey, how are you doin'? Long time . . ." As he talked to the familiar voice, with the familiar face in his mind, he realized that it had been an age since he had needed to resort to such a strategem. "Hey, beautiful," he had said, unable to remember her name.

On the eastern outskirts of the city Connie Barnes sat hunched over an electronic adding machine in the office of the Wheelwright Museum's elegant gift shop, the Case Trading Post. Whenever a new shipment of Indian jewelry or pots or whatever arrived, the shop called Connie to make an appraisal to confirm the shipment's value, as required by the insurance company. Connie, who had grown up on the Hopi reservation in a thoroughly traditional household, had gone on to the University of Arizona and studied to be an accountant. (Her Anglo father, a construction worker named Jeff Barnes, had long since disappeared.) After a couple of years in a small accounting firm in Santa Fe, she had set herself up as an appraiser of Indian artifacts, combining the cold eye of the CPA with an intuitive and ancient feel for such things that went beyond analysis. Her fingers flew over the machine's buttons, adding a column of figures for the third time, when the phone rang. She picked it up with a kind of relief.

"This is the Case Trading Post," she said in a voice slightly lower than her normal alto. "Connie Barnes speaking." There was silence on the phone, and Connie heard the distant hum of the museum's air-conditioning system, only now beginning to force cool air into the office.

"You heard that Walt Meyers is dead."

"Yes, Mo, everyone here at the museum is talking about it."

"Well, we're innocent of the crime, aren't we? They said it took place around eleven, and as I recall . . ."

Connie unaccountably felt the sticky outbreak of perspiration on her forehead. She laughed.

"Not that he didn't deserve it," said Mo.

"Mo, that's terrible. Nobody deserves it."

"Everyone's been telling me today that I'm terrible for telling the truth about Walt. But yeah, you're right. He didn't really deserve it. I told him he shouldn't live there."

"What are you doing, Mo?" she asked. The air-conditioning, gathering strength, dried the perspiration from her forehead.

"Hah—hah. I got that piece of marble figured out."

"What . . . ?"

"You'll see."

"You've been promising me an eagle for six months."

"Seven. I've been counting. Can't rush these things, Connie. You know, my old tequila-drinking buddy at the Santa Fe P.D.? Ramirez? He says his people haven't found any human spoor in Meyers's joint. Well, of course someone broke open his head and messed up the place, but there's no sign of the perp. No tracks. No prints. Nothing. It's like it happened of its own accord. You better tell those ladies over there to batten down the hatches. There's a phantom loose in Santa Fe, out messing up artifacts, hah—hah—"

"That's not funny, Mo."

"I know it." He sighed. "Nothing much is these days. Well, I'm off to my marble. You know, Connie, I wonder if anyone is going to mourn for Walt Meyers. You know, really mourn."

Three

From Santa Fe to what is called the Big I in Albuquerque—the crossroads of routes I-25 and I-40—takes about an hour if the speed laws are minimally heeded. The Big I, though well enough marked for most people, does call forth its share of last-minute lane changes and not a few accidents in this most accident-prone of states. Willie had made the trip many times, and without thinking, found himself in the proper lane to swing west onto Route 40, his 1971 Ford pickup wheezing to gain speed after the turn.

Willie Blaine headed west through the night, west where the dreams of youth have always had their draw, but the place where the sun also sets. Somehow, along Route 40—which replaced a long stretch of that boulevard of dreams, Route 66—the new dreams haven't materialized either. Well beyond the western city limits of Albuquerque, out in the desert, lie the disheveled and dry reservation lands of the Laguna and Acoma Indians, barren and raw wasteland where only Indians could chant up some value. Willie's truck groaned through these desolate regions.

Beyond lay Grants, jerry-built on the dream of wealth from

the mining of uranium, another typical western boomtown, only radioactive, and even before the collapsing prices and fortunes of uranium zapped Grants, it had always seemed to Willie a depressing place. The old truck strained on.

Ahead of Willie, beyond Grants, lay Gallup, New Mexico, Degradation Capital of the Indian World, where border Navajos get drunk; then Holbrook, Arizona, Fossilized Capital of the Petrified Forest; and eventually Winslow. Home. Route 40, Willie complained to himself, was nothing more than a long string of nothing punctuated by little accumulations of crud. The (mostly) all-music, all-night radio program blared out self-pitying and teary complaints on the part of country boys left behind by lovers and by life, and Willie Blaine was having none of that. He was a winner. He had beat the goddamned system. He knew the answers.

A few miles past Grants the road rises through a long high-way cut, the walls of which reflected back to him the noisy death rattles of his truck.

"Shit!" Willie said out loud, pulling the wheel leftward to avoid some old man wobbling along the shoulder like a phantom in the dead of night. The pickup fishtailed into a skid; Willie pulled out of that and immediately into another. His glands flooded. He couldn't breathe, his heart was in his throat, and he was covered with sweat. The engine strained and Willie knew it was dying. What the fuck do I do now? he asked himself. He thought of his cargo, wrapped in a green plastic garbage bag and buried beneath half a yard of sand in the bed of the truck. What the hell do I do if I crash right here in the middle of nowhere at one o'clock in the morning?

But the back end of the truck straightened out and the engine didn't die, and they labored loudly up the hill.

He made it home to Winslow, halfway across the state of Arizona, before the sun got there. He pulled up to the fence in front of the gray stucco house he rented from an old Chicano, Sanchez, who smoked cigars and would arrive to sit on the front porch—*his* front porch, for chrissake—just sit there without a word, to make it easier for Willie to deliver his check for the rent. Three hundred and forty-five dollars a month, thought Willie—robbery. He stomped on the emergency break pedal and stormed up the concrete path. Inside, he kicked a child's toy out of the way and, removing his clothes, collapsed into bed beside his wife, who snored slightly in the odd gloom that precedes dawn. Willie suddenly felt profoundly sorry for himself, but he slept.

Not long afterward, the sun blazed through the window, and Willie, half awake, pulled the sheet over his head, noting that his wife was no longer in bed. Two hours later, having slept again and having reached the end of a long creepy corridor with no doors anywhere in sight, he panicked and woke again, and heard knocking at the screen in the living room.

"Yeah?" his wife Cheryl said, probably from the kitchen.

"Yeah?" she said again, and he heard her Kmart flip-flops flap against the bare floor.

"Huh?" she said, sounding surprised, even alarmed.

"FBI. Willie Blaine live here?" It was a nasal voice, like a New York accent. Holy shit.

"Uh, yeah. So . . . ?"

"Is he home now?"

Holy shit, Willie repeated to himself, a kind of prayer for his wife to use her head.

"No. He's . . . uh, no."

"Tell him I stopped by." The screen door squeaked, opening.

"What's this?" asked Willie's wife.

"It's my card. Just tell him I was here."

The screen door thumped shut. Blaine's son whined, presumably left foodless in the high chair.

"Probably," the New York accent continued, "probably he won't get around to calling me, but I'd like him to have my card. A keepsake. Tell him he can Scotch-tape it to his ass."

"Huh?"

"Which is grass."

"Huh?"

"Just tell him I stopped by, Mrs. Blaine."

Willie lay under the sheet fuming.

"Willie?" The flip-flops approached. Flap, flip, flap.

"Yeah?"

"Wake up, Willie."

"I'm awake, I'm awake." He stuck his head out from under the sheet. "Jesus, Cheryl, your bathrobe is half open. Was that fucking fed looking at your tits?"

"Willie, what do they want?"

"Looks like they want to cop a feel of my wife's tits, that's what."

"Willie, I'm scared."

"Come here."

"No, Willie, I'm scared."

"Of this?"

"Willie, I'm not some squaw. We aren't doing that now. Jeez. I mean, the FBI . . . that's serious."

Their son whined again.

"I'm coming, I'm coming," called the woman. Flap, flop, flap.

"Okay, okay," said Willie. "Feed the kid and then start packing. Just take what we need for us and the kid. We gotta get out of here. I've got to talk to some guys first. Have we got any coffee?"

"You mean leave? Just leave everything?"

"We're going to L.A. Soon as I talk to some guys."

The bar was an inky red, a windowless place where the sun never shone directly and where the passage of time had been exempted. Two Navajos slumped at a table, and a couple of bar stools were similarly occupied, when Willie Blaine let the door shut behind him and stood letting his eyes adjust to the gloom. In his mind he heard the voice again with its mocking Noo Yawk accent. Tell him to Scotch-tape . . . Bastard.

A guy in a windbreaker and curly hair got up from the far end of the bar and headed for the dank interior where a dim sign glowed in red letters: RES ROO S. Willie Blaine crossed the room, nodding at the two Navajos, who averted their eyes, and mounted a stool.

"Hey," said the woman tending bar. She had a garish slash of lipstick that looked black. "You're early."

"When are we gonna do it, huh, Agatha?"

"Maybe when you grow up," Agatha said offhandedly. "Want a beer?"

"Come on, Agatha, I know I turn you on. Lookit, your nipples are sticking up under your shirt."

"Dream on, little man. That's the air conditioner does that. You want a beer or not?"

"Yeah."

Agatha drew from the Coors Lite tap and slid the glass across the bar. Blaine took a gulp.

"Hey," he said. "I'll be right back. Gotta use the phone."

He swiveled on the stool and stepped lightly off, heading for the phone that hung on a wall just beyond the broken restroom sign. He grabbed the receiver and was about to punch the buttons when he saw a hand-lettered sign:

THIS PHONE IS BUGGED, SCUMBAG, LIKE YOURS

Willie Blaine's forehead burst into sweat. "Shit!" he said, and slammed down the receiver and tore off the sign. The guy in the windbreaker. Willie rushed to the bar.

"Who was that guy down there?" he demanded.

Agatha crossed her arms under her generous bosom.

"Down where?"

"The guy who was at the end of the bar when I came in."

"I don't know. Some guy. Ordered Mexican beer. Hey, you didn't finish your—"

But Willie was gone in a quick burst of morning as the wooden door swung open and then shut behind him. Agatha reached for the phone down behind the bar and punched in some numbers. While she waited for the connection, one of the Navajos approached the bar.

"Your mother must've been a weaver, sonny" she said, "the way you're walking."

The Navajo put his glass on the bar and smiled. One front tooth was missing. Agatha sprayed the thin yellow liquid from the Coors Lite tap into his glass and said into the phone, "He's outta here, sweetheart. Didn't even drink his beer." She hung up. "That'll be a dollar thirty, toots."

To stem what was incipient hysteria, Willie Blaine reminded himself that he was just as well-educated as anyone in all of Winslow fucking Arizona—graduate of the University of Oklahoma—and needed to fear no brain out here, especially some eastern accounting degree nerd out of the College of the Sacred Sisters of the Holy Blood. Noo Yawk. Brooklyn, maybe. FBI jerk. He screeched around the low brick wall that separated the bar from the Gulf station next door, leapt out of the pickup and headed for the pay phone. Reaching in his tight jeans pocket for coins, he saw another piece of paper Scotch-taped over the buttons:

MEYERS GALLERY (505) 989-4221. DIAL 1 FIRST, SCUMBAG

"What the *fuck!*" Willie shrieked, and broke out into a whole body sweat. He fled back to the truck, thinking shit, shit, shit, and then thinking, I'm thinking shit? I'm dead. I'll never shit again. Killed. The engine rumbled into life, and instinct took Willie straight out into the street without an accident while local traffic swerved and men in farm caps bellowed obscenities. A moment later he stopped in front of his house and turned off the ignition. He walked up the cement path to the cluttered front porch and reached for the handle of the screen door.

"You look terrible, Willie."

Blaine spun to his left. Seated on the cement floor among his son's plastic toys, all in primary colors, was the curly-headed man in a windbreaker—the guy from the bar.

"What is this?" demanded Willie, knowing what it was.

"You are a very bad boy, Willie," said the man, leaning back comfortably against the railing, wrists resting on his knees, a terrible smile showing two crooked front teeth.

"What do you want?"

"Yeah, you're really a lousy example for that little boy in there."

"Who are you?"

"Me? I'm Big Brother, the Angel Gabriel. Nemesis, Willie— yours. I know where you go. I know what you do. Who your friends are." The man stood up. He was thick-shouldered, a bit taller than Willie, maybe five-ten. "You don't have many friends, do you?"

"This is my house," said Willie, short of breath. "You can't—"

"You pay three hundred forty-five a month for this dump, Willie. Rent. It's not your house. Your wife wears a B-cup bra, when she wears one. You get less than twelve miles a gallon on that old wreck you drive, and the IRS is waiting for you to come up with the $2,350 you owe 'em from last year. You're a month behind on your phone bill—a crummy fifty-eight dollars. You're losing it all, Blaine. And that Mexican girl you've been screwing, the one works down at the dry cleaners? She works for me. You really set a bad example for that little boy."

"What do you want?"

"Want? Want? I don't want. I've got."

"You don't have anything. . . ."

"Want to bet, scumbag?"

"So you got something, arrest me."

"Let me tell you something, Willie, you schmuck, the FBI has changed. No more nice accountants and lawyers. For this kind of stuff they hire guys like me and say, Hey, take care of it. The courts are slow, some kind of situations the evidence is slippery, so take care of it. I'm a guy with a lot of freedom of action, and you know what else, Willie, you schmuck?"

Willie reached for the handle of the screen door. "What?"

"Your wife cheats on you. If I was your wife, *I'd* cheat on you." The man swung off the porch and walked lightly down the cement path, and Willie Blaine's nervous system turned into the biological equivalent of bread pudding.

Ten minutes later Larry Collins walked into the Winslow, Arizona, police station. He shucked his windbreaker and slung it over his shoulder as he approached the desk sergeant, a preternaturally thin man with white hair and more lines in his face than a raisin.

"That little shit Blaine is going to run," said Collins.

"So what good will that do?" asked the old sergeant.

"It's movement, action . . . carelessness, maybe, panic. Have you got a—"

"Don't sweat it. Wilson is watching the place for you. He'll let us know."

"Thanks again."

"You got a message here." The old man held up a piece of pink paper. "Called in a couple hours ago from your people in Albuquerque."

Collins took the paper, saying, "Christ, what do they want . . . *Damn!*"

The old man looked up.

"Walter Meyers was killed."

"Yeah, I know. I read the message. Who's Walter Meyers?"

"Look, I gotta go to Santa Fe. Damn. What's his name,

Wilson? Tell him to stick to that little prick Blaine like super-glue. Wherever he goes."

"Wilson can't officially leave the county."

"Hey, Charlie, it's important, real important. If Blaine splits, I gotta know where he goes. Give Wilson a little paid vacation or something, okay?"

"It's real exciting working with you federal big shots."

"Okay, Charlie, okay?"

"For you, okay."

Larry Collins raced out of the station, gunned his Chevrolet and headed east. As he left the outskirts of Winslow on Route 40, the speedometer read seventy-six and he flicked on the radar detector he had bought out of his own salary check. Another lead dried up. Dried up? Dead and gone, a leaf in the wind. Larry Collins, special agent for the FBI, mourned the death of Walter Meyers, really mourned it.

Not that he gave a damn about the dead man in Santa Fe; he was no sentimentalist. It was merely that the man's death was an impediment. *Impetuous* was a word that had occurred all too often in the performance reports Collins's superiors would write. *Loner* was another, a serious pejorative in the team culture of the FBI.

When he was a gregarious freshman at Fordham University, considering a career in teaching, Collins's parents, who owned a 7-Eleven in Brooklyn, had been mowed down by a thief with a cheap automatic rifle. Larry Collins finished Fordham as a lonely student of sociology, with a minor in various forms of socially approved violence. After graduation, he thought about a career in the U.S. Navy SEALs, but joined the FBI instead. Burning with an incandescence that pegged him as a potential maverick, he got the highest grades in every course at the training program in Quantico, Virginia, and then took off like a heat-seeking missile in a Turkish bath. Reprimanded three times in four years for overzealousness of one sort or another, and once more two years later, he had undergone four years as an instructor back in Quantico. But then a unique problem arose on the FBI's horizon, one calling for a loner, a free-lancer. So Larry Collins, much chastened, had been plucked from the boredom of teaching the arts of self-defense and thrust in the midst of Indian country in the southwestern desertlands where everything is far away, even the sky, and people used to the urbanized eastern landscape can feel profoundly ill-at-ease. Not Collins. He barely noticed the landscape, so narrowly focused was his internal guidance system.

The highway east—Route 40, with Holbrook about forty-five minutes ahead—was straight, flat, skimming through land seared white in the sun, featureless landscapes so slow to change that he bit his lip, this impatient Brooklynite clamoring inwardly for justice. Any justice. He pressed the Chevrolet to a frame-joggling eighty-eight miles per hour—federal business, however recondite—and ate up the miles, still not quite aware that he had wound up in one of the last American refuges for the habitual elbow thrower.

F o u r

Police sergeant Anthony Ramirez stood in the middle of the main room in the Walter Meyers Gallery in Santa Fe, his arms folded across his chest. He surveyed the wreckage. Pots lay around the floor, many of them cracked, many shards scattered here and there. An old kachina mask lay in one corner, its face looking helplessly up at the ceiling. Indian pouches, head-dresses, moccasins, bundles—these were strewn around the floor. Ramirez looked again for a pattern in the chaos, a pattern that might point to a purpose. He had studied archeology in college, drawn less to the physical artifacts themselves than to the puzzles and patterns they presented, the ways in which old junk, cast aside by its users, could take on a meaning from the very manner of its discard. Oddly, the gallery's walnut display stands, gleaming from careful polishing, seemed to be all in place, including the central pedestal where once, a discreet label said, the Zuni mask now lying on the floor gaping at the ceiling had rested. There was no way to tell what, if anything, was missing. That would have to await the inventory, a tedious affair, what with the sheer quantity of stuff in the gallery.

It had been the tedium of archeological fieldwork—along with the death of his father, leaving the family in a financial strait—that had driven young Anthony Ramirez out of a life of scholarship and into police work. He was grateful that he would not have to participate in the inventory: this would fall to the assistant manager and the representatives of the insurance company—of course, under close scrutiny by the Santa Fe P.D. But even so, without an inventory it did not look to Ramirez's eye like a burglary. It looked more like some form of heightened vandalism—as if an angry wind had swept through the place.

"Sergeant," said the officer who appeared in the doorway. "There are people—"

"Who?" asked Ramirez, impatient at the interruption of his reveries.

"Miz del Massimo and one other woman."

"Okay," said Ramirez.

Marianna del Massimo, assistant manager of the Meyers Gallery, was a figure widely recognized in the city for the very reason that, in a place where people tended to present themselves to the world in ways that drew attention, she managed to do it masterfully by an un-Santa-Fean tactic: understatement. Ramirez had seen her around town, always tailored, her mid-length ebony hair simply coiffed, her clothes subdued, lit only with an accent of simple but expensive jewelry, the perfect gold pin, the lovely pearl necklace. There were, along with her aura of understated grace, quiet stories that she was the widow of an Italian prince who had died in a racing car accident, and stories as well that there had been no such prince, and that her name had been Mary Massey when she grew up somewhere in northern New Jersey. Such stories arise as if by spontaneous generation in a spot like Santa Fe, especially if, as a matter of tactics, they go undenied.

Marianna del Massimo entered the gallery with the dignity of the bereaved, dressed in black, without a shred of jewelry.

She was followed by a woman Ramirez recognized at once: broad-shouldered, with a cascade of matching black hair, also attired in a somber suit.

"Miz del Massimo? I'm Sergeant Ramirez."

"Sergeant, thank you. This is Constance Barnes, the appraiser for the insurance company. She'll be helping me inventory . . . all this." She gestured with a small movement of her hand.

"Yes," Ramirez said. "I know Miss Barnes. Hi, Connie."

A loud voice sounded from the entrance.

"I'm with the appraiser, officer. She needs me, can't function without me."

Ramirez smiled. He heard the officer quietly protesting.

"Oh, come on, officer. I'm not going to scramble the evidence in there. I wouldn't want to mess up Tony Ramirez's meditations on the crime. I'm just going to stand there and give the appraiser, the official appraiser, a little moral support at this very difficult time."

Ramirez stepped into the entrance hall. "It's okay, Arnold. He can come in. Hi, Mo."

"They say you got yourself a hell of a mess in here," said the big man, stepping gingerly into the building. "Maybe you can help me through the mine field, so's I don't mess up the provenance of your evidence."

Ramirez took Mo by his beefy forearm, bristling with blond hairs, and led him to a spot near the wall in the main room.

"So what's it look like in here?" Mo said, standing erect as a spear.

Ramirez described the room, and the emergent pattern in his mind, and then asked, "Why are you so interested?"

"I'm not," Mo said. "I'm just here to give Connie moral support."

"Don't bullshit me, Mo. Why are you trying to snoop around here?"

"Tony," Mo said, "let me explain to you about that—hah—

hah. See, you and me, we're sure as hell going to wind up talking about this anyway, while you're buying me the drink you owe me, and I figured I might as well step in here and get a sense of things. You know, so I'll know what you're talking about." The big man sniffed loudly.

"That's also bullshit," said Ramirez softly as the del Massimo woman approached him. "But I'll find out what ant is bugging— Yes, Miz del Massimo?"

"Sergeant, when may we start? I'm really terribly anxious to see what's missing."

"Right now is good," said Ramirez, and the two women settled themselves in the office, murmuring. The assistant manager, del Massimo, seated herself before the computer on Meyers's desk, and her fingers rippled over the keyboard.

"Where did it happen?" Mo asked.

"The killing?"

"Yeah."

"In the little anteroom behind the office."

"Can we go there?"

"There's nothing to see there. I mean—"

"Hah—hah—forget it, Tony. Not important."

"It's okay. Here. I'll lead you there."

Bowdre sniffed the air as Ramirez steered him through the mess, into the office, and through the wooden door into the anteroom.

"What are you doing, sniffing like a dog?"

"Two old dogs," Mo said. "One sniffing, the other a Seeing Eye dog. You know the old saying, two dogs are better than one. That's an Anglo maxim."

"That's Anglo bullshit," said Ramirez. Mo sniffed. "What do you smell?"

"Blood, dust, garlic—that's you—and something else. Pepto-Bismol." Bowdre leaned toward the policeman and whispered, "And if you ask her, you'll find that the royal widow lady uses just a tiny bit of Opium."

"Opium?"

"Perfume, Tony, *perfumar*. A strong scent designed originally to overcome other scents. Don't they teach you boys anything at the police academy?"

"Why don't you run along now, Mo? The captain said he was going to stop by in a little while. . . ."

"Say no more. Captain Ortiz is a fine man, if a bit conventional for my taste. I can find my way out now. This place gives me the creeps. Always did." Ramirez walked along with the sculptor. "Ever been to Gettysburg?"

"The battlefield?" Ramirez asked.

"Yeah, Civil War."

"I never been east of San Antonio."

"Gettysburg gave me the creeps just like this place. All those dead people. I don't know why anyone would want to collect all this dead old Indian stuff. Christ, it's all stolen, nothing but pain, loss—you can feel it." Reaching the entrance, Mo strode out into the sunlight. "Ah, Father Sun. See you, Tony."

"Adios."

The policeman watched his large friend pause on the sidewalk, sniff the air, and set off to the east, shoulders back, facing blankly and defiantly ahead. Later, later, Ramirez reflected. In good time he would find out what T. Moore Bowdre was up to in the Meyers Gallery. Sergeant Ramirez was a patient man with an abiding faith that there were patterns to events, and that the patterns had a tendency to assert themselves. One merely had to wait.

Meanwhile, Ramirez had another task. He crossed the anteroom of the gallery and through the main room to the office.

"Miz del Massimo? Could I have a word with you?"

The slender woman looked up, and Ramirez couldn't tell if it was irritation at being interrupted or nerves, but her face reddened for an instant.

"Yes, of course."

"Out here, maybe . . ."

She stood up, touched her hair, and followed Ramirez out of the office into the gallery.

"Yes, Sergeant . . . ?"

"Ramirez."

"Sergeant Ramirez. What can I do for you?"

"Well, I know this is a difficult time for you, for everyone, and this is just a formality . . ."

Marianna del Massimo smiled. "Oh, yes. You want to know where I was last night."

"It's a routine we follow, Miz del Massimo."

"I understand, of course. Last night I had dinner at the Café des Artistes."

"The new place, just opened over on . . . ?"

"Yes, my friends, the Bellamys, Jill and Jack, own it—he's the chef—and I went there with some friends for dinner."

"About what time was that?"

The woman shifted her weight from one leg to another and frowned at the floor. Ramirez admired her slender figure. "We got there about seven-thirty, and I guess we finished around ten."

"Ten?" Ramirez said sharply.

"Yes. Then my friends went on home and I stayed to talk to Jill and Jack. In fact, my idea was to introduce them to a better scotch than they were serving. I brought in a bottle for them from the car and we sat around in the kitchen until, oh, I'd say well past midnight—almost one. Talking about the joys and woes of the restaurant business. Then I drove home. Very slowly."

Ramirez smiled and nodded.

"You could, of course . . . ask them," said the woman.

"Yes, ma'am, I will," Ramirez said apologetically. "It's part of the routine."

"I understand. Is that . . . ?"

"Oh, yes, that's fine," said Ramirez, looking at her.

"Okay?" she asked.

"Uh, well, just out of curiosity . . ."

She smiled. "The scotch? It's called Old Sheep Dip." She laughed and turned toward the main room. "Really, that's what it's called."

Ramirez, no scotch drinker, was nonetheless pleased with this detail.

Walter Meyers had been a most meticulous man, handling the record-keeping with the same deft precision with which he would hold a priceless Mimbres pot, leaving nothing to chance, never failing to note just how and when something had come into his collection and how and when it had moved on to a buyer. He even left in the files exquisite little pencil sketches of the items that came into his possession, sketches that captured, almost cartooned, whatever unique features the artifact had. And these sketches greatly eased the burden of Marianna del Massimo and Connie Barnes as they began matching records in the files with what was to be found, either intact or in pieces, in the Meyers Gallery.

"Why didn't he just use Polaroids?" asked Connie after Marianna had explained the system. "They're faster. And the insurance companies are used to them. Or a video camera?"

"He didn't like photography," Marianna said. "He thought it was stupid."

"Stupid? Photography?"

"Yes, it simply records everything that's there, without any emphasis, without understanding. That's what he used to say. But he could draw something, like one of these pots . . ." She held up a white pot with fanciful black lizards on it, a classic Mimbres pot worth $17,500. "With a line or two, or a little bit of shading, he could emphasize what was special about it. For him it was a kind of mnemonic device. But for someone who isn't really familiar with this kind of material, like an insurance company, they all look alike, and so does a sheaf of photographs. But see, these drawings, look, you can spot the drawing of this pot without even thinking, out of that whole pile of drawings."

She fanned out a dozen drawings like playing cards and extracted a sheet. "Here. See?"

Connie took the sheet from her and held it up, glancing at the Mimbres pot with its lizards. "I see what you mean," she said, smiling. "But it still seems like a lot of unnecessary work."

Marianna looked away. "He was very deft, very quick. And he really wasn't in any hurry. He loved these things, God, how he loved them. He used to hold them in his hands and turn them in the light. He'd put them on his desk and watch them. It was something nearly carnal, you know, between him and these objects."

Connie put a check mark next to an item on her list and said, "Then what about selling them? Did he mind selling them? If he, uh, loved them so much?"

Marianna smiled at her. "Of course not. He was in it for the money, after all. We all are, in this business. We're not the same thing as museum curators, Connie. He was a pimp, and these were his whores. And he was a very good pimp."

"I almost threw up when I thought about it," said Connie. She was seated in the shadows across from Mo Bowdre in a booth along the wall at Tiny's. "It sort of brought the whole thing home to me—no rationalizations. That's just what he was doing. Selling off our things, our beloved things, our sacred things, like so many . . . whores."

Mo leaned across the table at her. "Still think he didn't deserve it?"

"Oh, Mo, that's different."

Mo sat back and blew some air from between pursed lips. "I don't see why. It wouldn't surprise me at all if whoever killed him did it for that very reason, to end the profane and profaning career of Walt Meyers, then messed the place up to make it look like a burglary. Did you and Her Royal Eyetalian Highness find anything missing?"

"Nothing conclusively missing yet. But we've got at least a couple of days' worth more work." Connie dipped a corn chip into the dish of salsa, clicked off a piece with her teeth and chewed it. "But why would someone who cared enough about these things—and you mean an Indian, right?—why would someone like that then go ahead and break all that stuff? It's Indian too."

"You're asking me to explain the mysteries of the Native American mind? Me, a redneck from Lincoln County? Say, listen here, do you think that woman was ever really married to a nobleman from Verona, or is she just one of the self-invented around here?"

Connie suddenly felt irritated. "Aren't we all self-inventions?"

"Now don't you go and get all defensive on me, woman. Under this worldly disguise I've invented for myself lies the soul of a small-town gossip. And I'm just curious about Her Highness. What's she going to do now, for instance? Who gets the Meyers Gallery now that the little twerp is dead and gone? Maybe he said in his will that he wanted all his stuff buried with him in some massive sarcophagus. Did you find a will in there?"

"Are you two happy here?" asked Emma, the waitress, who had materialized by the booth.

Willie Blaine seethed at the injustice, the downright incompetence, of the whole goddamned world. His wife Cheryl and their little boy sat as far away from him as they could manage in the cab of the old pickup, both of them sniveling, watching him with eyes full of fear. He glowered through the windshield into the setting sun, a half hour from Flagstaff. Six hours. Six hours it had taken, with Cheryl asking dumb questions and the kid whining, sitting around the fucking gas station in the sun, wondering if he was going to make it out of town before they caught up with him—they, the frigging feds, that prick in the windbreaker, the old Chicano looking for his rent check, the phone company, the cops, the IRS, all of them, he could feel them all breathing down his neck while he waited for the big stupid redneck bastard to fix the steering on his goddamn broken-down memorial to ripoff artist Henry cocksucking Ford. So now they were out of Winslow, maybe out of the entire mess, but the truck was wheezing, hardly gaining on the old volcano called San Francisco Peaks that loomed on the horizon. With a little luck it was goodbye Arizona, goodbye Indians, goodbye to all that shit. He looked over at his wife.

"Jesus, what are you crying about? We're getting out of all that mess."

"I'm scared."

"That's great. You're scared, so the kid is scared. So everybody's sniveling. What are you scared of?"

"Why are we running?" his wife asked. "Why did the FBI guy come? Where were you the last two days till you came home?"

Willie took a deep breath. He should explain. "Okay, we're running because we're out of money and everybody's after us for it. We're gonna make a new start. In L.A. The frigging fed came because they think I was involved in stealing stuff from the Hopis, you know, masks, that kind of stuff. They suspect anyone who ever worked there, coaches, teachers, construction guys."

"I wish you had stayed being a coach. Part of the government, the Bureau of Indian Affairs and all. It was nice."

"Nice? working for those guys, it was like a bunch of Nazis. Anyway, it was them who fired me, remember? So? What the hell, I like it better being a trader." He smirked.

"Were you?"

"Were I what?"

"Stealing."

"No, I wasn't stealing," he mimicked. "I don't steal stuff. I buy stuff and then sell it. Legal transactions. Where the hell do you think our money came from?"

"Okay, so where were you the last couple of days?"

Willie thought about the cargo, still wrapped in a green plastic garbage bag under the sand, beneath a half a ton of crap that Cheryl couldn't bring herself to leave behind.

"None of your business," said Willie. His wife tightened and looked out the window, chin jutted in an unmistakable sign of defiance.

"We're getting out at Flagstaff."

"Who, what?"

"Little Billy and me. We're getting out at Flagstaff. You can go to L.A." She stared straight ahead. "You can go to hell."

"Okay, okay," said Willie. "I was in Santa Fe. Making a deal. The best of my life. I'm not kidding. Fantastic deal." He smiled at the thought. "Cheer up. We'll be rich when this one is over. Rich in L.A."

His wife watched the highway before them.

"We're getting out at Flagstaff," she said.

"Oh bullshit," replied Willie Blaine, figuring the odds.

Larry Collins had spent more than an hour at the FBI office on Grand Street in Albuquerque, checking with the agents there and assembling some information from the files, so it was past five o'clock when he came over the last rise and saw the outskirts of Santa Fe spreading toward him from the blue-green mountains. The sight was a relief from the monotonous, colorless rolling hills and mesas, sand, and rock dotted here and there with scrubby, stunted trees the size of bushes, which extended for miles on either side of Route 25 out to treeless gray mountains and mountain ridges on the east and west horizons. Larry Collins had begun to notice the landscape, and it bored him. A New Yorker, he thought any landscape was pointless, especially one that was so utterly vacant and tortured.

As he came down an incline, his Fuzzbuster blinked frantically, its red eye looking alarmed, and Collins intuitively hit the brakes, feeling guilty. Then he glanced around and saw a TV station to his right and grumbled to himself about electronic pollution. He took the Cerillos Road exit, and by the time he reached the SFPD's building, which lay on the outskirts of the city, Captain Andrew Ortiz, whom the people in Albuquerque had said would be his contact, had gone home for the day. The desk sergeant, sitting lumpily at the window like a tired racetrack teller, asked him if he wanted to contact the captain at home.

Collins thought it over.

"Nah. I'll see him tomorrow." He asked directions to the Walter Meyers Gallery. The sergeant drew a little map on a sheet from a phone pad. The gallery was a block north of the plaza.

"It's closed down, you know," said the sergeant.

"Yeah, I heard about it."

"That why you're here?"

"Yeah, federal business," Collins said.

"Or otherwise, why would . . . ?"

Collins grinned. "Right, otherwise why would I be here? Tell Captain Ortiz I'll be here about eight, okay?"

"There are two men stationed at the gallery," said the sergeant helpfully. "Weldon and Baca."

"Thanks. I'll tell 'em hello."

A few tourists were standing around the gallery beyond the yellow tape, gawking at the two cops who stood near the door, hands behind their backs, looking bored. It was a low-roofed, stucco building like a pueblo, like every other building in town. Collins eyed it from behind the wheel of his Chevy, stared at the sidewalk café next door and, beyond that, the boutique called Earth Maven, which had a lot of silvery T-shirts in the window. He headed for a motel on the outskirts of town on Cerillos Road, not far from the police station. On the seat beside him was a file labeled MEYERS, full of stuff he had Xeroxed in Albuquerque. He wanted to read through it again, carefully. Especially that stuff about Meyers's brief career almost two decades ago as an archeologist in the National Park Service.

Samantha Burgess found a parking place in the bank lot near the plaza, and gave the dignified old Hispanic attendant a dollar. She was a bit early. When Audrey had called the day before from Washington, D.C., to announce that she would be in Santa Fe on business, they had agreed to meet for drinks at La Fonda, the big tourist hotel on the plaza, and then go on to dinner. Her ex-roommate from Reed College was one of those management/personnel consultants who sell psychobabble to corporations—a lot of b.s., Samantha thought, but she looked forward to getting together anyway. Samantha, though a Santa Fean for only two years now, already had absorbed the locals' avowed disdain for the plaza and all its swarming tourists, its galleries and with-it shops gaping hungrily for Texas and California dollars. Still, some of the best shops and galleries *were* to be found on the plaza, and in spite of its local rep, it was a beautiful place—the old facades, the trees and grass in the park in the middle, the abrupt changes from sun to shade.

She stopped on San Francisco Street, just east of the plaza, to look in the window of White Feather Gallery and fantasize again about one day owning a Bowdre. Peering through the glass, she saw big gleaming bronze cats caught in mid-hunt—probably mountain lions, she thought—along with a familiar abstraction that somehow said bison. Farther back in the huge room was a standing figure in a robe, a figure that looked at the same time strong and broken, threatening and tragic. It was Bowdre's Franciscan, which, as Samantha well knew, had caused a storm of controversy and protest when it had been presented as part of a Columbus-inspired celebration. Some outspoken Indian groups did not appreciate its strength, its majestic quality, and some outspoken Hispanic groups did not like what they saw as the deadness of its visage. Samantha mused on the politics of art, but then noted with sudden alarm that the huge grizzly bear, rising up on its back legs, was no longer there.

A woman of exaggerated elegance stood inside near the front entrance, beside an antique inlaid desk. She looked more like a model for *Elle* than a salesperson. Samantha thought about going inside and asking her who had bought Bowdre's bear. She decided not to. She'd never see the sculpture again in any event, she thought sourly, as she became aware of someone standing a few paces away, looking at her. She peered at his reflection in the polished glass of the gallery's big front window. Short. An Indian. Still looking at her.

She turned and glanced at the Indian, a young guy in a cheap shirt and jeans. Not, evidently, drunk. He looked away and glanced at her again.

"Excuse me," he said in a quiet voice. "You live here?"

Samantha looked back in the gallery window. Maybe he'd go away.

"Excuse me," said the soft Indian voice again. "Can you tell me how to find Canyon Road?"

"Where are you from?" asked Samantha, a bit surprised at herself. She knew better than to strike up conversations with anyone on the street, especially Indians, who usually went on to ask for money. But his round face seemed open, innocent.

"Hopi," said the Indian. "My sister lives on Canyon Road. She's my clan sister, you know? She's staying with this guy." He pointed into the gallery with his lips. "With the sculptor." He looked at Samantha and smiled fleetingly. "I got something for her."

Samantha explained how to get to Canyon Road, went over

it again while the Hopi nodded, and said "Take care" automatically. She watched him disappear around a corner and then turned, heading for La Fonda. Probably Audrey'll want to eat dinner at the Coyote Café, Samantha sniffed to herself. The Coyote Café, though internationally known, is the kind of place that real Santa Feans never go.

"What's your interest in this, Collins?" asked Captain Andrew Ortiz. A tall, trim, lugubrious man in plain clothes, he was seated behind a gray metal desk in a small, bare office at the SFPD. To Collins's left, in a metal chair, sat the sergeant named Ramirez, also in plain clothes, who watched him with brown eyes that seemed amused. Collins was hunched down in his metal chair, legs crossed, with one ankle resting on his knee. "Aren't you pretty far afield from northern Arizona?" the captain asked.

"Okay, yeah, it's like this. A year ago, a little more than a year ago, the Hopi Indians lost some of their most important religious objects. They didn't lose them, they got stolen. These aren't just masks and that sort of thing. They're even more than altar pieces. You know about that stuff? Altar pieces that they use in special priesthood ceremonies? Well, these things are even more . . . more what? Powerful than altar pieces. The Hopis say they're immortal. They just can't be made again, you know?"

The captain nodded. "We heard about that. Real crude-looking. A couple of sticks with some paint on them. There was a report circulated a few months ago. Yours, I guess. You think Meyers was involved?"

"I'm fairly sure of it, but wait, let me go back." Collins looked at Sergeant Ramirez, who continued to gaze at him. "See, the Hopi religion is at a standstill. Without these things—they look like sticks to you and me, but to the Hopis they're gods, deities, and poof! they're gone and that's the end of this particular priesthood for the Hopi. It happened one other time, back in 1978. Four of 'em got stolen, one of 'em came back, don't ask me how. Anyway, now it's another priesthood that's crippled, in another one of the villages."

Collins looked around; the two remained expressionless, the way cops do.

"The Bureau assigned me to these things. Just these objects. Four months ago. The point is to get 'em back. If we can find the bastards who took 'em, fine, we'll nail them good, stick 'em with the Archeological Resources Act, well, you know all that crap. But my real job, as I see it, is to get 'em back. Anyway, I've got a pretty good idea of several of the steps along the way—can't prove anything, of course, these bastards are slick as hell. There's a guy in Winslow, used to be a coach at the BIA schools at Hopi, I'm pretty sure he was in the loop. I think he passed them on to a guy in Phoenix. And I'm pretty sure they were here, and that Meyers was involved. I was going to . . . well, I figured I could pin it down, but now the bastard is dead."

Collins paused.

"He's not the first one, either. The guy in Phoenix died last month. Weird as hell. Brand new pickup, you know, one of those jobs with everything on it, and I mean brand new. Drove it out of the lot one afternoon right after he bought it—for cash, twenty-seven thousand in cash—and the next thing you know, he drove straight off the highway and down an embankment. Broken neck. Nothing wrong with the truck, nothing, no sign of stroke, heart, nothing. Just drove off the road."

Ramirez cleared his throat. "Do you—uh, do you believe in . . ."

"Hey, Sergeant, I grew up in Brooklyn. I went to college. I took science courses. I believe in cause and effect, just like everybody else, you know? I don't know from refried beans or piki bread about Indian religion, just what they tell me. I believe in police reports, huh? So what killed the guy in Phoenix, I don't know yet. Anyway, it looks like this guy Meyers was in the loop—maybe the final seller to the final buyer, so that's my interest in this."

Captain Ortiz leaned forward. "Of course, we'll help in any way we can. Ramirez here is in charge of our investigation. He'll cooperate however you need him. Let me ask you, what are these things worth? I mean on the market."

"God knows what somebody'd pay for them," said Collins, looking almost surprised. "The ones in 1978, I heard figures like seventy-five thousand, that's probably low. Hell, I don't know. Today? These ones? Maybe a quarter of a million. Plenty to kill some guys for. Just think, for a quarter of a million bucks you can own your own gods. Izzat sick or what?"

The captain stood up. "Okay, it's all yours."

Collins stood up and stuck out his hand. "I appreciate it. The sergeant'll keep you up to date."

Mo Bowdre stepped out of the cool shade of his covered patio into the warmth of the courtyard. The early sun heated the back of his neck and he stretched luxuriously. He listened to the breeze blowing through the trees beyond the wall, picked out the other familiar sounds, the rustles, the twittering of birds, placing them on his mental map. In the big oak tree that grew in the yard next door, a black-headed grosbeak called *eek*, *eek*. A towhee *chink*ed from the bushes near the house. A hummingbird whirred noisily back and forth in irritable uncertainty about trying the sugar water that hung by the portal.

In his mind's eye, where it was not always dark, he felt an eagle emerging, its fierce and implacable eye the focus of the universe. An old memory. He recalled a golden eagle, sitting imperiously on a fence post near his boyhood home, its feathers ruffled in the wind, rattling almost. He saw the eagle stare at him from its obsidian pupil and then, almost languorously, take to the air with obvious indifference. For Mo, this eagle of his memory represented the entire world of light and vision, snatched away from him so long ago with such indifference. He wished he hadn't promised Connie an eagle, the quintessential seer, the frowning eagle eye so crucial a feature, a bird defined by the quality of its eye.

Mo had never sculpted anything so airy as a bird, so fragile.

He became aware of a disharmony somewhere outside his mental vision. Something was not right, some sound, a nearly inaudible hiss. He took a step back into the shade of the patio and listened. It came again.

He lunged to his left, two steps, reaching out with both hands, clutching a fleshy neck, and hauled a person, a man, out of the hammock, holding him dangling above the ground.

"Who the hell are *you*?" Mo roared, setting the birds to making scratchy calls of alarm. "Who *are* you?"

The man emitted a gargling, choking sound, and Mo set him on the ground, still holding him by the throat.

The man gasped. "Darrel," he said. Mo's nose was swept with the sour smell of last night's wine on the man's breath, a lot of wine.

"What are you doing in my yard, in my hammock?"

The man named Darrel gagged and coughed and sneezed.

"Goddamn it! What the hell are you doing here?"

"I came . . . last night . . . I came to find . . . Connie . . . She's my sister." He coughed. "Clan sister. I'm Darrel. Hopi. Corn clan. I got something for her. Nobody was awake . . . and I came around here and . . ." He was having difficulty speaking without the full use of his larynx.

"And passed out in my hammock, huh?" Mo released the man's throat. He slumped, shuffled, and was still.

"Uh, yeah. Like that, you know?"

"Well, you sure as hell surprised me, Darrel . . . Darrel what? What's the rest of your name?"

"Quanemptewa. Darrel Quanemptewa. I'm from Kykotsmovi. Third Mesa. I think I'm going to throw up."

"Jesus Christ! Not here!" Mo yelled, shoving the man through the door and into a small half bathroom. "There!" Mo said. "In there." He closed the door and listened to the wracking coughs and heaves, and the splatter of vomit in water. "Thank God. He made it."

He heard the toilet flush, the water run in the basin, and stepped out on the patio. The bathroom door opened and Mo said, "Come out here, Darrel." He heard the man obey, coughing.

"Quit coughing," Mo ordered. "You make me feel guilty. Why the hell should *I* feel guilty? I don't feel guilty. You're the one that broke the damn laws of trespass."

"I . . . I didn't mean . . ."

"Forget it. Just quit coughing and gagging. I didn't grab you all that hard. Connie's not here. She's working, till late this afternoon, maybe this evening. When did you get here?"

"Last night?"

"No, to Santa Fe," Mo said impatiently. "What're you doing here?"

"I was lookin' for work, you know, got here yesterday."

"What kind of work?"

"Anything, for a while."

"So instead you went out and got drunk?"

"I don't feel—I don't feel, uh, real good, you know, right. Being here, you know, away."

"Well, you don't smell so damn good either. Go take a shower, get yourself cleaned up. You can't look for work smelling like vomit." He heard the Hopi open the door to the house.

"And Darrel? You may have noticed that I don't see. But I hear real good. So don't screw around in there."

The door closed and Mo stepped into the sunlight again. "There's hot coffee in the kitchen," he called, thinking to himself that he had never smelled vomit like that.

In the Meyers Gallery a uniformed policeman stood in the doorway with a bored look on his face, but, Marianna del Massimo noted, his eyes rarely strayed from her or the Hopi woman as they worked. He was a large man with a comfortable paunch testing his shirt buttons, a lot of shiny leather, and a dully gleaming black pistol prominently perched in a hip holster. Probably in his fifties, thought Marianna. Named Weldon. Officer Weldon, an Anglo. Going nowhere fast in a police force dominated by Hispanics. She glanced blankly at him, then averted her eyes when he stared back. She studied one of Meyers's clever little drawings of a Northern Cheyenne umbilical fetish, dated "1870s?" It was a beaded object about five inches long, resembling a lizard with stumpy legs, no doubt taken from some dead warrior before it was buried with him. Along with the supposed date, there was a notation that read 250/1400, meaning price paid (the low one) and price sought (the high one), with the transaction confirmed by the underlining. The Meyers markup, Marianna thought, with a little awe at the dead man's gall. But on the other hand, it was an exquisite piece. Whoever had sold it to Meyers for only $250 was simply stupid.

"I can't find this fetish anywhere," she said.

Connie sighed. "Well, just put it in the pile. It may turn up later."

Marianna admired the placid single-mindedness with which the broad-shouldered young Hopi woman, seated behind Meyers's ornate desk, plowed through the files in silence, sorting, matching, checking things off on a long computerized list. She looked again at the Indian woman's face: strong eyebrows above the coal-black eyes. Those astounding high cheekbones, the wide, lipsticked mouth. Almost coarse, Marianna thought, and taken individually, the features of this Hopi face would be seen as coarse, perhaps. But they came together in an inexplicable harmony, even grace, the white woman thought.

The eyebrows knitted together in a straight line. "What about this one?" Connie held out another file.

"I've looked high and low for it," said Marianna.

"Okay. Missing." The file dropped onto a stack of folders about three inches high. "What a lot of stuff," Connie said to no one in particular. The phone rang and she picked it up. "Meyers Gallery. This is Connie Barnes speaking . . . Yeah, sure." She looked up. "It's for you."

"I'll take it in—" said Marianna, then thought better of it. She reached over the desk and took the receiver. "This is Marianna del . . . Oh, hi. Yes, we're getting there . . . No, no, that's fine. No problem. Seven-thirty . . . Oh, please." Marianna listened with a broad smile. "Nice. Beautiful. Thanks. Yes. Goodbye." She hung up the receiver and looked at Connie. "That's Nigel. He's a dear. You know, Nigel Calderwood, the tenor at the opera."

"I've never been to the opera here," Connie said.

"Oh, you should come some night. You'd love it. Nigel would take us backstage."

Connie smiled perfunctorily, and Officer Weldon shifted his weight from one foot to the other. The women went back to work, looking up a few minutes later from their tedious chores to see Sergeant Ramirez approaching, trailed by a man in a navy-blue windbreaker and a head of curly black hair. He was introduced—Special Agent Collins from the FBI—without explanation, and at his request Connie reviewed her system for him. The agent listened intently and scrutinized several samples of Meyers's drawings for a long time, looking from one to another.

"Can you show me the piece, the thing that goes with this?" he asked.

Connie reached behind her and presented the agent with an orange and black pottery bowl. The agent studied it with hawk-like attention, then the drawing.

"Neat," he said. "Neat."

He took a ballpoint pen from his shirt pocket and began to doodle on a piece of scrap paper on the desk, drawing some odd-shaped things that looked like gnarled sticks.

"Did you come across anything like this?"

The women bent over the drawing, and Connie quickly drew back and looked away.

"Nothing," said Marianna. "Nothing like that at all. What are they?"

"A long shot," the agent replied. "You're sure?"

"Positive. I've never seen anything like that. Not here in the gallery, nor anywhere else. How about you, Connie?"

The blood had run out of the Hopi woman's copper face. She looked off into the middle distance.

"I `. . . I don't think I should have seen them. Even a drawing."

The agent put his hand to his forehead. "Oh, jeez. Are you Hopi, Miss Barnes? Oh, jeez, I'm sorry."

"You couldn't have known," said Connie.

"I could've guessed," said the agent. He snatched the doodle off the desk and stuffed it in his windbreaker pocket. "Damn! I'm really sorry. But, well, can I ask you a question, I mean . . . ?"

Connie looked up at the agent and clasped her hands before her on the desk.

"I would know if I had ever seen things like these," she said. "Only the priests . . ."

"I am truly sorry," said the agent. "This is a lousy thing all around. I'm really sorry if I—"

"You were doing your job," Connie said. "It's all right."

A baffled Marianna followed the agent and Sergeant Ramirez to the entrance.

"What *are* those things?" she asked.

"Look," the agent said, "there's already enough trouble. If you don't know what they are, you don't need to. I'm sorry to, uh—that I can't be more responsive. But look, if you see anything like this, you tell the sergeant here right away, okay?" He turned and went through the doorway into the sunlight.

Marianna stood watching the door close and thought how strange that an archaic expression came so readily to mind: the agent from the FBI had fled in confusion.

Outside on the street in the sun, Larry Collins strode along in agitation beside the silent policeman, Ramirez.

"Christalmighty!" Collins burst out. "I didn't think for a minute that she was . . . I mean, she's gotta be six inches taller than any Hopi woman I ever saw. Christ, she's almost as tall as you and me."

"Almost," said Sergeant Ramirez quietly, as he tried to memorize the exact sequence of words, the precise flow of information and noninformation in the conversation he had just heard. It struck him that the slender Anglo woman, widow of the supposed Italian sportsman and assistant manager of the dead man's gallery, had said that she had never seen anything like the objects the agent had drawn on the little scrap of paper. But Connie, the insurance company's appraiser, the friend of his friend, Mo Bowdre . . . perhaps in the emotion of the moment—she clearly was not supposed to see such objects, so complex is the religion of these Indians—she had not explicitly made such a denial. Ramirez filed away this perhaps accidental, perhaps perfectly innocent and explainable part of a pattern he was sure would emerge in due course. The slender woman with black hair, so fine, so delicate, the black eyes so deep, stuck in his mind. He shook himself back into the present.

"She is very big for a Hopi woman," said Ramirez. "Very tall. I should have told you. I wish I had thought of it."

The agent shrugged and Ramirez thought how strange a man this agent was, this special agent of the FBI. He was like static on the radio.

It was noon and the sun had burned through some high-altitude hazy clouds, leaving only a great white bank of moisture lurking around the top of San Francisco Peaks. The air was crisp and cool, and despite such beneficence on the part of nature, Willie Blaine was fed up. He couldn't stand it when his wife—whom he alternately thought of as a slatternly anchor around his neck, and as the one person in the world without whom he could not manage yet another day—shrieked at him. Crying, sniveling, moping? He could take all that bullshit, but the shrieking . . . He couldn't hack it. He always compromised when she shrieked, and then felt deballed.

God *damn*, had she ever shrieked when he ignored the first exit to Flagstaff and kept his foot to the floor while the old Ford shitforbrains pickup had humped it up the incline. So he had taken the next Flagstaff exit and came to a stop in an illegal parking space on the main drag and slowly he had turned to her and said, "This is bullshit, you know that, don't you?"

Cheryl responded with a snivel. Little Billy stirred in her lap and whimpered.

Jesusfucking A. Christ, Willie fumed to himself.

"You're not going to do this, Cheryl," he said.

"We're staying here," his wife said. "We don't need this."

"Whattaya mean, you're staying here?" Willie shouted. "Where? On the street? What do *I* do in the meantime? Whattaya think I'm thinking about all this, huh, Cheryl? Talk to me, for chrissakes."

So they had limped off to one of the countless cheap motels along the strip in Flagstaff and hunkered down for the rest of the day and the night, with Cheryl reluctantly, finally, letting her husband put his arm clumsily over her shoulders while little Billy breathed fitfully beside her, the whole damn family together, lying in the inefficiently air-conditioned room with the curtains firmly and thickly drawn against the night. Outside, engines revved, and semis rumbled by, and Indians and other flotsam wobbled past on drunken and long-forgotten missions. Willie, fitful and awake, alert to the intrusive noises of the world, pessimistically calculated the value and potential of his cargo out there, wrapped in plastic in the bed of his pickup, reckoning that no motherfucker would think to look under the sand, especially when Cheryl's goddamned bureau that had been her mother's and all that other crap was piled up on top of it.

And of course, as soon as he awoke, sweating and filled to his eyeballs with a headache, Willie Blaine ran right back into the buzz saw. There was Cheryl, sitting at the crummy little table about two feet from his pounding temples, with that pinched look on her face, saying, "I've called Charlene. Billy and me, we're going there."

Willie hated to wake up first thing in the morning with his wife with her mind all made up on some goddamned thing or another. It took him two hours even before he ate anything to talk her out of it. Having won, he finally stalked out, talking about reading the goddamned newspaper, and he hunched over a greasy fried egg and some overdone home fries, nervously turning the pages of the early edition of the Arizona *Republic*, looking for news maybe from Santa Fe.

Anyway, it was about noon, with a big white cloud hanging onto San Francisco Peaks just north of Flagstaff, when Willie impatiently waited for his wife to hoist herself up into the cab of his pickup.

"You really think you've got something this time?"

"No doubt about it. We're goin' to L.A., and they ain't seen nothing like this yet. All aboard."

The well-eroded gears whizzed and clunked ominously, but the old Ford pickup swung out of the parking lot.

Elsewhere in the lot, an engine started in a nondescript sedan and an officer of the law named Wilson, now more than a hundred miles outside his proper jurisdiction and assuming that he would get paid for this one way or another, said out loud, "Well, here we go again."

A few miles later, his quarry easily in sight two hundred yards ahead, Officer Wilson reached down for the radio transmitter to call his whereabouts in to Winslow.

"Charlie? The whole damn family is headed west out of Flagstaff. Do I tail him all the way to fucking California?"

The studio of T. Moore Bowdre was an old windowless mill house made not of adobe, but of stone, in the backyard of his place on Canyon Road. The mill house had once lain athwart the creek that runs down the canyon to this day, but its course had been altered two decades previously by a landscape designer, so Mo's studio was high and dry some ten feet from the tinkling passage of water over rock, which is supernal music in any arid land. Mo had enlarged the old north-facing door to facilitate the passage of large sculptures, but even with the door open, the studio was sunless and cool. A wren had taken up residence the past three years in a large and unkempt lilac bush outside the door, and Mo, while not in the slightest superstitious, nonetheless had come to connect this wren's song to his own creativity. When the wren sang his burbling song in harmony with the rippling of the creek, Mo could get to work. This morning the wren had been silent.

He put both his hands on the cold block of marble and, under its rough surface, sensed the tight directionality of its grain for what was it—the hundredth time? He remembered the golden eagle, perched on the post, wind ruffling its feathers, its body facing him, head turned sideways to cock one eye at him. He tried to feel the eagle in the block of marble—not, he thought, that there's an eagle in this rock. Not till I put it in there.

It was a meditative exercise, nothing more, no mystical crap about feeling the eagle already immanent in the stone. Just a kind of mind control, trying to transmit his notion of the eagle into the marble, the implacable perfection of its eye, the fierce curve of the beak. Mo sighed deeply, still caressing the marble, and was irritated. Distracted.

What the hell was he supposed to do with this Hopi "brother" of Connie's? This Darrel . . . Quanemptewa.

Something besides the intrusion bothered Mo, something about the kid. He couldn't retrieve it. He forced his mind back to the eagle, but it wasn't there. Gone again. He felt the familiar helplessness when Indians like Darrel simply turn up, basically lost, with nothing, no real plan, looking for work, looking for what? Sitting around silently, waiting for you to figure it out. Too polite, maybe too timid, to blurt it out, to simply ask. Talking around it endlessly. He wondered if that's what the Hopi men did, sit around all night waiting for the point of the gathering to emerge out of the silence and tangential comments.

Darrel *had* said he was looking for work in Santa Fe. Probably he wasn't looking for work. You want work, the kind he was probably up to, you go to Albuquerque, not Santa Fe. Well, Mo thought, that's uncharitable. Maybe the kid's a silversmith, a jeweler, looking for an outlet in one of the galleries. He felt badly: so many bedraggled, hopeful Indian craftsmen show up in the galleries, all nervous and hangdog, only to be turned away. He wished Connie was at home today, not down at that gallery. She'd take care of the kid, naturally enough, and he could concentrate on the eagle.

What *was* it about that Hopi kid that stuck just outside his mind?

There was a tap at the door.

"Come in," Mo said.

"It's me. Darrel."

"Yeah, come on in."

Mo heard the Hopi step into the mill house and go over to the big wooden bench where he kept his tools laid out in neat rows.

"Wow, these your tools, huh?"

"Right."

"They're really nice. Expensive, I guess, huh?"

"Not too bad."

"I carve kachina dolls," the Hopi said. "Some, you know. I sold a few."

"That's good," Mo said. "Traditional ones? Or those new jobs with the natural wood showing?"

"No, I don't like it that way. I do it the old way."

Mo shifted his weight from one leg to the other, getting impatient.

"That what you're doing here? Selling dolls?"

"I was thinkin' about it."

It was going to be a long day. In his mind's eye he saw his golden eagle languidly take wing and fly off, soon lost in the blue of the remembered oceanic sky.

Sunlight glowed through the two windows cut in the two-foot thick adobe walls of the office of Allen Templeton, attorney-at-law, and, had anyone been seated opposite him at his Taos-style, raw wood desk, the backlit lawyer would have appeared to be blessed with a halo. And had Templeton been aware of this iconic image, he would have smiled. On his desk before him was the last will and testament of Walter Meyers, a document he was familiar enough with, having drafted it only three months earlier, after one of Walt's incessant changes of mind. Meyers had seen fit to use his will as an instrument of revenge, to get even with whichever malefactor had crossed him at the moment. He had cut out of the will his only living relative, a nephew in Phoenix, and reinstated him through at least four cycles. Now, when it counted, the nephew was out. And while it would be months before the will was probated— and the circumstances of his death would obviously prolong matters even further—Templeton thought it appropriate to alert Walt's beneficiaries of the long arm of his influence, reaching out even beyond the grave. He punched out a number in the desk telephone, and asked the polite voice that answered if he could speak to Phillip Bleeker, please.

Phillip Bleeker was the director of the Wheelwright Museum across town, with one of the finest collections of southwestern Indian artifacts anywhere, an old and much honored collection. Long before the Indian pressure groups had set up a national hue and cry—the object being to bring their sacred objects and their skeletal remains home from such institutions—the Wheelwright had quietly begun returning certain objects to the local tribes, even setting up a kind of clinic, Templeton remembered, to help private collectors, afflicted with guilty consciences, to do the same. Templeton, whose attitudes about such matters had developed largely through his long association with Walter Meyers, thought that such concern was quaint. Also stupid.

"This is Phillip Bleeker."

Templeton explained that he believed it appropriate to alert the Wheelwright of a provision in Walter Meyers's will.

"Meyers! Oh, God."

"Mr. Bleeker, the man is deceased."

"Oh, yes, forgive me. . . ."

"To make matters brief and to the point," Templeton said, "I am sure you'll be delighted to know that Mr. Meyers felt strongly enough about the work of the Wheelwright to leave the museum his entire collection . . ."

There was a loud gasp.

". . . of Navajo medicine bundles. I believe there are about three hundred of them, mostly from the nineteenth century, though a few pieces are more recent."

"Jesus."

"Mr. Bleeker?"

"That son of a bitch," Bleeker said in measured and heartfelt tones.

"I beg your pardon?"

"Look here, Mr. Templeton, this museum has made a practice of returning things like that to the tribes. For ten years. We can't take these things. I mean, do we have to take these things? Goddamn it, this is outrageous."

"Well," Templeton said smoothly, "it is very difficult in this state to abrogate the wishes of a dead man as expressed in his will. And, of course, if the museum goes through the lengthy procedures of declining this bequest, then the material becomes the property of our beloved and efficient state government. I must say, Mr. Bleeker, this is the first time in my experience that someone has been unenthusiastic about such a bequest."

"Do you have any idea," Bleeker said, his voice rising, "what it costs in terms of staff time and money to repatriate things like this? Which of course we'll have to do. It's a matter of policy here at the museum."

"Well, of course, that's entirely up to you and your board of directors, what you do with my, ah, former client's generous bequest. I just thought you would like to hear about it promptly, Mr. Bleeker. I'll send you the precise details as soon as it's appropriate. Goodbye until then."

Templeton hung up and smiled broadly, still haloed by the sun. "All right, Walt," he said out loud. "Vengeance is yours."

While Allen Templeton, in his office across Santa Fe, set out to make three more calls, two of them out of state, to other beneficiaries of Walter Meyers's vindictive mind, Phillip

Bleeker stared at the receiver of his telephone as if it were an unexpected specimen of marine snail. Presently he put it down in its plastic cradle and buzzed the intercom.

"Verna," he said, feeling that something was sucking all the oxygen out of the air in his room.

"Yes?" said the intercom.

"Get me Claudia Peters in Denver, please." Bleeker touched the purple sugalite stone mounted in the silver clasp of his bolo tie, and breathed deeply. Seconds later the intercom buzzed and Bleeker picked up the phone.

"Claudia—" he began.

"I've got someone on the other line, Phillip. That man Meyers has—"

"You too?"

"It's sick. Sick," said Claudia Peters, chief curator of the Denver Museum of Natural History. "Call me back in ten minutes. Maybe there's something we can do."

Bleeker hung up and again the intercom buzzed.

"Mr. Bleeker," said Verna's voice. "There's a Mr. Collins here to see you. He says he's with the FBI. Shall I—"

"Have him come in, Verna," said Bleeker with a sigh.

He stood up and stepped around the desk as the curly-haired agent in a blue jacket and blue jeans entered, saying, "Mr. Bleeker, we talked on the phone a couple of months ago."

"Yes, I remember. About the Hopi deities. Still missing, I understand. Here, have a seat. What can I do for you today?"

The agent flopped down in a leather sling chair in front of Bleeker's desk and slung his ankle over his knee.

"I'm sorry to interrupt your day," he said. "I need you to tell me about Walter Meyers."

Bleeker sat down behind his desk and touched his fingers together before him.

"I didn't know him intimately, of course, but besides the fact, Mr. Collins, that Walt Meyers was an amoral, sociopathic, misbegotten bag of slime, what can I tell you?"

S i x

Sergeant Ramirez sat gloomily in a booth at Tiny's, staring past the salt crystals that lined the rim of his glass and into the lime-green margarita.

There was no particular word, no phrase, nothing specific he could put his finger on—just an overall . . . what? A cavalier manner. The old Anglo attitude was always there, especially among these second-generation or older New Mexico Anglos, like the lawyer Templeton. The Hispanic was treated as a functionary, not a person—a talking police uniform, not a man who was a police officer. How, Ramirez wondered, did such a man treat other Anglos of lesser standing? As functionaries too? It no longer produced any anger in the sergeant's gut, the way it had when he was younger, even when he was in the university, even in the graduate school, where there was an intangible condescension toward an Hispanic student of archeology—a kind of surprise that an Hispanic might be interested in such arcana, and in Indian arcana to boot. Hispanics were supposed to be a more or less self-centered group, a closed society, one of the Three Cultures of Nueva Mexico that coexist but never really meet.

Once out of the intrusively rationalist and materialist world of archeological science, however, and into the physically dangerous life of law enforcement, Ramirez had drifted back into his family's world, a world of emotion and faith. He had found himself eyeing the old familiar *santos* in the niches and mantels of his mother's home, the wooden, painted saints to whom she prayed for guidance and direct, practical assistance. She would pray to San Lorenzo, with his palm and chalice, to look out for her little patch of vegetables in the month of August. She would pray to San Antonio de Padua, embodied in her house by a tiny statue wearing the blue robe of the Franciscans, tonsured and clean-shaven, to help her find lost articles, even lost animals, like the time when the young burro she kept in the backyard for no purpose disappeared for three days—and then returned.

Ramirez had come to find this practice not entirely silly, even calming, habit-forming. The santos and the rituals and the gradual reenveloping of himself in at least some of the trappings of an old faith served to rid him of the anger or despair one logically felt as a constant witness to humankind's slurs on one another—and worse.

He didn't know which santo was authorized to come to the aid of detectives, so, sitting at the booth in Tiny's waiting for the wild agent from the FBI, he contented himself with an unspoken conversation with San Antonio de Padua. Presumably a pattern in events could become mislaid as easily as a hammer or a burro.

Ramirez's conversation with the saint ended abruptly when Larry Collins appeared at the door, peering with sunstruck eyes into the room. He spotted Ramirez and approached the booth.

"So what'd you find at the lawyer's?" he asked, sliding into the seat opposite Ramirez. "I think I'll have one of those. Looks good."

"I didn't know they let federal agents drink," said Ramirez with a straight face.

"You mean there's booze in that thing?" Collins said with a mock grin that revealed his crooked front teeth. "It looks like a green Shirley Temple." The white-haired Emma approached, and Collins said, "I'll have one of those. What the hell! So what did you find? The will, right? Tell me about it."

Ramirez reached under the table and lifted a leather case to his seat. "I've got a copy here for you. To begin with, he left four large groups of artifacts from his collections at the gallery to four museums, one of them here in town. All four museums are leaders in repatriating ceremonial stuff to the Indians. He left them all collections of really sacred stuff. It's about the nastiest thing he could do to them. It takes a lot of work, a lot of tact, time, even money, to get this stuff back in the proper hands."

"Why?"

"Indians are complicated."

"No, why them? Why these four museums?"

"The lawyer finally let it out that curators at these four museums had tried recently to have his ass, you know, bad-mouthed Meyers publicly, tried to help get him on illegal possession, that sort of thing. So he got his revenge, is what the lawyer called it."

"Cute," observed the agent. "Well, that's true to type." He thanked Emma as she carefully placed a wide goblet on the table before him and watched as he took a sip. He nodded. "Hey, there really is booze in here. Jeez, don't tell anyone." He looked around the room as Emma slid away. "What about heirs?"

"There was one heir," said Ramirez. "A nephew in Phoenix. A kind of latter-day hippie, hangs around those city-Indian gurus doing sweat lodges and all that crap. The will cuts him off at the knees. Not a thing. Not a cent."

"So what happens to all this guy's stuff, his gallery, his bank account? His gallery must be worth a fortune."

"The will says that Templeton, the lawyer, is to sell the gallery for the highest price he can get, the proceeds to be split one-tenth to him, and nine-tenths to—get this—America First, that group in Louisiana."

"Those white racist bastards? We're gonna have them out of business and half of 'em in jail in a couple of years, max."

Ramirez shrugged and went on. "But before that happens, you know, before they put the place up for public sale, there is an option to buy it for five million dollars, if the deal can be pulled off within six months after his death."

"An option? Who, what? Like a contract with someone?"

"No," said Ramirez. "It just says in all the right gobbledegook that if Marianna del Massimo can come up with the five mill in six months, and thinks the place is worth that much, it's hers. Templeton still gets his ten percent, and the kooks get the rest of the estate."

"So *there*'s a powerful little mix of motivation for you, huh, Tony? Christ, you need a computer just to add up the figures."

The door to Tiny's opened and was immediately filled with the frame of Mo Bowdre, who stepped inside and paused. Emma smartly detoured from a mission and whispered in his ear. Mo grinned and set forth in a direct line for the booth where Collins and Ramirez sat.

"Hey, Mo," said Ramirez. "Where's Connie?"

"I've been baby-sitting a twenty-year-old, down-in-the-mouth, out-of-work Hopi since this morning, and I need a drink. I deserve a drink. Connie is at home with him now and they're jabbering in Hopi, and that makes me feel left out—hah—hah—hah—so I will need two drinks. And no doubt your gloomy meditations on crime and the blackness of the human soul will give me an excuse for a third. Where should I sit?"

"Over there, next to Larry Collins, FBI. He's interested in the Meyers murder too. We're working together."

"Glad to meet you," Mo said, sitting down next to the agent. "Sounds serious."

"Did you know this guy Meyers?" the agent asked.

"Old New York, huh?" Mo said. "Yeah, I knew him. A little twerp. What's your interest in him?"

Ramirez nodded, and the agent briefly explained about the stolen Hopi dieties, while Mo sat motionless except to smile broadly at Emma when she put his beer on the table. When the agent was finished, Ramirez asked Mo, "You ever hear of those things?" Turning to the agent, he said, "Mo here is shacked up . . . living, with a Hopi. You know, Connie Barnes, the one over at the gallery."

"Christ," said Collins. "Small world you got here."

"Almost to the point of being stuffy," Mo said with a satisfied grin.

"A little bit small-town here for you?" asked Collins.

Mo shifted his bulk so as to face the agent, the opaque glasses fixed on him.

"Let me explain something to you," he said. "This is just about the only place in the world where someone like me can be what I want to be. Here I'm even what you might call a celebrity. Right, Tony? A weirdo who's allowed some pride, allowed to invent himself every day. If I was in New York—hah—hah—I'd be just another blind man tapping my way around the sidewalks. No, I like it here."

Collins stared for a moment at the dark glasses facing him. "Huh," he said presently and looked away.

Ramirez wondered if these two strange men were going to have a fight of some sort, or honor each other in the manner of two equally matched bulls. "What exactly do you want to know about Meyers?" he asked the agent.

"Okay, the guy had this reputation for dealing in stolen stuff, but he obviously wouldn't keep it on display there in his store, gallery, whatever. He'd have it somewhere else, some stash. I mean, they're not going to find anything over there in the gallery, those women. But the guy is a fanatic record-keeper, you know, all those little drawings he did for the record. Would he have done the same sort of thing for his illegal stuff? I mean, how compulsive was the guy? See, if he was compulsive, and he did have those deities stashed somewhere, then he might have a record, and maybe we can find that, and then maybe we can find the deities."

"That's a hell of a lot of contingency," Mo said. "Is your life always this, uh, subjunctive?"

The agent looked at him. "Hey, if I wasn't doing this, I might be just another fed, chasing bad checks around the sidewalks of New York."

Mo smiled broadly through his blond beard. "Meyers was as compulsive as they come. He probably counted the socks in his drawer every day when he was a kid. You know he started as an archeologist?"

Sergeant Ramirez raised his eyebrows.

"Yeah," Collins said. "With the Park Service. And what's interesting is that in the early seventies, he was detailed to the Hopi reservation to help them restore some old buildings for the bicentennial. He was out there for almost three years digging around."

"And," Mo interrupted, "since we're dealing with contingencies here, that might be the time when Walt Meyers learned about these deities, found out maybe where the Hopis kept them—they usually stow this sort of thing in some out-of-the-way shrine in the desert or the cliffs, whatever. So we can assume, maybe, that this is when the rich possibilities of a life of crime became a twinkle in his beady eyes."

"He quit the Park Service in 1977," Collins said.

"And opened his creepy gallery two, three years later," Mo added.

"So why," Ramirez asked, "would he wait almost fifteen years to grab these deities if they're so valuable? That is, if any of this crap is true."

"You've got to watch out for retired archeologists—hah—hah. Okay, he'd bet that no one else would find them, steal them. He'd need to develop his markets, his contacts, selling minor league stuff, then major league—"

"It's simpler than that," the agent interrupted. "Another set of these things was taken in 1978. Disappeared. It took the Hopis a couple years to ask for help from the cops, then us. We traced 'em here, there, finally to a gallery in Chicago, never could pin anything down. They vanished. We heard they got sold out of the country for seventy-five thousand dollars. If this guy Meyers was as smart as he was greedy, he'd want to wait—let things cool down, but at the same time let prices go up."

Ramirez leaned forward. "Problem. If the Hopis had already lost one set of these things, would they leave another set in some place in the desert where someone might find them? I mean, wouldn't they put 'em in a safe or something?"

"You'd think so," said the agent. "But they didn't. It was a different Hopi village, even a different mesa. All three mesas out there have got some real differences."

"And," Mo said, "tradition is tradition. If these weren't the most tradition-bound people on the continent, you guys wouldn't be chasing around the landscape after a bunch of deities. It's time for my second beer. Anyone want to join me?"

"You're really heroic, doing all this," Marianna del Massimo said as the two women stood outside the Meyers Gallery in the late afternoon sun. The stucco walls of the gallery glowed a reddish-brown, and a light breeze ruffled the leaves of a lilac bush that grew in a small garden near the entrance. Next door, several groups of people with various handsomely printed shopping bags at their feet sat at small metal tables on an outdoor patio, drinking margaritas. "I realize that you don't feel the same way about these things. . . ."

Connie shrugged wistfully and struggled to hold back the tears that suddenly welled up.

"It's got to be done," she said, and turned to leave. "I'll see you tomorrow. We'll probably be able to finish it up."

Marianna's condominium apartment was in a large complex on Bishop's Lodge Road, past the turnoff to the mountains, and by the time she arrived there, an incipient headache had turned into an eye-pulsing nightmare. Once inside, she took four buffered aspirin tablets, remembered to call Nigel Calderwood and beg off dinner with the tenor, and laid down on a sofa in agony.

She awoke with a gasp, not knowing for a moment where she was, then turned on the light on the end table. Her headache was gone, the only trace of it being a sour feeling in her skull. She collected her shoes from the floor and headed for the luxuriously tiled bathroom where, her clothes in a heap on the floor, she permitted herself a flagrantly long hot shower, emerging fifteen minutes later with a craving for something sweet.

Ice cream.

She hadn't had an ice cream cone for years. Scrubbing herself with an ample, pleasantly coarse towel, she darted into the bedroom and looked at her alarm clock. Ten-thirty—just enough time. Hastily dressing in slacks and a sweater, she bolted out of her apartment and to her car, and drove to the plaza, arriving in front of the Häagen-Dazs ice cream parlor on the plaza a few minutes before eleven. The plaza was largely deserted, all its other storefronts dark. She stepped out of the car and went in, returning to her car a moment later with two scoops of chocolate almond swirl in a sugar cone—pure heaven. She got in her car and sat, licking the ice cream eagerly, feeling restored and, at the same time, pleasingly illicit. She watched idly as the young man in the ice cream store locked the door and receded into the back of the store, the lights going out a moment later. Time to go, she thought, and put the key in the ignition, and her car flooded with light.

Two high-beam headlights blazed in her face, reflected from the rearview mirror, and she intuitively hit the button that electronically locked her car doors with a loud click. The truck—for that is what it had to be—was pulled up only inches away from her rear bumper. Where had it come from? Marianna asked herself, the icy tentacles of panic snaking into her innards. She could hear its engine idling, then she startled as the driver of the truck revved the engine, a low threatening rumble. No muffler. Kids maybe, fooling around. But the glands rejected this: Marianna, breathless, her chest tight, turned the ignition key, wondering what to do with her damned ice cream cone. She couldn't open the window to throw it out, not with a truck full of rapists right behind her . . .

There was a crunch of metal and her car lurched, her head snapped back. Marianna shrieked and the ice cream cone fell on the floor. She sensed a man near the rear of her car. Her engine stalled, and she reflexively hit the lock button again. It clicked dully and Marianna turned the ignition key. She heard the door of the truck slam as she pressed down on the accelerator and fishtailed away from the curb.

She hit the brakes to make the turn at the end of the plaza, and the truck roared up on her tail. She pulled the wheel to the left, too far, and the car leapt and plummeted over the curb, glancing off a lamppost as it thumped back onto the street. The truck swung around the corner on her tail again, and she looked down the street, out to Bishop's Lodge Road and—no, no way . . . She screeched into another left turn on the plaza, desperately searching for signs of life, practically blinded by the headlights and by tears of panic. No one in sight.

She slowed for the next turn and the truck rammed her again and Marianna shrieked. Blindly, she made the turn and glimpsed a man walking near a tree in the plaza's parklike center. She fumbled with the button that lowered the window, felt a rush of air as it opened, and yelled: "Help! Jesus, help! Call the police!"

The man paid no attention as she hurtled by, the nightmare

truck on her tail, its engine roaring maniacally. Another turn. I've got to stay on the plaza, she said to herself, stay in the open. The truck rammed her again, and again she cried out. Another turn. Marianna was sobbing, gasping for breath, and saw a couple emerge from a doorway onto the sidewalk.

"Help! For Christ's sake, call the police!" She headed into the next turn, saying "Oh God, oh God," and floored it, gaining some room, hit the brakes, swerved around the next turn, again and again, she couldn't count, the truck gaining, then falling behind, until she thought she couldn't keep it up. She saw the glow of a red light from a side street before she heard the siren, and looked up to find no headlights' glare in her mirror.

It was gone.

She let her car slow to a stop and put her hands over her face, shuddering violently.

When she looked up, a uniformed policeman was approaching her through the flashing red light from his squad car.

"Oh, officer!"

"Ma'am? You all right?"

She nodded.

"You want to turn your engine off, ma'am?" She did so, as another police car pulled up behind her. She heard the door open and the officer say, "Sergeant." Sergeant Ramirez appeared beside her car.

"Miz del Massimo? You okay? You're not injured, are you?"

"No."

"You want to just rest there for a while before we talk?"

"No," she said, breathing more easily. "It's okay." She described the appearance of the truck behind her, the chase, the disappearance of the truck. "It's like a nightmare," she ended, weakly. "I think I'd like to get out."

Ramirez reached down to open the door. "It's locked," he said. Marianna hit the button and Ramirez opened the door. "The rear end and the left-hand side of your car, pretty badly banged up," he said. "That's why I wondered if you'd been injured."

Marianna walked around the back of the car and looked at the severely dented and scraped metal. The rear fender was torn and folded backward; its edge had sliced a shallow groove in the tire, which was almost totally flat.

"My God," she said, shaking.

"I'll take you home, Miz del Massimo." He went over to the cop and they spoke for a moment, the cop nodding, getting in his car, while Ramirez returned to her side. "They'll take care of the car, get it to a garage."

Marianna thanked him, and, his hand lightly holding her elbow, he ushered her over to his car and opened the door. She told him where she lived and they drove out of the empty plaza in silence. He pulled up outside the apartment complex on Bishop's Lodge Road and shut off his engine.

"I'm afraid I should ask you a few questions."

"Of course. Can we go in?"

"Yes, ma'am."

When she had turned the key in the lock of her door, Ramirez said, "Here, let me," and preceded her into the apartment. Marianna was suddenly cold with the thought that the chase might not be over. "There'll be an officer here in a few minutes," said Ramirez quietly. "She'll watch the place tonight. Just a precaution."

"I think I'm going to have a drink."

"Good idea. Settle your nerves."

"You?"

"No, ma'am."

Marianna poured herself a scotch, neat, from a decanter, took a small sip, and sat down on the sofa, her elbows on her knees, huddled like a refugee. Ramirez sat opposite her in an easy chair, wondering if her glass contained Old Sheep Dip.

"Did you get a look at the truck, Miz del Massimo?" he asked.

"No . . . I . . . just the headlights, I couldn't really see . . . I think it was light-colored, maybe white. No muffler. I just . . ."

"Of course."

"I think there were two of them. I think one of them got out of the truck and then got back in when I started my car."

"You didn't get a look at him?"

"No, I'm sorry."

"You didn't see what direction they went in?"

"No, no, they just vanished. They were gone as suddenly as they showed up. Like a ghost, like a dream." She shuddered, and took another sip of scotch. "I'm sorry."

"Don't be," said Ramirez. "It's a terrible experience. You did good, just keeping away from them."

"I panicked," Marianna said. "I realize I should simply have driven to the police station instead of . . ."

"Well, that might have worked," said Ramirez with a slight grin. "But you did good." There was a tap at the door. Ramirez stood up. "We'll put out an alert. Light-colored truck, two guys in it. You never know." He crossed to the door and let a uniformed officer in, introduced her to Marianna and said, "She'll be out here. Don't worry. Try to get some sleep. We can talk again tomorrow."

"Thank you, Sergeant."

"Can I ask you one more question?"

"Yes, of course."

"You did real good there, keeping away from that truck as much as you did."

"Oh, I see," Marianna said. "Yes, my husband taught me to drive. He raced cars. In Europe."

Ramirez smiled and said, "Good night, Miz del Massimo. I hope you get some rest."

Mo Bowdre had turned down the offers for a ride home from Tiny's. Instead, he walked the long familiar route that took him through residential streets and alleys and finally up the incline of Canyon Road to his wooden gate. He smelled the night smells, lilacs, fruit-tree blossoms, auto exhaust, and listened to the sounds—TVs and clattering dishes from the houses, the occasional far-off siren, the low rumble of cars juiced up to provide more than mere transport, the fragments of family squabbles. His head began to ache, instant hangover from too much beer, the price of living through that damned explosion maybe. He made a conscious effort to avert his mind.

He thought of Walter Meyers, imagining him crumpled on the tile floor. He thought how fragile a life is, how easily . . .

He wondered why he was so damn curious about Meyers's death—which in fact was none of his business. Sculpture was his business, and he hadn't done anything about it for days now except to oversee the casting of those horses down at the foundry while that reporter woman asked him dumb questions.

Without feeling sorry for him in the slightest, Mo pondered the chilly loneliness of Meyers's existence, summed up in his will. Ramirez had told him about it. Except for his pathetic vengeance on four museums, there was nothing to do with his entire life's work except to sell it off and give the money to some bunch of political kooks. Maybe the kooks were running out of money; maybe *they* did it. More than likely, Mo thought, that wild hair of an FBI agent was right. Meyers probably had been involved with those Hopi deities, though nobody could prove it. That would be a perfectly good reason to step on that crooked little insect. Someone trying to get them back. A Hopi? Somehow that didn't sound right. Someone who was in the loop and realized he had been screwed, that Meyers would make the big dough? Like the guy in Phoenix that Collins had talked about—bought himself a $27,000 pickup for cash, which was about ten percent of what Collins said the things might be worth. But of course the guy in Phoenix was dead too. The one in Winslow, the ex-coach, apparently headed for California with the FBI on his tail? Collins had seemed nervous about that, about not personally watching the ex-coach.

Who else? Maybe someone out of the loop altogether, someone who wanted to get into the loop. The del Massimo woman? He couldn't imagine her splitting open somebody's skull . . . but on the other hand, if she got those things and sold them, there would be most of the down payment on Meyers's gallery. On the other hand, Ramirez said she was accounted for that night. . . . Well, the hell with it, Mo thought. I'm an artist, not a damn detective.

But it stuck in his mind, like a chigger under his belt, and he kept turning it over and over until he reached his front gate, and remembered that the Hopi kid, Darrel, was no doubt there.

The Hopi kid was there, Mo discovered when he entered the house, but asleep on the sofa, his breathing quiet and regular. Mo tiptoed into the kitchen, took an apple from the bowl on the table and bit into it, thinking how lousy out-of-season, imported apples were. He proceeded silently down the hall and into his bedroom, reaching out to feel the light switch on the wall and noting that it was off.

"Hi, Mo," said Connie. "Did you eat?"

"Tiny's finest, plus this plastic apple. You've had a long day."

"Yes."

"So what's up with Darrel?"

"He's lost. Confused." Mo heard her roll over in the bed. "He says my mother told him to tell me to come home."

Mo felt dismay sweep over him like cold sleet.

"Home? What for?"

"There's trouble in the village. You know. Disagreement, gossip, arguments."

"There's been that kind of trouble in the village for a thousand years," Mo said.

"It's over those . . . uh, those things. Arguments."

Outside, a siren sounded distantly in the night. Mo sat on the bed and asked, "Is this a good time to—"

"I'm wide awake," Connie said.

Mo thought about the fractious Hopi, always some kind of esoteric disputation under way. He had heard how even Robert Redford ran into a buzz saw trying to film some novel out there. A bunch of traditionalists had tried to put a stop to it.

"Traditional versus progressive?" he asked.

"That's part of it. The old priests say they can't do the initiations without those things. The young ones want to do them anyway. But it's worse. Two clans. Each one is accusing the other, that one of their members stole those things. It's very bitter and a lot of bad stuff is happening. . . . My mother wants me there . . . for support. You know, moral support."

"Witchcraft?"

"Well, that always can be a part of these things."

"Now, let me guess here," said Mo. "Your clan is one of the two." Connie was silent. "And Darrel here is one of the guys who's under suspicion." More silence. Mo put his hand on the small of the woman's motionless back. "Well, that's just about the worst goddamned thing I can imagine."

"Yes. It is."

The night was shattered by the telephone ringing. "Jesus Christ!" said Mo, disgusted, and picked it up. "Hello?" he roared. "Oh. Oh. Hold on a minute. I'll see if she's awake."

He whispered, "It's Marianna del Massimo. You awake for her?"

"I'll take it," Connie said, and Mo headed for the bathroom.

When he emerged a few moments later, Connie told him about the wild chase in the plaza. He whistled tunelessly and said, "Well, it looks like someone thinks she's got those things."

"Oh, Mo, that couldn't be. She wouldn't—"

"Why not?"

"Probably it was just a bunch of drunks out on a—"

"That's one explanation, of course. Well, old Ramirez'll figure it out. Him and that crazy rocket-powered FBI agent. So what about your going home?"

"Marianna said she'd be at the gallery early. We can finish up tomorrow afternoon, I think."

"Well, that's fine. Just fine. I'll pack our things while you're at work and we can be there by midnight."

"Oh, Mo, you don't—"

"I need a break, woman. This sophisticated city life is getting me down. Creative juices as dried up as a witch's . . . whoops. You're smiling, aren't you?" He stood up and began to undress.

"You know," he said, "that's the only thing in the whole damn world I miss not being able to see."

S e v e n

So everybody's heading west all of a sudden, Sergeant Ramirez thought to himself, leaving me here to find the phantom of the gallery. Mo and Connie were off that night to Hopiland on some kind of "family business." Right after Connie finishes up her report, Mo had said.

"And it'll probably surprise the hell out of you, Tony," Mo had said on the phone that morning. "Hah—hah. It doesn't appear to have been much of a burglary. One or two things are missing, or at least they found records but no objects. Nothing particularly valuable got ripped off. Lotta stuff got wrecked, of course. You know that. Connie says that a bunch of stuff they thought was missing turned up—he'd moved it into his apartment in the back. Probably stuff he wanted to fondle. You know, that guy was as weird as a snake with three ends. Say, what d'you make of all that stuff with Her Eyetalian Highness last night? Think it was just your garden-variety random violence and mayhem?"

Ramirez had not answered. Instead he had asked, "How long you gonna be on the rez?"

"Hell, I don't know. Long as it takes."

Ramirez was silent. Then he said, "I cleared up one mystery around here."

"Congratulations. What?"

"Miz del Massimo *was* married to a racing car driver."

"How did you—"

"Superior detective work, what else?" said Ramirez. "Have a safe journey." He hung up.

Shortly after that conversation, Larry Collins had slid into Ramirez's little cubicle of an office and flopped down on the metal chair.

"Well, I'm off," he said.

"Off?"

"To Sedona."

"Sedona, Arizona?"

"Yeah, greatest little resort town in northern Arizona. That schmuck Blaine, he got all the way to Kingman, made a phone call, and then headed back east. He's hunkered down in Sedona, prowling around. He's up to *something*, and he's the only live lead I got these days, so I'm gonna go and scare some more shit out of him. You know what I'm looking for here, right?"

Ramirez did, and so he was now standing in the small apartment behind the Walter Meyers Gallery, studying the walls and the bookcases, the floors, the niches, looking for something he might have overlooked before, or more likely for something that had never existed.

Collins apparently didn't think that the woman in the gallery office, working with Connie Barnes, constituted a live lead. But it would explain a lot . . . if he could only imagine that slender and seemingly fragile woman bringing some kind of implement down hard enough on a man's head to split it open. She didn't seem the type. On the other hand, she sure as hell could drive a car. But not fast enough to get from Café des Artistes to the Meyers Gallery in minus an hour from the time she left the restaurant.

Ramirez studied the lines of grout between the orange Mexican tiles of Meyers's floor, knowing it was a waste of effort, just like most of the time a graduate student might spend pottering around some well-worked archeological site. The likelihood of there being some hidden crack, some spring device, some secret cache with all the evidence . . . but nothing ventured, nothing found, he thought to himself. Ramirez felt stupid, but he continued his examination, trying to look with fresh eyes.

"It's beautiful, isn't it?"

"What, what?" said Willie Blaine, wrenching himself from an important train of thought.

"The light. On those rocks. It's so . . . red."

Willie looked at his wife Cheryl and followed her gaze to the towering mesa a half mile off, which the late afternoon sun had lit like a Chinese lantern. It was called Cathedral Rock, one of the many huge red buttes and mesas for which Sedona was renowned—red rock country. Willie could remember driving through Sedona years ago when it was nothing but a few corny western-type geegaw stores along a short strip of road running beside Oak Creek, but now it was Ree-fucking-zort City, full of probably a million fat-assed tourists and retired geezers trying to look healthy.

Houses were creeping up the sides of all the red rock mesas, and Willie, who considered himself a wilderness buff even though he hated most things that crept or crawled, thought that maybe if they put cyanide in the drinking water, they could get rid of all these people and the place would be beautiful again. Pretty soon, he thought to himself indignantly, they'll put a goddamned tennis spa on top of Cathedral Rock. Or maybe they'll let the weirdos build a church on it.

For those of a mystical bent of mind, Cathedral Rock already had what might be thought of as ecclesiastic standing, being one of Sedona's seven power centers, or vortices, from which concentrated cosmic forces are said to be emitted in ever-widening concentric rings, bringing peace to the world. Sitting in the park along Oak Creek that afternoon, Willie had seen several obvious fruit-loops making their way along a trail on the other side of the creek, earnest pilgrims to the vortex, and his mind had filled with derision.

He was bored, impatient. He hated just waiting around.

"It's like there's a light inside it," said Cheryl, and Willie looked over at her, both charmed and irritated with her child-like appreciation.

"It's the sun, shining sideways through all the atmosphere. Takes the blue light out and leaves red. So what d'you think red light is gonna do to red rocks? Turn 'em green?"

"It's beautiful," said Cheryl dreamily, her face burnished gold by the same atmospheric physics. Nearby, the light gleamed and dazzled in the ripples of Oak Creek, which slid calmly by in near silence. Willie eyed his wife with interest. Billy was asleep in the cab of the pickup some fifty yards away.

"We could do it," he said.

"Huh?"

"Right here. Now."

Cheryl, who had hiked the skirt of her blue dress up over her knees as they sat on the sandy bank of the creek, tugged it down. "Willie, this is a public park."

"But we're the only ones here."

"What about those people who've been walking by over there? They'll come back."

"Nah, they're over there at that big rock, praying, watching for the moon, jerking off, who knows?"

Cheryl giggled and Willie nuzzled her neck.

"Willie," she protested.

A hundred yards downstream, in a willow thicket along the creek's edge, a recently hired recruit to the ranks of the FBI observed Willie and his wife through a pair of binoculars. He had replaced the "off-duty" cop from Winslow that morning. Voyeuristically, he watched Willie press his wife down onto her back and put his hand on her upraised knee. He saw Willie startle violently and swivel his head to look across the creek. The agent swung his glasses and saw two women standing on the opposite bank of the creek, holding hands, staring at Willie and his wife. Lowering his glasses to take in the entire tableau, the agent saw Willie leap to his feet and shake his fists at the two women, who turned and fled behind some boulders along the trail. Willie's wife was by now on her feet, heading for their truck. Willie turned and raised his arms, face to the sky, hands outstretched in the universal gesture of those who feel the entire burden of an unjust universe.

The agent ducked back into the willow thicket and headed for his car, praying that Agent Collins would arrive soon and relieve him. This was not at all the sort of thing he had had in mind when he joined the FBI.

The headlights of the truck picked up fractured yellow cliffs as Connie guided it down the steep incline into Keams Canyon, home of the Bureau of Indian Affairs' Hopi Agency. She could see a few house lights below and to her right. Mo was sitting erect as a ramrod in the seat, but she knew he was dozing. They had managed to get an early start, and so they had reached this eastern end of the reservation by nine o'clock, hurtling along the highway through the Navajo lands west of Gallup. Connie shared the uneasy feeling most Hopi have when driving through Navajo country, particularly at night. Several centuries of resentment between the two tribes underlay much of this sentiment, disputes over the use of the land, as well as sheer cultural differences, all of which made getting along an uneasy proposition at best. But with that peculiar empathy that grows up for barely tolerated neighbors, many Hopis were infected by the Navajos' fear of the night. On Navajo land, at least, the night was full of hostile shades, witches, wolfmen, danger, and while these phenomena were not part of the Hopi demonology, the Hopis respected them enough to fear them.

Ahead, west of Keams Canyon, lay more familiar devils. Connie eased the truck into the intersection and turned west, accelerating slowly.

"It's okay, I'm awake," said Mo. "Keams Canyon, huh? You made good time."

"No more," said Connie. "The Hopi cops are real tough on speeders." To the west she could see lightning flashing in the utterly black, starless sky.

"Thunder out there," said Mo.

The flashes of lightning on what would have been the horizon grew brighter, more frequent, as they headed west through the night along Route 264, the two-lane road that winds through the mesas that define the center of the Hopi homeland.

Ten minutes later Connie noticed that there were no lights where they should be, sprinkled around the bottom of First Mesa: the town of Polacca was dark. The storm had taken out the power, always a fragile system at best. High up on First Mesa, where the ancient village of Walpi brooded, a place where there was no electricity, she noted a couple of lights— Coleman lamps, the traditional people winning out in the storm. The lightning ahead, maybe twenty miles off, rippled green in the night like northern lights gone mad.

"It looks like we're headed right into it," said Connie. Once abreast of Polacca, the truck lurched in a sudden shot of wind, and raindrops began striking the windshield. Connie put on the wipers, low, but they were soon overwhelmed by the heavily spattering rain and she turned them up. "It's going to get hard to see," she said.

"Want to pull over, wait it out?"

Connie shook her head, then said, "No."

She could hear the thunder now, over the sound of the engine, the rain and wind, and the frantic slapping of the windshield wipers. It was nearly a constant rumble, punctuated with louder cannon shots, and the lightning, much nearer, lit up one part of the sky or another at any moment. The truck rocked in the torrent of wind. Halfway across the flat desertland to Second Mesa, they plummeted into the heart of the storm and Connie jumped as a massive column of light erupted not more than twenty feet from the road with a throat-constricting crash.

"Jesus, *that* was close," said Mo.

"Right next to us."

Another violent stroke on the other side of the truck, green lights all around, a nearly continuous din, the metallic odor of ozone; the windshield mostly awash, the wipers providing only instants of vision; the truck shuddering; another titanic stroke, and another. Knuckles tight on the wheel, tight to aching.

"Damn storm had to choose the road, didn't it?" Mo shouted.

"If we keep going," Connie shouted back, "we'll be through it sooner."

"Long as you can see the road."

"I can see it enough."

The vicious pounding of earth continued, huge quadrants of the sky blazing, columns of light blasting the near desert as the truck began the long, curving ascent up Second Mesa. Every few yards water cascaded over the cliff in violent cataracts and poured across the highway and over the precipitous edge. By the time they had reached the top where the land flattens out, the lightning was behind them, the rain now just a constant and gentle patter on the windshield. Another few hundred yards and the rain too had stopped. Connie flipped off the wipers.

"Whew," she said.

"Tell me, was there any time back there when you were a bit—well, say scared?"

"The whole time. I'm still shaking. You?"

"It reminded me of the mine for a moment. Long time ago. That's a fairly unusual storm for this time of year, isn't it?"

"Very," said Connie, spotting the lights of the Hopi Cultural Center, the tribe's motel. Running the generator, Connie thought. "I've never seen a storm like that out here, so violent."

"Too much of a good thing," Mo mused.

"Those floods," said Connie. "They'll wash out a lot of corn-fields." She fell silent, considering the trials of her people. She could visualize the young corn plants, so green and fresh, planted four paces apart in the sandy dry washes, needing only a brief rain or two in the whole season—now being dug out and washed away by the torrents of water pouring over the sand. There was always something—not enough timely rain, too much, some unforeseeable event, something that seemed to spring from outside the prayers, from beyond the ceremonial round, something to try the patience of the people.

A few minutes later the lights of Kykotsmovi sparkled in the night about five miles ahead. Kykotsmovi, a relatively new village, part of the fallout from the now nearly legendary split at old Oraibi just after the turn of the century, when that ancient village fell asunder in two factions, a somber and not wholly explained period in Hopi history. In fact, a split with many explanations, none of them complete, behind which lurked the bitter mysteries of the secret priesthoods with their unknown ceremonies and their dimly perceived functions. The weight of those nearly century-old decisions still hung over the three villages of Third Mesa which had come about by a process of painful social meiosis.

Those old events, Connie thought, that she had heard bits and tatters of from her parents and grandparents and had read about in the anthropology books—somehow, she felt, they lay at the root of all of Hopi life, even her own life, even when she was in Santa Fe. Up there above Kykotsmovi, sulking on its finger of the mesa, the old village of Oraibi slowly shriveled from its former preeminence, one day perhaps to become another ruin in the landscape in the endless cycle of Hopi history.

"Welcome home," said Mo. "It's different, huh?"

"Everything's different here." She drove on in silence. "And as they say, always the same."

They swung into the road that led to the village, turned at the trading post and bounced along a dirt road to her mother's home, a two-story house her brothers had built for her some years ago, a place where she would have room to take care of their aging father, the widowed and now frail patriarch of the Eagle clan.

"Well, here we are."

"Glad to be home?"

"I'm always glad to be here," Connie said, "and I kind of dread it. You know?"

"I can guess," said Mo Bowdre, stepping out of the pickup and sniffing the piñon smoke in the air with a sense of contentment. A few semiferal dogs barked somewhere in the village. He was a welcome visitor here these last few years, with none of the problems, no responsibilities. For him it was easy. He stood by the truck until Connie came around and walked ahead of him to the door of her mother's house. She knocked and, as her mother's high nasal voice said, "Come in, come in," she opened the door and entered.

"Hi, Mom; hi, Grandpa," she said. Mo came in behind her. Her mother was seated at an oilcloth-covered table in the big kitchen, weaving strips of multicolored yucca into a round traylike plaque. A television set was on, a gray flickering—the late NBC news out of Flagstaff—and Connie's grandfather was watching it, half awake, seated in a worn old easy chair. He looked up and smiled, nodding his head happily.

"You're home, you're home," beamed Connie's mother, putting her yucca strips aside. Beaming even more, she said, "Oh, you brought Mo too."

"Hello, Melanie," boomed Mo. "Do I smell *na'quivi* over there on the stove? Hopi stew? Hah—hah—hah."

In his easy chair, the old man laughed in wheezes.

"Evening, Emory," said Mo.

"He's always hungry, Connie," said her mother. "Don't you feed him enough?" She laughed, a high giggle, as she got up from her chair and headed for the stove.

"Does he look like he's starving?"

Her mother Melanie laughed again. "Sit down, sit down," she said. "You've had a long drive. You must be tired."

Willie Blaine stood under the branches of a cottonwood tree in the dark, next to his tent. Overhead, the sky was flecked with diamond and a light breeze set the new cottonwood leaves to rattling gently. Willie heard Johnny Cash take his turn singing about reincarnation, some camper playing the tape deck. Willie thought about previous lives and those to come, figured not for the first time that it was bullshit, but a good song—here came Kristofferson's version—and decided one life was enough. He wished he didn't have to wait around so much for all these assholes. He wished he didn't have to wait around outside Sedona in a campground; the damn town had gotten so frigging chichi, he couldn't afford the cheapest motel. He wished this part of his life would hurry up and get over with so he could be rich in L.A., get himself a place near the ocean, drink rum drinks at noon while Cheryl toasted her fanny in the sun on the patio, start a new life—maybe a little gallery, something, a little movie production company, what the hell.

"Willie?"

It was his wife Cheryl, inside the tent, about to complain.

"Willie? I hate this."

Willie moved toward the tent's entrance flap.

"What do you hate, Cheryl?"

"Living in this tent. I can't find anything. It's uncomfortable." For a moment Willie thought of going in the tent and tying his wife up, hog-tying her, with a gag in her mouth. He swallowed and folded his arms over his chest.

"We're not *living* in a tent," he said. "We're just spending a night in a tent."

"Just one night?"

"Look, Cheryl, we gotta stay here until I get my call. Maybe one night, two nights."

"How are you gonna get a call in this campground? There's no phone here."

Jesus H. . . .

"Cheryl, for chrissakes, think. In the morning, I go to the pay phone at the gas station just down the *motherfucking* road about *two* goddamn miles and call, and if the guy isn't there, then I try again. Until the sonofabitch is there. Do you get the picture?"

There was silence from the tent.

"Cheryl? Do you see?"

More silence. He opened the tent flap and stuck his head in.

"Ouch, Christ!" he yelled as something metal struck his forehead and clattered on the ground.

"What the fuck . . . ?"

"Don't you talk to me like that, you prick. I'm not stupid."

"I'm going for a walk," Willie announced, holding his forehead.

"Willie?"

"I'll be back, I'll be back, though Christ only knows why," he said, and he walked beyond the cottonwood tree, across a scrubby field, feeling profoundly sorry for himself. He looked up at the sparkling black velvet sky, then back at the few glows of light in the campground. He put his head back, opened his throat and howled. Feeling better, he returned to the tent and lay down on his back next to his wife.

"Was that you?" she asked.

"Me what?"

"Howling?"

"Some fucking dog," said Willie. "Maybe a coyote. Nothing to worry about."

"I hate it when you talk to me like that, like I'm—"

"Forget it, will you. Look, I'm under a lot of stress. Go to sleep."

Sometime later Willie made a decision. It was easy.

Cheryl was snoring, his son Billy was sniffing liquidly, and Willie was feeling imposed upon, claustrophobic in the tent. He imagined himself in a deck chair next to a tiled pool with water the color of those travel ads for the Caribbean. The pool was sunken into a patio overlooking the Pacific, fresh sea breezes whispering in the exotic evergreens, a rum drink in one hand, the other lying with proprietary indifference on his wife's round ass in the sun. . . . But it wasn't his wife's. It was a new, fresh, silken, mysterious . . .

So Willie got up, checked his watch—it glowed 10:35 in radium green—and slipped out into the night. Opening the door of his pickup, he put it in neutral and pushed mightily until the truck began to roll down the slight incline toward the highway. He hopped in and coasted down to the campground entrance, stopping there to start the engine. Willie, feeling not good, not terrific, but *launched*, headed down the highway to the Circle K, the telephone, the future. A phone call, maybe two, and then . . . hey, he would be free.

Free!

Elated, Willie carefully kept a few miles an hour below the speed limit until he saw the anemic lights of the Circle K come into view. He bounced into the parking lot and came to a stop next to a van with Minnesota plates in front of the store's glass window. Dumb shits, Willie thought, putting all those signs and posters in the window. Just asking for a robbery.

The door of the Circle K opened and a couple emerged, both wearing T-shirts that advertised CELESTIAL PEACE, both in blue jeans and athletic shoes. The man wore a brand-new straw cowboy hat.

Vortex pilgrims, Willie guessed. The woman came over to

the passenger side of the van while the man went around to the other side. The woman was nervously tearing open a Clark bar.

"Want to play with my celestial piece?" asked Willie sociably.

The woman turned and stared expressionlessly at him, and the man paused on the other side of the van. She had large blue eyes.

"Fuck you, creep," she said, and opened up the van door.

"Yeah, creep," said the man.

"Hey, buddy," Willie called. "You know why cowboy hats are like hemorrhoids?"

The man opened his door and began to get in the van.

"Eventually," Willie explained, "every asshole gets one."

As the van snarled backward and bustled out of the lot, Willie stepped lightly out of his truck, breathing deeply and feeling good in his rib cage.

The store was empty except for the salesgirl who had her back to him behind the counter, where she was shuffling stuff around on the shelves. Willie took the measure of her hips under the tight denim of her jeans and felt randy as a goat. Presently she stood up and turned to face him. Willie beamed charmingly.

"Hi," he said. She was a knockout, shiny brown hair, olive skin, nice rack of melons.

"Yeah?" she said.

"Can we talk?" Willie asked. The woman took a step backward, and Willie kept smiling. "See, I'm with the FBI, and there's a couple, you know, like Bonnie and Clyde, they go after places like this, and we think they may be here in Sedona. Pretend like they're fruit-loops—"

"Look, buster, you wanna buy something or what? My friend back there," she gestured toward the back room with her head, "he's part Navajo and part Apache. He's six-eight, weighs two thirty, and he's got a chip on his shoulder, 'specially about guys with your color skin. You want me to wake him up? Hey, *Al*!" She smiled at Willie, with fine little white teeth.

Willie broke out into a sweat.

"I need change for the phone," he said, thrusting a dollar bill onto the counter.

"Never mind, Al," she called as she opened the register and dropped four quarters on the counter. Willie scrabbled them up and went outside, swearing, hearing the woman's high-pitched giggles.

The phone booth was in the adjacent parking lot, a gas station that was closed for the night. Willie shut himself in, pulled a piece of paper from his shirt pocket, put a quarter in the slot and nervously dialed a local number.

"L'Auberge de Sedona," said a highfalutin voice.

"Room 612, please," Willie said in imitation.

The line buzzed a few times and then a man said: "Yes?"

"This is Blaine, I've called a couple of times about . . . well, about some business."

"It's late," the man's voice said.

"Look, I'd just like to have a brief word with Mister—"

"He's not here."

"Not *here*? He told me to call him when I got to Sedona. We got business."

"What's your name again?"

"Blaine. Willie Blaine. I talked to him just—"

"Oh yes, Blaine. He told me that if you called, I should tell you that he's in Tucson."

"Tucson?"

"Tucson."

"But—But where do I reach him—"

"You can try the Pima Inn." And the line went dead.

Willie slugged the phone with the palm of his hand and the entire booth rattled.

"Shit! What does that bastard think I am, some kind of yoyo on a string?"

He stormed out of the booth and into his truck, and headed south into the night.

Mo Bowdre sat at the kitchen table, sated with mutton and hominy and salt, and content to listen to the women talking in Hopi, not more than five or six words of which he understood. It was a language both fluid and occasionally guttural, with a lilting inflection, and it washed around him like a warm, quietly bubbling stream. Occasionally he would hear an English word in the flow: *Saturday, triba' council, Winslow.* And sometimes the stream would eddy into laughter—the mother's high-pitched giggle. Presently, Mo heard the old man, Emory, murmur something in Hopi and shuffle across the room.

"Ha-kee, ha-kee," Melanie called out. "Wait." She went over to the door and went out after her father, reemerging a moment later.

"He's goin' over to the kiva," she explained. "There's a dance this weekend, long-haired kachinas. He likes to be there when they rehearse. He learns all the new songs, even though he's too old to take part."

Mo smiled, and the women resumed their conversation, long and serious exchanges but flowering every now and then with sighs and, less frequently, giggles.

Mo thought about the old man, wondering when he'd get too old even to descend the ladder into the underground chamber. What was he now, mid-eighties? What that old man has seen in those years, Mo thought. They probably didn't get automobiles out here till he was in his teens. Now he can sit there watching the news on TV. He wondered what impression the news made on the old man's view of the world, a view so totally focused on the daily, weekly, monthly, yearly round of ceremony and ritual that had been going on here hardly changed at all for about a thousand years.

The old man had told him one day a couple of years ago about how the old clans had gathered from all over the place, destined to arrive here on these mesas, one after the other. The Bear clan was first to arrive, being the leaders. They would know when they had reached the right place when they saw a star that shined during the day. And when they got to Second Mesa, there was a star in the sky shining so bright they could see it during daylight, so they stopped there, just below the mesa on top of which the village of Shungopavi now sits.

Almost immediately there had been some sort of squabble, as Mo remembered the tale, and one guy had come over here to Third Mesa, starting the village of Oraibi, which still glowered on the mesa above where he was sitting. The fractious Hopi, Mo thought: a string of disagreements and dissension unbroken to this day.

"Your archeologists," Emory had told him, "used to say that us Hopis got here around 1250, you know, A.D. Then they pushed it back to 1150, found some stuff below one of the plazas. But I can tell you just when we got here. When those Bear clan people got here, they saw that star in the daytime. Well, I was readin' something, and it said the Chinese people saw a star just like that—shined so bright they could see it at noon. And they wrote it down on their calendar, 1050 A.D. Same thing, see? Same star. We just didn't have that kind of calendar in those days."

Twelve years before William the Conqueror saxed the Angles, Mo thought. Why not? He stood up and said, "I think I'll sniff the air a bit."

He went out and stood leaning on the fender of his truck, wondering how Connie managed to live in two such opposite worlds. Like breathing water and breathing air. Idly, Mo toyed with the idea of cultural amphibians and got nowhere. He went back inside, to the sound of dishes being washed, and a half hour later he was lying in bed next to Connie, who breathed almost silently, and he wondered when it was going to hit the fan . . . if it hadn't already and he just didn't know it yet.

*   *   *

It was a few minutes after eleven when Larry Collins drove past the empty lot of the Circle K, lonely in the greenish wash of light, and headed for the campground. He turned into the dirt drive and eased up the slight incline, parking alongside a red van. He saw the van's occupant twitch, startled, and look over at him. Collins held up his thumb, shut off the engine and stepped out of his car, closing the door quietly behind him. He leaned in the window of the van and said, "I'm Collins. You're free. So where are they?"

"Back there," the man said, pointing over his shoulder with his thumb. "In the blue tent." Collins spotted a shape over by a tree.

"Where's Blaine's truck, that old Ford?" he asked abruptly.

"What?" The man spun around. "Shit! Where is—"

"Jesus Christ, you let him just drive off?"

"They were in the tent. All zipped up. For an hour. I went over and listened to them sleeping. . . ."

"And so you thought you'd catch a few z's yourself, huh?"

"But I would've heard . . ."

"Not if he pushed the truck down the hill, jeezus! You stupid . . ." Collins took a deep breath.

"I'm—"

"Never mind the sorry shit. Get on the radio and tell 'em to put out a description of Blaine's truck. Think you can do that?" Collins set off at a run for the blue tent.

As the agent in the van was finishing his report on the radio, a long rising howl of pain and despair pierced the night.

E i g h t

Nigel Calderwood awoke with a smile on his face and a tingle in his loins. The sky was beginning to lighten through the window, and he could make out the slender form lying next to him in the unfamiliar bed, a bed blessed beyond all beds, the bed of his dreams.

Long before his provincial critics had noticed it, Nigel Calderwood's forty-seven-year-old tenor voice—never of the first rank—had begun to lose its timbre. Noting this, and staring down a precipitous slide into failure and a penurious old age, Nigel had reacted exactly the way anyone of diminishing talent and limited options would. He panicked. Then he had bought himself time by substituting technique for talent, artfulness for art, and began a rushed search for a lifetime sinecure—that is, a rich woman. And so Calderwood, now in his second season as second tenor at the Santa Fe Opera, had fixed his dreams like a laser-guided missile onto the slender frame of Marianna del Massimo, the woman of mystery and at least financial promise, if not great wealth, who was attractive (in a slightly pinched way) to boot. With all his charm and subtlety, he had offered her his soul. And lately she had accepted it. He had arrived at her door last night with twelve yellow roses which, just before the consummation Calderwood had so eagerly hoped for, she had brought from the living room and put on the dresser with a girlish giggle.

And here he was at dawn, lying next to this sumptuous flower of a woman, an entire new (and secure) life opening up before him like petals, as the sun turned the sky behind the mountains a glorious shade of peach. Calderwood could almost hear the grand musical accompaniment.

Marianna stirred and smiled, her eyes still closed. She stretched luxuriously, pushing her hair from her face, and Calderwood stared at her in the dawn light the way a newly crowned king might stare upon first seeing the crown jewels.

"Good morning," she said sleepily and opened her eyes. They fluttered shut. "Nigel," she said softly, as if to herself.

"My life is yours, in service," the tenor said grandly.

She opened her eyes again.

"You've certainly done a good job of that so far," she said, reaching for him.

An hour later Calderwood was seated at the table in Marianna's small but superbly equipped kitchen, sipping his second cup of coffee, when Marianna emerged from the bedroom in a trim black business suit.

"Do you have to go to the gallery today? I thought it was closed."

"It is. I'm going to the bank."

Calderwood raised his eyebrows.

"I need to find out what kind of money I've got to come up with."

"Ten percent, I should think," said Calderwood. "About a half million."

"No, less than that," said Marianna. "They make special arrangements in this state for Hispanics who want to get into business."

"Hispanics?"

Marianna smiled. "My maiden name was Chavez. You didn't know that."

"How wonderful," said Calderwood brightly.

"But I don't look Hispanic, right? Except for the black hair?"

"Well, I was about to say . . . in fact, I was *not* about to say . . ."

"My stepfather," said Marianna, picking up an expensive lizardskin briefcase from the floor. "He adopted me and my sister when we were infants. So all I need are some old records, like my college transcript. Which are right here in this case."

"Beautiful, my dear, beautiful," the tenor said, thinking what good and clever hands he was in.

At seven o'clock in the morning, Larry Collins sat in a coffee shop across from one of Flagstaff's inexpensive motels, fatigue closing in on him like the water pressure in the deep ocean. He stared at the little detergent slick on the surface of his coffee, and it was as if he were staring down a tunnel. Blaine was off, God only knew where. His wife and kid were stashed with a friend—Charlene? Charlene Ferguson—a few blocks away, apparently the only friend Blaine's wife had in the whole damned world. Poor woman—blown through life like a leaf in the wind. After she'd stopped howling in the tent, the kid crying, she had cried and blubbered something about it being her fault, she shouldn't have thrown the can of soup at him, then she got mad and called her husband a lot of names she didn't learn in Sunday school, and then had just about collapsed in self-pity and despair. She didn't have a nickel, didn't have a thing but what was in the tent, all her stuff was in the truck, her mother's bureau, her only thing from her mother . . .

Eventually Collins had gotten her to the point where she would answer his questions. He had told her that he would find a place for her to stay until things got cleared up, and so she had mentioned this Charlene in Flagstaff, and that seemed to calm her down some. At least she wasn't stuck in the middle of some campground with no money, no food, no clothes . . . No, she didn't have any idea where Blaine might be headed. No, no idea even why they had turned around at Kingman. Willie had made a call from a pay phone outside of town and had come back to the truck furious and said they were going to Sedona. They had been going to L.A. and Willie had some deal he was going to make there, she didn't know what it was. She burst into tears again, and Collins waited until she stopped and asked her what he thought was an unemotional-type question—what was in the truck, could she remember? She mentioned things like furniture, a few pieces, and the bureau, and swore at her departed husband, a couple of suitcases, Willie's toolbox that he always kept in the truck, bolted down and locked. And sand.

"Sand?" the agent had asked.

"It was a pain in the butt," the woman had said. "I kept telling him to shovel it out, it kept blowing in the rear window when we were driving. You know, the rear window won't shut all the way, and this sand kept blowing in out of the back, get in your teeth, your hair."

"Why did he have sand in the back of his truck?"

"He got some to make, you know, cement. He was going to build a wall in the backyard, but he never did." She had burst into tears again, presumably at the thought of all the things he had not done, or never would now.

The subject was changed a few more times, and she told him that he had been trying to reach someone here in Sedona, called a couple of times yesterday from the pay phone down at the gas station. No, she didn't have the faintest idea who the guy was. It was a guy? She guessed so. No, she didn't have any idea at all what kind of deal Willie was working on. He just said it was a big one.

Around and around it had gone, with nothing more emerging, so Collins had driven her and the kid to Flagstaff and they had waited until dawn in an all-night eatery, the kid asleep in her arms, and then she had called her friend. She had never asked why the FBI was looking for her husband. Collins had told her that she shouldn't leave Flagstaff, go anywhere else, without letting the FBI know. He had handed her his card after he wrote the local field office's number on the back.

"And if he shows up? Calls?" she had asked quietly.

"Well, Miz Blaine, we're trying to find him."

The woman had looked down, then straight into Collins's eyes. "If I hear from that prick, I'll call you. You can count on it."

She had thanked him for taking care of her, and he had watched her walk into the house and shut the door. Now he stared bleakly at his coffee, put a dollar on the counter, drove over to the police station and caught a couple of hours of sleep on a cot in one of the empty cells.

When Connie Barnes woke up, she remembered that she had been awake many times during the night, off-balance, irritated, clumsy, tangled, disappointed. But she had slept deeply for a while, and now could see the beginning light through the window. It had been a habit of hers to wake up to the light and smile, at least inwardly, to be grateful, to rejoice regardless of whatever else might be going on. So she set aside her gloomy feelings and prayed to her father, the Sun, now reaching the highest house of the year. She needed to straighten her legs, and bumped into those of the big man. He sighed, made room, and dropped a heavy forearm over the sweeping curve between her waist and hip.

"You awake?" she whispered.

"Nope." He breathed on in the steady rhythm of sleep.

She wished he could see. She wished he could see the light on the mesas when they turned copper in the evening, or thin precious white-gold at dawn. She wished he could see the colors of the kachinas, red, green, white, yellow, their serious beaks, their kindly, godly eyes, as they danced in the sun in the plazas. She wished this great rough-hewn man could see the clouds arise in the west when the kachinas danced, and tore themselves off the mountain, and see the ribbons of rain connecting the sky and the red and purple earth, the rain moving across the desert, touching here and there. She wished he could look in the clouds that scudded low over the cornfields and see the faces of her ancestors, the white and gossamer. . . . Maybe he could see all that, she thought.

His way.

How is it, she asked herself, that I love this white man so? This blind white man?

Because he sees so well?

Because he sees me.

She nestled against his round, warm stomach, and continued her orisons to the Sun, now peering over the mesas to the east.

At seven o'clock in the morning, Willie Blaine pulled out onto Route 10, south, to Tucson. His eyes were sandy with sleeplessness but he was exhilarated, proud of his handiwork. The Oldsmobile handled like a dream, a fuckin' dream, and he noted, glancing down, that it had almost a full tank of gas. Mr. Glen Greene of Mesa was a thorough and careful sort of person, not taking the car to the airport only to come home and find it low on gas. Willie's elbow hung out the window in the early rays of the sun, the window he had broken and then had managed to roll down. He flicked on the air conditioner—what the hell? Cool down the fucking state of Arizona with Glen Greene's gas. Thanks, Glen baby. The whole state is grateful to you.

Hours earlier, even within minutes of leaving Sedona, Willie had realized he'd have to jettison the truck before dawn, when his wife would wake up and start howling like a pregnant cat sitting on a spike, calling the police and God knows what. He was only a couple of hours away from Phoenix. Before he got to the main highway, he began to peer at the sides of the road, and jammed on his brakes when he found what he was looking for. He bounced off the road up a dirt track a few feet, turned off the track into a field behind a stand of trees. He shut off the engine and the headlights, jumped out of the cab and, holding the side of the truck, went around to the back and climbed in.

"Ow, shit!" he'd said, barking his shin on some goddamned thing. He reached down and took the hard plastic suitcase in his hand and pitched it into the night, hearing it thump on the ground. He threw out several more familiar objects, the accumulated junk of his marriage, feeling a rising satisfaction. Then there was the bureau, the fucking bureau, the keepsake, the only thing Cheryl had from her battle-ax of a mother, the old bag, mean as snake, God how he had hated that woman. Willie had heaved the bureau onto its four legs. He got around behind it and pushed it out of the truck with a breathless giggle rising in his throat. There was one more thing, a huge overstuffed canvas suitcase. He hurled that off the truck. Then he pulled his old army surplus duffel bag closer to the pile of sand that lay up against the cab, and dug around, extracting the green plastic garbage bag, which he stuffed into the duffel. Sitting in the sand, with his arm resting on the duffel—his plans worked out perfectly in his head, and a mental list of what he would need from his toolbox—he had allowed himself to sleep, sufficiently uncomfortable that he knew he would wake up in a couple of hours max.

At six-thirty in the morning he'd pulled up at the gate of the long-term parking lot outside the Phoenix airport and took a ticket from the slot. A wooden bar rose, and Willie went on the prowl, eventually noticing that another early bird in a not-too-new maroon Oldsmobile Cutlass was nosing around, looking for a space. Willie stopped his truck and watched the Oldsmobile creep into a space. A man got out nervously, closed the door and hurried off toward the pedestrian exit carrying a briefcase. Willie parked his truck, grabbed his duffel from the back and walked over to the Oldsmobile. Within three minutes, he had seen that the guy had left his parking ticket on the dashboard, and that there was no obvious security system on the car. He broke the window on the driver's side, ripped out the glass shards and rolled it down, hot-wired the car and was approaching the sleepy-looking attendant at the exit gate. He stuck the ticket and a dollar bill out the window, looking distractedly in the other direction. "Forgot my damned airline ticket," he said. The wooden bar rose, and he drove off looking for Route 10 south, thinking, Okay, I got three days, at least, before I got to trade this fucker in for another model.

Now, headed south under the white pall of Phoenix smog, Willie felt completely liberated, the new man. The flat, parched lands stretched away toward the ripsaw mountains all around, blue in the haze. Talk about fucking up an entire area, Willie thought. He looked with disdain at the poorly irrigated fields here and there, crummy little plants gasping for water. Ten years, Willie thought, and they'll have to move all these jerks out of here. He wondered happily where all the lardasses would go when Phoenix ran out of water, when the last goddamned lawn sprinkler fizzled and went out. Send 'em to Bangladesh. Plenty of water there. The warm breeze filled the car, mingling with the cold air from the air conditioner, and he settled back in the comfortable velour seat and flicked on the radio. There was a low sound barely audible over the sound of the wind. He turned up the volume and a zillion violins scraping away like fingernails on the blackboard burst forth in his ears.

"What the fuck!" Willie said, and punched the scan button. "None of that public radio faggotry. Not for Willie fuckin' Blaine." He glanced over his shoulder at the duffel bag on the backseat. *"Yeah!"* he said.

A little before ten Willie swung off Route 10 onto Speedway Boulevard in Tucson and came to a stop at a red light behind a huge electric-blue pickup with a bumper sticker on it that

said: GOT A GUN FOR MY WIFE: GOOD DEAL. Willie smirked.
Tucson is my kind of town, he thought, and looked around for
a gas station. He spotted one a few blocks farther on, pumped
five dollars of lead-free and asked the woman in the booth
where he could find the Pima Inn. She looked at him strangely,
then told him the directions. Not all that far. Couldn't have
chosen a better turnoff. Things were going his way.

Finding his way through a rich residential district with low
houses set among enormous cacti and alien-looking trees nestled behind walls, Willie pulled up before the Pima Inn, which
looked simply like the most elegant home in the area, with the
biggest wall.

Two things suddenly struck him. The reason why the woman
in the gas station had looked strangely at him was because he
didn't look like the sort of person who would be going to the
Pima Inn. There was a simple and understated sign as the only
indication that it wasn't in fact a private residence, and a sign
across the street offering parking space to the inn's guests and
tradesmen. Well, that could be handled, Willie thought. But the
other realization was that he would have to leave his duffel bag
in an unlockable car with the goddamned window rolled down,
or lug it around with him. Be cool, Willie baby, he thought to
himself.

He pulled across the street into the inn's lot, a thickly hedged
dirt and gravel place landscaped with cacti. He switched off
the engine and thought briefly, then stepped out of the car and
casually looked at the other cars in the lot. A number of them
had open windows, so maybe this was the sort of place where
people were so wealthy there weren't any thefts. On the other
hand, where else would you go if you . . . Well, maybe the
place is watched. He didn't see anybody watching. Maybe these
were all rental cars and there was nothing in them and the
people didn't give a shit if some creep snatched their car, hey,
just order up another one from fucking Hertz. He weighed the
odds, then reached in the back door of Glen Greene's Olds-

mobile and gently shoved the duffel down on the floor in front of the backseat. Things were going his way, he thought.

He crossed the street and stepped into the bright hallway of the Pima Inn, looking both ways and finally spotting the desk to his left. Down a high-ceilinged hallway to his right was what seemed to be the entrance of a dining room, and a couple of geezers in reddish cotton pants and polo shirts came out. They looked like overfed eastern bankers on vacation, and they were followed by their wives, in casual but costly dresses. Posh City, thought Willie, and headed for the desk, behind which stood a pleasant-faced young man who looked Willie in the eye and said, "Can I help you?"

It isn't like the guy thinks I'm some kind of terrorist, Willie thought, but he's sure as hell cautious.

"Blaine Delivery Service," Willie said. "I got something for one of your guests."

"Blaine? Are you new?"

"Uh, what? New? I don't know. I just work for them. I guess they are new."

The young man behind the desk looked at him without expression.

"It's for Mr. Robert Breeden," Willie said.

"Breeden." The clerk looked at Willie. "I'm sorry, we have no Mr. Breeden visiting here."

Oh, for chrissake, thought Willie. The fucking runaround. He despaired. "Look, it's very important. I mean the dispatcher said it was urgent. Are you sure this guy Breeden isn't here? Can you check again?"

"I'm sorry but—"

"Maybe he's registered to come, you know, a reservation."

"Let me look." The clerk looked through the register. "In fact, a Robert Breeden is scheduled to arrive later this afternoon." The clerk looked irritated. "Yes, this afternoon. You may leave the package here for him and we'll see to it that he gets it."

"Well, uh, no, it's . . . He's got to sign for it."

The clerk looked like he had smelled a fart. "Our guests expect us to take care of such things in their behalf. You can—"

"No, sorry. Blaine company policy. I'll come back. This afternoon, you say?"

"After four-thirty," said the clerk firmly.

"Okay. Hey, thanks," Willie said, at his most ingratiating, and left, hoping that no slimebag two-bit Tucson hustler had gotten into the Oldsmobile under the nose of whatever snooty fucking watchman was supposed to be keeping an eye on things.

The bag was still there, where he had left it, and Willie got in the car and pondered what he would do for the next six hours. From where he sat, all he could see was that mountains surrounded the place, a city built in the desert. A real desert, Willie thought, and a fucking hot one at that, and he began to feel claustrophobic.

Sergeant Anthony Ramirez was thinking about a time he had gone over the border into Mexico with some friends—one evening a few years ago while they were all in graduate school. They went over across from Bisbee, Arizona, into a seedy little border town called Naco, nothing but ill-lit houses along ill-lit streets, with a few barren bars where the convention seemed to be no more than three customers at a time. Ramirez, whose family had lived in New Mexico for generations, felt oddly alien in Mexico, and for a brief while it had upset him. Then they had come across a little street carnival with a couple of broken-down rides and little black-eyed kids darting around like fish in an aquarium, and some scratchy loudspeaker playing mariachi music, and Ramirez had gotten into the swim of it.

There had been a sad-eyed teenager manning one of the booths—nothing but a piece of wallboard with hundreds of balloons tied to it. The trick was to take the kid's four darts and break four balloons in a row—but the catch was, one of his friends found out, that the darks had to stick in the wall after the balloons were broken. The companion had broken four balloons, but two of the four darts had bounced off the wall, and the kid had told him he didn't get a prize. So Ramirez had decided to have a try, even though he wasn't normally able to shed enough reserve to act stupid in public. Looking at the old and throughly beat-up darts—they had to be twenty years old—Ramirez had an idea. He leaned over and briefly honed each point on the macadam surface of the plaza. The sad-eyed kid looked upset. Then Ramirez, forgetting his natural reserve altogether, reared back like a major league pitcher and, without aiming except in the general direction of the wall, broke four balloons in a row: pop, pop, pop, pop. The darts all stuck solidly in the wallboard. The sad-eyed kid looked like he was about to fall apart.

One of Ramirez's companions said, "I don't think anyone's ever won this thing. Look at that kid's expression."

And from the battered appearance of the plaster trophies— mostly penny banks in the form of Mickey Mouse heads with white scars and lesions all over them—Ramirez imagined that his companion was right. He went off in triumph with a battered Mickey Mouse head, only to feel so stupid with the silly face grinning out from under his arm that he put it down on the sidewalk next to a bunch of kids fooling around near the carnival, and walked away.

He remembered the night in Naco now because it reminded him of the FBI agent, Collins. Collins seemed to be the sort who always just reared back and threw the darts in the general direction . . . no especial target all worked out, just stand up and throw and see what happens. Now he was off chasing that ex-coach around Arizona. Maybe it would work, Ramirez thought, but he couldn't see how. Darts and murder were different games. But then, Collins wasn't all that interested in Meyers's murder, Ramirez reminded himself. He was interested in those objects that he assumed Meyers had had, and for which Collins thought Meyers had been killed. A lot of conclusions to jump to. What had his friend Bowdre called it? Subjunctive.

On the other hand, why not? Ramirez had spent the better part of the morning following an iffy path; in particular, seeking something interesting, noteworthy, even telling in the records of Meyers's telephone calls for the last six months. Patterns. The man had an astonishing phone bill, close to three thousand dollars a month—more than Ramirez's monthly salary.

The phone on Ramirez's desk rang and he picked it up. "Ramirez."

"Yeah, this is Collins, I'm in Flagstaff. We lost the guy. Blaine."

"Lost him?"

"Yeah, I'll tell you about it some day. Dumb recruit, he's gonna wind up manning the eight-hundred number on 'Unsolved Mysteries' if I have anything to say about it, which I won't. Shit. Blaine could be anywhere within five hundred miles by now."

Ramirez was silent.

"So," Collins said, "what d'*you* know today?"

Ramirez explained that he had been looking through Meyers's phone records. "You'd think he was the Secretary General of the United Nations or something. Germany, Spain, Singapore, all over the place."

"So did you find anything interesting?"

"Well, for one thing, I think it's pretty interesting that he called Singapore at eleven o'clock every Tuesday night for three months. It's a restaurant."

"Great. That's a lot of help. Anything else?"

"Yeah. About two months ago he called a number in Winslow about once a day for five days."

"Blaine."

"A pay phone at a Chevron station."

"That was Blaine."

"Then a couple weeks later, the same pattern of calls to a gas station outside Phoenix."

"Okay, then what?" the agent asked hastily.

"Well, nothing like that again. Then for a couple of weeks before he was killed, he made a bunch of calls to some numbers in southern Arizona. New ones. New on his records anyway."

"What were they?"

"I'll tell you, but what's interesting is that those two weeks are the only time in three months that he *didn't* call the Singapore number." He paused. "Then he called Singapore the night he got killed."

"That's great, Tony. Great. That's probably the final destination. But . . . well, later. Whoever the guy is in Singapore, maybe he went to Arizona and then back to Singapore, right? Now tell me . . ."

Ramirez went on to explain the calls to southern Arizona. There were three calls to a Tucson museum. ("Get this, a *wildlife* museum.") And there were three to the unlisted number of a private archeological foundation in Patagonia.

"Patagonia? Jesus . . ."

"It's a town in Arizona," Ramirez said. "South of Tucson, about forty, fifty miles."

There was a long pause on the phone, and then the agent said, "Well, that's where I'll go look for Blaine, down in Tucson."

"Blaine? What makes you think *he's* there?"

"What else have I got to go on? Thanks, Tony. I'll call you later." The line went dead.

Ramirez put his receiver down in the cradle and shook his head. More dart throwing.

Willie Blaine was discouraged and bored. He had found a Mexican dump to eat an early lunch in, sodden tamales, some rotten fucking meat, maybe beef, and a pile of rice and beans that would've sunk Mark Spitz in his Olympic prime. What else could he afford but crap? For now. He had sat in a creaking booth near the window to keep an eye on the car. Pretty soon the little Mexican waitress who wouldn't look him in the eye shoved his bill at him and he had to leave. Everybody seemed in some kind of goddamn rush in Tucson.

Afterward, he had driven aimlessly around town for an hour or so, getting honked at by all the assholes who knew their way around all the goddamn road construction and couldn't care less about tourists. Oh yeah, Glen Greene had Arizona plates. Well, anyway, a stinking rude bunch of rubes and smartasses. So he had wound up driving all the way east on Speedway Boulevard, through some open lands with a few fancy houses, and then it ended outside some park full of these giant cactus plants twenty, thirty feet tall. He read about them on a little sign next to a dirt trail that led away from the parking lot toward the mountains that rose up before him, hemming him in.

They were called saguaro cactus, and to Willie they looked like big green dicks, the straight ones did. Some of the others had little arms sticking out, looked like crosses almost. Willie smirked at the thought of the Spanish friars—they'd mentioned them on the smug little signs at the entrance—arriving here on their stupid mules to save souls for Jesus and Mary and seeing this big fucking confusion of crucifixes and peckers that the gods had arranged for them. Musta driven those guys nuts, Willie thought with satisfaction.

Now Willie sat in the shade of one of the big saguaros— one with arms—and he was bored, waiting for four o'clock, when he could set out for the Pima Inn. It was three-thirty. He decided to get there early and see if he could spot someone arriving who might be this guy Breeden.

After lunch in the doughnut store across Cerillos Road from the police station, Ramirez had had a thought. Bored by inaction, he would throw a few darts as well. He walked back to the station and approached the young officer who worked as a secretary for Captain Ortiz.

"Hey, Maria, how do I get ahold of a Tucson yellow pages?"

She had smiled and disappeared into a large storeroom, returning in moments with a thick telephone book, both white and yellow pages.

"Gracias, Maria." He bowed. "You will go far in law enforcement."

In his office he had thrown the book open to "Hotels," and for several minutes he studied the advertisements, checking off about a dozen. On the third call he had hit paydirt. Having introduced himself and explained the urgency of the matter— a homicide investigation—he asked if the hotel had entertained anyone from Singapore in the previous month. And the hotel manager, without hesitation, said yes. Ramirez was elated— what good fortune, thank you San Antonio de Padua—but his enthusiasm drained away when the manager explained that it was a ninety-three-year-old Englishwoman who lived part of the year in Singapore, part in England, and who visited Tucson once every three years to see her grandchildren. The Englishwoman was totally deaf and had to be pushed around in a wheelchair.

The fifth call turned up another unlikely candidate, another old woman, this one an octogenarian with Parkinson's disease, who traveled with three small dogs and a sixty-year-old maid. After two more calls, Ramirez was exasperated and ready to quit. He dialed one more number. Having been put through to the manager of the Pima Inn and having explained himself, he again asked if the hotel had entertained a guest from Singapore in the past month.

"Oh, certainly," the voice said, evidently a young man. "Mr. Breeden. Mr. Robert Breeden."

"From Singapore?"

"Yes."

"Can you—"

"He's a sportsman, a hunter. He was here to donate some
... ah, trophies to the wildlife museum."

Ramirez's lips pulled back in a grin.

"The wildlife museum," he said.

"Yes, that's what I understand, sir."

Ramirez asked some more questions and scribbled down the
replies in his notebook, hanging up the phone in triumph. He
stared at the scribbles—chiefly an address—and then scratched
his head. He stood up and went to find Captain Ortiz, to find
out what the hell he should do next.

Within minutes the Albuquerque field office of the FBI had
what it needed, and only moments later a technician in the
Hoover Building in Washington was feeding the information
into a globe-circling system of satellites and lasers, and within
yet a few more moments information was in the Albuquerque
field office to the effect that not only was there no such person
in Singapore as Robert Breeden, so far as local and international agencies could discover, there was no such address in
the city-nation of Singapore as had been provided Sergeant
Ramirez by the manager of the Pima Inn with such confidence
in the quality of his guests.

The electromagnetic spectrum had rippled for a brief moment with the name Breeden, and then took up other matters,
just as the phone rang in the Santa Fe P.D. offices and Ramirez
learned the bad news from Albuquerque. From then on, that
afternoon, the world became nothing more than a series of
fading messages for Sergeant Anthony Ramirez.

He had already asked the agent in Albuquerque to radio
Larry Collins and tell him of the great new find: the guy from
Singapore was named Robert Breeden and he had stayed in
the Pima Inn a couple of weeks before the killing of Meyers.
Collins would, Ramirez imagined, be astounded, and go there.
He mentioned also to Albuquerque that the guy had donated

some hunting trophies to the International Museum of Wildlife. Make sure, Ramirez had said, you tell Collins that.

No sooner had he gotten off that call when another came in. It was the manager of the Pima Inn, sounding flustered and apologetic.

"Sergeant Ramirez?"

"Yes, Ramirez here."

"Thank heavens I got you. Right after we talked, you know, just a few moments ago, I discovered that Mr. Breeden had made a reservation yesterday to stay here a few days."

"When?"

"This afternoon, beginning today, for three days."

My God, thought Ramirez. We've got him.

"But he called. Or somebody called for him. They canceled the reservation."

"When?"

"An hour ago. About an hour. Do you want the exact time? We have that, of course." Ramirez waited. "Three thirty-three. But there's more. He left . . . well, whoever called left a message."

"A message? For who?"

"For a delivery service."

"What? What delivery service?" asked Ramirez.

"Well, that's the strange thing, Sergeant. This whole thing is a bit strange. . . ."

"Please go on."

"Well, none of us had heard of this service, we looked it up, called information—"

"What's it called?" Ramirez snapped.

"Well, you see, a man came by twice today, once this morning and once this afternoon about four-thirty, just a few moments ago, and said he had a delivery for Mr. Breeden. He said he was from Blaine Delivery Service, or Company, or whatever. Never heard of it . . ."

Ramirez's eyes lifted to the ceiling, and the ballpoint pen dropped out of his hand, clattering lightly on the desk.

"Excuse me, but what was the message?" he asked, feeling a kind of epiphany coming on.

"Well, that's the problem. The desk clerk wrote it down, you know, when Mr. Breeden or whoever called in to cancel, wrote it on a message card and—"

"And the guy from Blaine came and picked it up." The trumpets fizzled.

"Uh . . . yes."

"And you don't have a record of it."

"No." There was silence, and then the manager said, "It was a telephone number."

"Does the clerk remember?"

"I'm afraid not. But it was a local number. Seven digits. No area code."

"What did the guy look like, the one who picked up the message?"

"Well, Sergeant, the clerk—it was a he, a very good man, by the way—he said that the delivery man looked . . . grubby, was his word."

"Good, good, but did he mention what he *looked* like, you know, features, that sort of thing?"

"A very nondescript sort of person, apparently. Medium height, medium build, blond-to-brown hair—short hair, by the way—dressed in blue jeans and a . . . shirt. Nothing distinctive. I'm sorry we can't be more helpful."

"You've been very helpful. We'll talk again. Probably some FBI people will be around. We appreciate your help."

Ramirez hung up.

Okay, he thought to himself. There's this guy Breeden from Singapore, gives trophies to some wildlife museum in Tucson, may be the guy Meyers used to call every Tuesday—in a Singapore restaurant—and called the night he was killed. This guy Breeden, or somebody, makes reservations for him to stay at the Pima Inn tonight, cancels at three-thirty, leaves a phone number for some nonexistent delivery service named Blaine, which is the name of the coach Collins is after. This guy Breeden doesn't exist in Singapore under that name, and his address in Singapore doesn't exist. While this non-Breeden is in Tucson the last time, Meyers calls two numbers in the Tucson area, one of which is the wildlife museum non-Breeden was in town to give trophies to—this being the period when Meyers did not make his regular Tuesday night calls to the Singapore restaurant.

Ramirez shook his head, bet himself that the number left at the desk for the Blaine Delivery Service, or Company, was the wildlife museum. What were the odds? Bad. He decided not to bet. Bets were noir, he remembered someone saying: black. Some French thing. He called the FBI office in Albuquerque with the latest news, asked them to contact Larry Collins with it, left his home number in case Collins wanted to talk to him, and then sat wondering if the international telephone system could trace how many calls might have come from Singapore to New Mexico two nights ago, no, more likely three nights ago. Four nights ago, Meyers had been killed. Two nights ago Marianna del Massimo had been chased around the plaza by a pickup, a light-colored pickup.

Ramirez was beginning to like throwing darts wildly and energetically in the general direction of things. Maybe Collins was getting to him.

Willie Blaine slammed a quarter into the slot of the pay phone and yanked the door of the phone booth shut as a semi rig the size of Mount Rushmore thundered past. He punched out the numbers from the precious little message card the clerk had handed him apologetically, and he listened to the *fucking* imbecile machine ring three, four, five times. He was about to try stuffing the receiver into the slot after his quarter when there was a click, a pause, and the robot voice of some machine-bitch came on saying that this was the International Museum of Wildlife in Tucson, Arizona, the hours were from ten in the morning until four-thirty in the afternoon seven days a week, admission three dollars for adults, a dollar fifty for children under twelve, if he needed information about how to reach the museum push one, if he needed to reach anyone on the staff and knew their extension push . . .

Willie slumped against the glass of the phone booth. He held the receiver of the phone in both hands. He raised it over his head. Then slowly, calmly, he hung it up while the robo-voice droned on, a thin, grating whine like a gnat he could just make out over the sounds of rush hour traffic on Speedway Boulevard.

N i n e

Mo Bowdre was perched happily on the side of the pickup bed, his internal organs rattling like peas in a whistle. Beyond the whining grumbles of the engine and the thump of the big wheels on the dirt, he heard the ancient *creeeee-e-e-e*, a descending note, the cry of the eagle. It was somewhere off to his left, behind them, back over the cornfields they had just left.

"Hear it?" he asked.

"Mmm," the old man assented. Connie was driving the pickup, her grandfather Emory sitting on the floor in back, leaning against the cab. They hit a rut and Mo swayed and heaved with the bucking of the pickup. The sun was still hot, shining directly on the right side of his face. Mo thought of asking if that were not good news, this big bird soaring out over the fields where two months earlier Emory had dug holes with his stick, explaining every step to his great-grandsons, and planted the seeds he inched along beside him in his coffee can, dropping them down into the earth's moist places beneath the sand. He thought better of intruding on the old man's thoughts. Emory would say whatever he wanted in his own time.

The air somehow felt thicker to Mo, denser. Not the dust

roiling up from behind the truck. Maybe he was getting a bead on atmospheric pressure. They were more than a mile above sea level here, and he'd been told once by some engineer that the reason why it felt so good when you got off the plane in Albuquerque from the East Coast was that there was five percent less air pressure bearing down on your shoulders than at sea level. Maybe he was turning into a barometer.

Mo was happy lurching along in the pickup beside this old man. Happy not so much to be part of an alien world, but happy simply to be lurching along in the truck with the old man, with nothing to do but sense the season, the place, the old ways of doing things that had not changed for so long— not a part of it, but not left out either. If there were sense to the world, Mo thought . . . and then let the thought die. There was no sense to the world.

At least not that you'd want to hang a hat on.

He thought of the block of marble in his studio, the old dank mill house where it was cool and sheltered from the entire world. How am I going to get an eagle, he thought, out of that block of inert marble? A big clumpy piece of rock?

"I'm trying to make an eagle out of marble," he said over the bumping of the road and the truck.

"Well, that's okay," said the old man. "You carve good."

Distantly, Mo heard the *creeeee-e-e-e* of the eagle again, far off behind the truck.

"You hear that?"

"Oh, yeah, I heard it."

The truck heaved and pitched over the road, and the old man was silent.

"I'm tryin to remember things," said the old man.

Mo turned his face toward the old man.

"How so?"

"You know, remember things. Pictures in the mind. I re-member when . . ." His voice drifted off. "When I used to run

out here after school, we didn't have no trucks then, none of
that, and I'd come out here on foot after school and see the
eagles. They would be waitin out here, you know, and I got to
know 'em, watch for them in their places."

He fell silent again.

"They're still here," he said. "Back there."

"The one we heard?" asked Mo.

"There was two of 'em back there."

"Over the field?"

"I don't know about that. Around out there."

"Beautiful," said Mo.

"Yeah, that's how I remember them."

Mo was silent.

"I'm gettin like you," the old man said.

Mo lurched as the pickup hit another rut, nearly pitching
over the side.

"You okay?" he asked.

"Still here," said the old man.

"So you can't see the eagles anymore?" Mo said.

"Can't see nothin anymore. TV's the same as a radio."

Mo sat on the edge of the pickup bed, rolling with the
lurches, not knowing what to say, feeling awkward for the first
time in a long time.

"Well," he said.

"Like you white guys say, it's a pain in the ass," said the
old man. "Isn't it?"

"Hah—hah—hah. Now isn't it just that?" said Mo. "But
you get used to it." He paused. "Sort of."

"It's more work."

"Right."

"That's the Hopi way," said the old man. The pickup
bounced along the dirt track, descending slowly into what Mo
guessed was a dry wash, then heaving up out of it.

"You think it's gonna rain?" the old man asked.

"Air feels heavy."

"Almost," said the old man. "But I don't think so. It don't rain when we got troubles here."

Or it rains too much, Mo thought, recalling the storm he and Connie had driven through only last night. The old man stayed silent as the pickup bounced through the desert.

When they reached the paved road through Kykotsmovi, the sun had begun to fire up the sky west of San Francisco Peaks, which sat on the horizon, a constant focus of Hopi attention though a hundred miles away. It was there that the kachinas dwelled, rehearsing the bringing of rain and accepting invitations from the Hopis between December and July to come and dance the villages. As they would do tomorrow in Kykotsmovi's plaza as well as several other villages.

Before he went into Connie's mother's house, Mo pulled Connie aside and said, "I didn't know Emory had gone blind."

"He hasn't been able to see very well for a couple of years. But then all of a sudden . . . it happened real fast. Three months."

"Well, he sure seems to get around well for a recently blind man," said Mo. "I couldn't keep up with him in that cornfield."

"He knows that cornfield, every inch of it. He's been planting there for years, decades."

"Still . . ."

"He's a very traditional man," Connie said. "He only has to know a few places. His home. His field. How to get to the kiva. That's really all he ever saw."

Mo hadn't thought of that.

Inside, Connie's mother, Melanie, put a large bowl of Hopi stew on the table. Two vast pots of stew were simmering on the stove, filling the house with moisture and the earthy aroma of mutton. Except for the small fraction they ate for dinner, the rest of the stew would be taken to the plaza tomorrow morning and reheated in the house of one of Melanie's clan sisters to help feed the seventy-odd relatives and guests who would stream through the house to be fed while the kachinas danced.

"Sit down, sit down, eat," Melanie said in a distracted way. The two blind men sat at either end of the table, the two women across from each other, talking in Hopi. Emory was silent.

In the ripples and eddies, Mo caught the word "Darrel," and when a pause came, he asked, "Where *is* Darrel? I forgot all about him. Did he make it back here?"

Darrel had left Santa Fe a few hours before Mo and Connie yesterday. He had said he had to get back to practice in the kiva for the dance.

"Yeah, he got back," said Connie. "He went to the kiva last night, right, Grandpa?"

The old man wheezed.

"Then today," Connie continued, "he went out to the field— his father's field, about a mile out beyond Grandpa's. Both our clans' fields are out that way."

Melanie said something fast in Hopi, mentioning Darrel. She made a sound Mo had learned to associate with trouble: *eeee-e.*

"Yeah," Connie resumed, "my mom was telling me Darrel's dad came over before we got back. He said Darrel was going to spend the night at the cornfield. Didn't want to go to the kiva tonight, didn't want to take part tomorrow in the dance."

Mo broke a rule he had set for himself when among the Hopi and asked a direct why-how question. "How come?"

"He said he didn't feel right. You know, his heart wasn't in the right place. He didn't want to be, what do you say, an obstacle. You know, in the prayers and all."

Melanie again said something in Hopi, something gloomy, ending again with, *eeee-e-e-e.*

"It's real complicated, these things," said Connie.

"I'll bet," said Mo, and lapsed into silence while the women continued to talk desultorily through the meal. Mo didn't need to be told that there was more to it than what he had just heard, but even though one direct question had succeeded, he knew that patience was the best policy. He would hear in due time . . . he would hear no more and no less than the Hopi wanted him to hear. Just by sitting around over the past few years on visits with Connie, he'd been told some things by the old men that the anthropologists who have swarmed over the mesas for generations have never imagined. Mo wondered what *he* would say if some ethnographer showed up in his house and started asking a whole lot of questions.

Lies, he easily concluded, and laughed to himself.

Darrel Quanemptewa stood as still as a scarecrow next to his father's field in the red light that filled the western sky and washed the sandy desertlands pink. Behind him, to the west, the mesas lay on the horizon like sleeping animals, inert, and beyond and out of sight, the villages where his kinsmen prepared for the dance tomorrow. The old lands stretched away around him, laden with the meanings his people invested in them, meanings from old stories that he had been told over and over, stories that he thought he understood, but meanings also that he had yet to find. Nothing stirred, not even the young leaves on the cornstalks, although he heard the low hiss of an evening breeze from the west.

Then he heard the guttural squawk of a raven out on its last evening patrol, and saw it soar up over the low rise across the field, oily black, glinting red. It circled upward and then descended toward the corn plants in the field, paying Darrel no heed.

"Hagh!" Darrel shouted. "Go away. There's nothin' for you here yet."

The raven circled up nonchalantly and arrowed over the rise, leaving the world motionless. Darrel contemplated the notion that he was nobody, a pinprick in the universe, merely a point in infinity, the way his science teacher might have said it, a point without identity or meaning. Even the raven had not noticed him until he shouted. He felt a familiar tightness in his stomach, the craving he had determined to stand off this night, make a new beginning, purify himself. . . . But for what? If he had no meaning, if he had no place in the universe, if his world had been stripped away from him like a bandage . . . Hadn't his grandfather said as much? Without really saying it? But Darrel knew such things, the locutions and circumlocutions of old men, how they pointed the finger without really pointing.

Darrel knew at once one thing that was expected of him, though unspoken: to bow out, not to take part. And a good thing too. All those endless recountings in the songs in the kiva, the songs commemorating the meaning of Hopi life, the prayers to the kachinas to come and join the celebration of being of the world and its creatures, butterflies, raindrops on the cornstalks . . . It all cut like a hot knife, and the blood of shame oozed from the wounds. For Darrel knew they were no longer for him, these things, and so he hated them with fear, and his stomach tightened, a curious lightness to his limbs, and he walked across the sand to his pickup, reached under the seat and took out a bottle of Thunderbird wine. He took his first swallow standing beside the cab of his truck, then vaulted into the back and sat with his feet dangling over the open tailgate, watching the red deepen in the sky to night.

Children and dogs darted here and there in the plaza as the sun rose higher, drawing the shadows back across the dusty ground to the east. People, mostly teenagers, began to appear on the roofs of the one-story houses that formed the plaza, some standing, some in cheap aluminum porch chairs, others sitting with their legs dangling over the edge. Women in shawls bustled out of the houses, carefully placing porch chairs around their entrances. There was a fresh breeze blowing in from the west, stirring up the dust from the plaza floor. A few white people, men and women in sunglasses, stood near one of the entrances to the plaza—really just an opening between two houses—looking indecisive. One of the women wore a wide-brimmed straw hat which put her face and neck entirely in shadow.

Connie led Mo to one of the chairs outside her aunt's house and they sat down. Melanie emerged from the shadows of the house into the sun and sat beside Connie. The ring of chairs around the edge of the plaza began to fill up, mostly with women—all in shawls—and a handful of old men. Most younger people chose to assemble on the roofs. Connie and her mother talked quietly in Hopi, and Mo caught the sound of a familiar word, *bahana*, meaning a white person.

"Are you talking about me?" he asked.

Connie laughed. "No, my mom was just pointing out some white people over there at the other end of the plaza. They look confused."

"You mean you people still're letting stray white folks into these things? Hah—hah—hah."

"More people, more prayers," Connie said. "But one of those ladies is going to get a surprise." Mo cocked his head. "She's wearing a big hat. The kachinas are going to tell her to take it off." Connie and her mother giggled.

Mo stirred. "It used to be a custom among my people, and it still is some places, for women to wear hats when they went to church services."

"Right," Connie said, "but among your people, church services aren't for rain. The kachinas think a hat is something like an umbrella."

"I see," Mo said. "Well, I'm sure glad you explained that to me. Why don't you explain it to that woman?"

"The kachinas will, or maybe the clowns," said Connie, and she and her mother giggled again.

Presently, a drum thudded loudly, and in the sudden silence

a rattle sounded. A loud, low moan started up, like the wind blowing through a distant cave, and the kachinas entered the plaza in a long file, chanting, the drum banging, turtle shells on their legs clop-clopping together, sleigh bells clanking, rattles in their hands scratching—short kachinas at either end of the line, the purest of the pure—and an old man with a red band around his gray hair sang out prayers and directives, walking up and down the line, sprinkling white cornmeal on the dancers, feeding them the food of spirits. For twenty minutes the kachinas—their multicolored faces turned slightly up, the long black hair hanging down in front of their necks, ringed with evergreens—chanted and moved in unison, turning this way and that, moving in single file around the plaza to take up new positions, turning . . . and the plaza was filled with ancient and orderly cacophony.

Throughout the day the kachinas alternated periods of dancing with periods of rest somewhere outside the plaza, and people came and went, many drifting into the houses to be fed, usually in silence, and then returning into the sun. The white woman with the big hat had at one point found herself faced with a fierce-looking man painted in bright colors and masked, who waved a sheaf of yucca leaves at her threateningly, and she fled the plaza, certain that the Hopi spirits had looked into her soul and found her unworthy. A Hopi woman had taken pity, explaining that the kachina only wanted her to remove her hat, and she appeared back on the edge of the plaza hatless and pink-faced.

In the course of the day, Mo ate in four different houses around the plaza, it being the courteous thing to do, and by late afternoon, with the sun streaming hot out of the western sky, he sat almost hypnotized by the astounding, monotonous rhythms of the dancers and the insistence of the unintelligible songs and the fullness of his stomach. He let his mind go free, and soon found himself in the strange position of seeing himself floating through, above, alongside evergreen trees, heading up a ravine through which white water roiled, tumbling over rocks. He was above the trees, looking down their straight shanks, seeing at their very tops the little light green shoots striving even farther upward, the same kind of shoot with which the trees had begun when they sprouted from the earth. How odd, Mo thought. You need to look down on trees to see their purpose. He continued up the ravine, higher, above the treeline and among the rocky scree, to a small mountain lake that was the blue of the sky, then white as a cloud passed over it. He began to lose sight of the lake, the cloud, but that's okay, he thought, I know where it is now, and he was in his chair in the plaza, the sun hot on his cheeks. "Beautiful," he said, and Connie looked at him strangely.

"Where have *you* been?" she asked.

"Out and around," Mo said quietly, adding, "hah—hah."

North and west of the village of old Oraibi, there is a dirt hemisphere, a turnout on the side of the highway, for which there is apparently no particular purpose, except that as with all such places, some people pull off the road there to dump stuff out of their cars and pickups—packaging from the junk food stores an hour away in Tuba City, bottles, cans. It is an unprepossessing little spot, as a result, and without much of a view. It is a half mile to the edge of the mesa, where there is a view out to the pastel stripes of the Painted Desert and, beyond, to San Francisco Peaks. Most people passing through the reservation don't stop just anywhere and march around what signs have warned them are Hopi lands. So, except for its occasional use as a mini landfill, the little turnout on the highway sees little use.

It was here that Darrel Quanemptewa left his pickup, having swerved off the road at the last moment, bouncing to a stop, practically blinded by the late afternoon sun. He stumbled over the lip of the fill dirt and almost fell as he plunged down the embankment to the scrubby land, holy land—it was all holy, sacred, profaned, fouled, vengeful, reeling land, and Darrel tripped over a rock and fell into the sand, chest heaving, listening intently for his pursuer, hearing only his own breath. Slowly, ever so slowly, so as not to be noticed, he turned his head and squinted, looking behind him with one eye, seeing the two great eyes, the grinning visage peering at him over the edge of the dirt turnout. The pickup didn't move, and Darrel pulled himself to his feet and stumbled on, knowing . . .

He headed for the edge of the mesa, toward the secret spot, the cold place, where fire became ice, where the caverns were, caverns of ice, and the sun was red and growing before his eyes, filling them with water, and branches lashed his legs, and he was walking in the water, the water swirling around his legs. He had to get to the edge of the mesa where he could . . . call out on his knees, seek . . . But the water was rising as he ran, stumbled, reeled, and he couldn't bear to look behind him, no, not where the . . . He stopped and bent over, wanting to wash his hands in the water, but he couldn't find it, and stumbled on. A great rock loomed up beside him, vibrating, a spiral glowing red on its face, and Darrel screamed and veered away, heading for the edge of the mesa, with the water clawing at his legs, shoving him sideways, and he struggled to the place and stood on the edge, knowing he would need to turn around and stare.

He shut his eyes.

He breathed deeply three, four times, water running down his face from his eyes, and turned to look at the serpent in the flood.

He felt himself wrenched upward, off the land, alone and without meaning, and silently he fell, without protest, hurtling through the air and the metallic sunlight, fetching up in a broken heap against a boulder far below the edge of the mesa, now free to become a part of the holy, sacred, profaned, and vengeful land.

"Where was your grandfather today?" Mo asked, sitting contentedly in the kitchen, nursing a cup of watery coffee.

"He likes to spend the dances down where the kachinas rest," Connie said. "It's a way these old men can take part."

Idly, Mo played with the notion of baseball teams letting the decrepit old veterans from the thirties and forties hang around the locker rooms, maybe even expanded dugouts, when the door banged open and a Hopi woman ploughed in talking like a machine gun. In the rapid spray of words, Mo heard "Darrel" repeated. There was a great howl from Connie's mother. "Oh, God," said Connie, and Mo felt her stand up. There was more rapid-fire talk, more moans, crying. Amid the chaos, Mo smelled a curious odor, and it grew stronger—an oddly familiar smell, but he couldn't place it. Pungent.

Connie said into his ear, "We've gotta go. You be all right here for a little while?"

"I'll be fine, but I'll be better if you'd tell me what the hell is going on. Not that I can't make a stab at the general idea."

Connie said something in Hopi and the door closed. "I told them I'd be right along. They're going to Darrel's mom. Darrel's dead. They found him below the mesa over past Oraibi. A guy was driving from Hotevilla and recognized his truck beside the road. So he followed his tracks over to the mesa edge and saw him down below."

Mo put a hand on Connie's arm. "What happened?" He felt the arm shudder. He shouldn't have asked the question. She would tell him. "Okay, I withdraw the question. What's that I smell?"

"Smell?"

"Yeah, something in here really smells different."

"It's bear root."

"Oh," Mo said.

"It's the root of a plant you get up in the mountains. It's a kind of protection. You chew it."

"A protection," Mo said. "So maybe Darrel didn't just get drunk and fall off the cliff, huh?"

"Maybe it was that," Connie said. "Maybe it was different. More than that." There was silence. "The other night, in the kiva, when Darrel got home, his grandfather told him some things."

"What things?"

"Well, they were all talking about those things—the things that got stolen, you know—and Darrel's grandfather explained what happens to someone who does . . . who would do . . . who profaned those things." Connie shuddered again. "I should go and help."

"Okay."

"You okay?" she asked.

"I'm fine, fine. Just fine."

"But . . . ?"

"I don't like asking questions out here, none of my business, all that, but . . ."

"What happens? In the Hopi way of thinking, you disappear, you stop existing. They see to it." She touched his shoulder. "I'll be back." The door opened and closed.

They? thought Mo Bowdre to himself in the suddenly silent house. Maybe, he thought, if he was patient enough, he'd find out who *they* were.

Nobody, he noted, had offered him any of that bear root. Maybe us bahanas are immune.

Three old men, as bent as vultures, sat in the gloom of the kiva around the dying embers in the pit under the ladder. Overhead, through the opening in the roof, a few stars glistened in the sky, but they were not being consulted this night. The old men spoke in familiar riddles, allusions that were reassuring if, at the same time, ominous, tying current questions to the esoterica of the past, indeed spanning time as if it did not exist as a coefficient in the affairs of mankind and its history. Emory listened intently, always aware that there was more to be discovered as these more learned men of his generation recounted the stories that held meaning, holding up the experience of the people as if it were a crystal, turning it in the light to capture its rays, to read its rainbow of truth, however faint. They were speaking of Palatki, a former staging area in the gathering of the clans, an abiding place long before the Hopi had seen the star glowing at noon. They spoke of the old man who had called in the plumed serpent to bring floods that would cleanse the village of its overwhelming pride and corruption. The water serpent.

"But who," asked the old patriarch of the Badger Clan, in a highly ceremonial version of the Hopi language, "made this decision? A rabid boy. That is not the same thing."

"Good father," began the Bear clan leader, who, as such, held the office of *kikmongwi*, the religious leader of the village, "the meaning lies beyond the thing that was done. Whomever of us did this, it is done."

Emory noted that the Bear clan man had left the blame hanging, even though Emory's own relative had presumably paid the price out on the mesa.

"So that is ended," the kikmongwi concluded. "We have offended the Chiefs of the Four Corners, they have spoken, they have taken themselves away, and we begin again, to learn new ways to honor them, to find better ways to be righteous. Those ceremonies are gone. You must tell the priests that this is how it is."

There was a long silence. A lingering ember hissed in the little pit in the dirt floor.

"What do you say?" the Bear clan leader asked, and Emory knew the question was for him.

"We will explain this," he said presently, "but the troubles are not yet over." He felt a chilly hand on his shoulder and willed it away. He envisioned the moldering village on the mesa above him, Oraibi, and the times he had been told of as a boy when the soldiers came to Oraibi and the people shrieked at one another and the fear and anger in their faces, and the faces were those, too, of his children. This theft, this death today, this series of events, the rift it was engendering—these were, Emory thought, just another part of something more ancient, more ineffably part of the uncontainable forces ranged against his people; perhaps all people, he didn't know.

He stood up, holding on to the ladder, and sighed. "The troubles are not over," he repeated. It was time for him to leave these two more learned men to themselves, a good thing. For he was tired and the world was far too heavy now. He shuffled around to the right of the ladder, circled out from it and approached it from the other side, slowly pulling himself up into the night air.

Emory breathed deeply and stepped off the kiva roof onto the dirt path that snaked around the underground structure, down an incline and toward the road. Wordlessly he prayed for the kikmongwi, who was trying to heal his people, his children, and Emory found himself thinking of the strange bahana, the FBI man, what was his name? Something like . . . He couldn't remember his name. He picked his way along the dirt track, recalling how the FBI agent had visited the old men themselves to talk about the theft. He talked very fast, many of the old men had not been able to follow, but later they had reconstructed what he had said. He had said that his only desire was to get them back so the Hopi could decide what to do with them. He had seemed to understand that they were now profaned by having been seen by others, but he said that he agreed with the old men. They should come home.

He was a sincere bahana, Emory thought. A kind of warrior. Emory's clan had been a warrior clan, protecting the people, staying on the boundaries. . . . A lot of these things were changing now, he thought, wondering who the enemy was. In the old days . . . Utes, Navajos, Apaches. Then bahanas. Now . . .

Ourselves, he thought. Always ourselves.

What, he wondered, would the FBI man be able to do?

Calling. Callings. *Collins.* There. Collins. Good. The old man neared his house.

"Is that you, Emory?"

It was Mo, Connie's man. An in-law of a sort. Sons-in-law were always right in what they said, according to Hopi custom, so Emory decided to ask Mo about the FBI man. They were both bahanas, after all.

"The ladies," Mo said. "They're still off taking care of Darrel's family."

"I been thinkin'. There's an Eff Bee Eye man out helpin us with some things. Collins. You know him?"

"Yeah, I do." Mo considered the actual odds against his happening to know the agent out of the millions of people in the Anglo world. In the small and narrow world of the Hopi, he mused, everyone knows everyone else, and Emory simply thought that is how it is everywhere. "Emory? You ever been to Las Vegas, Nevada? Someday I'm going to take you there. Hah—hah."

Emory didn't understand, but he laughed good-naturedly.

Ten

As the two-lane road begins its curvilinear rise out of the cheerfully seedy west side of Tucson into the Tucson Mountains, newcomers are often momentarily surprised by the appearance outside their right-hand window of a vast and severe building designed to look like a medieval castle—or at least someone's approximation of a medieval castle. It is stark, gray and imposing. It is properly remote, lying beyond a stream—and a parking lot. Its barren high walls are crenellated. Near its entrance an oversized bronze cheetah woodenly surveys the area. It seems completely two-dimensional, a shotgun wedding of Old Europe and the phony storefronts of the Old West—in stone. It is the most, perhaps only, foreboding-looking building in the Tucson area where the general style (if one exists at all) can be thought of as happy-go-lucky. Most people in Tucson know little about the castlelike building to their west besides the fact that it is the International Museum of Wildlife. Beyond that, a questioner will be greeted with a slightly bewildered shrug.

Even Willie Blaine, who pulled up into the parking lot at nine o'clock in the morning with everything in his life to gain from whatever lay within its walls, was struck by the building's awesome and bizarre pretension.

"Sickos," said Willie out loud. "Whoever these guys are, they're sickos." He got out of the Oldsmobile and reached in his pocket to touch the key from the locker at the bus station. Safe and sound, he thought, safe and sound. Make the deal, give the clown the key, take the money and hop on the bus. Outta *here*! No fuss, no muss, no . . .

He ducked back into the front seat of the Olds and looked at himself in the mirror. Hair okay. He had pulled out a pair of brown slacks, a clean shirt, boots, and a bolo tie with a silver clasp, wanted to look businesslike—who knew what the hell he was going to have to cope with? Had his first shower in two, three days, practically no water pressure in the fucking fleabag that had cost him forty-nine dollars, for Christ . . . Well, he'd slept well, had gotten a shower out of it. He was ready.

It had to be pushing ninety degrees already, and Willie sweated under his arms, wishing he didn't sweat so much, especially under his arms. He stepped onto the narrow bridge that crossed a stream some fifteen feet below and paused to look at a handful of ducks that busybodied around in the shallows. Carefree little assholes, he thought, and headed for the unwelcoming entrance to the museum. Inside, he was enveloped in what seemed to be a huge cavern. There were a couple of small lights in the high ceiling above him. His heels clumped on a marblelike floor. Off to the right he saw another light source. He took off his sunglasses and the cavern resolved itself into a huge empty hall, to the right of which was what appeared to be a reception desk with a guy standing behind it, and beyond that some kind of store area. Straight back from the hall he stood in was a long corridor, lit every twenty, thirty feet by some kind of overhead spotlight. The silence was intimidating.

Jesus, thought Willie. This place'd shrivel the pecker of Superman's kung fu instructor. He decided to explore the store area before making his move, maybe find out what kind of a dump this was. To get to the store area, he had to pass the information booth and the guy behind it, who was screwing around doing something, looking in the other direction. Softly he walked past the desk, and the guy turned his head slowly. Greaseball, blond hair slicked back, bland face. Willie nodded and the geek said, "Good morning. You can go in the bookstore free, of course. Museum admission is three dollars."

"Great," said Willie. The bookstore, if that is what it was, was also out of scale, a large, dimly lit room—yet more overhead spotlights that didn't dispel the shadows, but only served to emphasize them—with several rows of elegant wooden shelves that were mostly empty. There was a bunch of books about birds, mostly pheasants and that shit, and a section on big cats. There was another section called "China," which had some books about pandas. Willie found a shelf given over to what appeared to be a series of yearbooks and, looking closer, saw that they were trophy hunters' records. So, Willie thought, this is a place for those assholes who go out and line up lions and gazelles and blow 'em away with those big fucking cannons. Not the goody-goodies who mope around about spotted frigging owls and six transparent fish in some damn cave. Okay.

Willie hitched up his bolo and sauntered over to the geek at the desk, who looked up blandly.

"Name's Blaine," said Willie. "Nice place. New?"

"We've been open for two years," said the geek.

"Yeah, well, I've been in Africa since—it's been three years now since I've been home. A lot has changed."

"Yes."

"A friend of mine—Robert Breeden? He said I should stop by here. He has something for me." Willie almost choked.

The geek beamed. "Oh, yeah. Mr. Breeden. You're a friend of his?"

"We go back a ways," said Willie.

"Well, you're a bit early. Mr. Breeden is expected at eleven. There's a luncheon for him. At noon."

"Eleven, huh? Well, why don't I check back around then," said Willie, withdrawing toward the cavernous entrance hall.

"You can have a look around, if you'd like, Mister, uh . . ."

"Blaine."

"On the house."

"Thanks, thanks a lot, but I've got to—have to make some calls. See you later." He put on his sunglasses and strode through the hall toward the entrance.

Out in the sunlight Willie Blaine put his shoulders back, breathed in deeply and said, "Bingo."

The call came through direct from Washington, D.C., at eight forty-five in the morning. Some loyal soul in the J. Edgar Hoover Building, following up on business. Ramirez, his hair mussed from a restless night, stood in his narrow kitchen, scribbling on an empty paper bag from the supermarket. He had made an attempt at a pleasantry, to the effect that the FBI never slept, never even took off time for church, and the voice at the other end had not reacted one way or the other.

"This is Sergeant Ramirez?"

"Si, yes, yes."

"In response to interrogatory number six-five-oh-eight-one-oh from Albuquerque dated eleven June, there were two incoming calls from Singapore to northern New Mexico from your time six A.M. Tuesday, six June, to six P.M. Wednesday, seven June."

"Two calls?"

"That's what I said. Shall I proceed." It was not a question.

"Yes."

"The first was made on Tuesday morning at ten your time to Al Fatima, an Arabian horse farm in Taos. The call originated from the household of the horse farm's owner, who apparently calls at least once a week."

"Yeah, okay, and the other."

"The second call in this period originated from a restaurant in Singapore"—he gave the name and number, the same place Meyers had called—"and the party called a number in Espanola. Ortega's Bar. This was at five thirty-eight your time on Tuesday afternoon."

"Any more?"

"Those were the only two calls."

"No, no. Anything else about the call to Espanola? Duration?"

"One minute and fifty-six seconds."

"How was it paid for?"

"Charged to the line where it originated."

"Anything else you can tell me?"

"It's raining here."

"Hey, listen, thanks—"

The line went dead, and Ramirez fixed himself a pot of coffee. While it rumbled and burped, he took a long shower, thinking about Ortega's in Espanola, a dump, a place where Hispanic lowlifes demonstrated their courage and turned DWI into a code of honor. Thought they were some kind of modern nobles, obliged to show off.

So now, at nine-fifteen on Sunday morning, Sergeant Ramirez, wrapped in a towel, stood sipping black coffee and wondering if he should make the call. Was it too early? It was, after all, Sunday morning. Why was he sweating it? It was police business. Darts. He dialed the number.

"Yes?"

"Miz del Massimo?"

"Yes."

"This is Sergeant Ramirez. I'm sorry to bother you, Sunday morning and all, but I've learned something about the other night, when you were—"

"Yes?" she said eagerly.

"Could I talk to you, uh, come over to your—"

"Of course. In an hour?"

"Yes, ma'am," Ramirez said. "An hour."

An hour later Ramirez was seated on the white sofa in Marianna del Massimo's living room, looking at the view of the mountains from her window.

"How do you take it, Sergeant?" she called from the kitchen.

"Oh, black, please, thank you."

Marianna emerged, bearing two large mugs decorated with Mimbres lizards. She was dressed in white slacks and a flowing white cotton shirt. The official mourning period was over, Ramirez thought to himself, at least here. She set one of the mugs down on the low table in front of him and sat down in an easy chair.

"So," she said. "The Santa Fe police never sleep?"

Ramirez smiled to himself, and had unofficial considerations in his mind. "I'm sorry to bother you on a Sunday," he said, "but it seemed important. You see, we have some information that suggests—it suggests only, there is nothing certain—but those men who chased you on Wednesday night in the plaza . . . ?"

"Yes?"

"They may not have just been, you know, random troublemakers."

Marianna put her coffee mug on the table and leaned back in her chair. "What makes you think that? May I ask?"

"Oh, of course. It's really a hunch, a policeman's hunch." He looked up and smiled narrowly. She smiled back. "A few details in a pattern," he continued. "It's really vague, tenuous."

"Well, Sergeant, can you give me some idea . . . ?"

"I'll have to be, you know, vague too. See, we've been tracking phone calls from a person who might have an interest in the Meyers Gallery, and he called a place where the kind of guys hang out who could have—"

"Someone with an *interest* in the gallery?"

"You know, in buying some stuff."

"Oh, a client."

"Yeah, I guess so."

"Can you tell me who?"

"Well, no ma'am. I can't. Not now."

"I ask because the gallery's business will have to continue, once . . ."

"Oh, I understand, Miz del Massimo. I'm sure this will all be okay in a while, soon as this is, uh, over. The reason why I brought it up is because there is an outside possibility, as I said, that the other night might have been deliberate. Done on orders. So there are two questions I wanted to ask you. The first is, can you think of any reason why someone would want to bother you, scare you, anything like that?"

Marianna looked at Ramirez over the lip of her coffee mug. Her eyes seemed to be smiling at him.

"This sounds like something on television," she said. "Is truth as banal as fiction?" She raised her eyebrows. "Forgive me, Sergeant. I wasn't mocking you or making light of your . . . concern. At all." She sipped from the mug, and put it down. "No, I can't think of any reason on earth why anyone would want to terrorize me. Some client of the gallery? I can't imagine a reason." She paused. "You know of course about Walter Meyers's will."

Ramirez nodded.

"I do hope to be able to raise the money to buy the gallery. I love the business. Perhaps there's someone else who wants to buy it, someone who is lurking out there, who knows about the option Walter put in his will for me. Would that be a reason for such a . . . ? To try and scare me off, so the gallery will go up for public sale?"

"Possible," Ramirez said. "Do you know of any of the gallery's clients who have that much of an interest?"

Marianna thought. "No. Not offhand. No. I think it must have been one of those things, Sergeant, just a bunch of hoodlums out wilding. . . ." She sounded to Ramirez like someone trying to convince herself.

"Well, the other question I wanted to ask? The other night, when it happened, we put a police officer outside, you remember . . ."

"I certainly do. It meant a great deal to my peace of mind."

"Well, all we have is this vague business with the phone call to a place where that sort of person hangs out, and if you thought there was some risk, you know, from your standpoint, we could have someone watch out for you . . . for your peace of mind."

Marianna watched Ramirez intently as he talked. When he was finished, she smiled at him.

"Sergeant Ramirez, this is probably not the sort of thing that someone is supposed to say to someone like you, I mean, a policeman, but you are very sweet to be so concerned. I really appreciate it." She leaned forward. "But I really don't think . . . well, I just don't feel that I'm in any danger from anyone associated with the gallery. So thank you, but no. I'm okay."

"Okay," Ramirez said. "That's good, that's fine. I just wanted to make sure. . . ." He stood up. "Thanks for the coffee. Now you can have a little peace, huh?"

She shook hands with him at the door, and he went down the outdoor staircase wondering if he had done the right thing in the first place, or made a fool of himself and the Santa Fe Police Department, or if he had learned something.

And upstairs, standing with her arms folded, looking out the window as Ramirez pulled out of the parking lot and headed south back into town, Marianna del Massimo wondered exactly what the sloe-eyed detective had been up to, and if she had responded properly to whatever chess game he had in mind. She wondered about the mysterious caller, and decided to look at the telephone records in the gallery on Monday. She needed not a half-million dollars, as Nigel had suggested, but a quarter of a million—thanks to dear old Ramon Chavez, who had married her mother.

She crossed the room and picked up the telephone, poking the buttons deftly.

"Hello."

"Nigel. It's me. What are you doing tonight?"

"You, I hope."

She laughed. "What would you think of tea?"

"Tea," he said.

"Foursies."

"Lovely. With scones and all?"

"Yes."

"And honey?"

"Yes." She laughed again.

"Four-thirty all right?"

"Fine."

"I'll see you then," he said.

Marianna hung up the phone slowly. *It's so nice,* she hummed to herself, *to have a man around the house. Especially when some son of a bitch is out to get you, maybe kill you.* She decided not to wait till Monday. She would run down to the gallery and have a look at those phone records today. If the SFPD could figure them out, certainly she could.

The manager of the Pima Inn was an ambitious man who had studied the manners of the wealthy—especially the old wealthy—the way some people study computer programming or fine cooking. He now knew the lingo, indeed it had become a part of him. Indeed, so isolated was he, so much of his time spent serving the inn's well-to-do clientele, that he had come to expect the world to conform to his narrow preconceptions. He was tingling with excitement over the call he had received from an agent of the FBI, following up on a conversation he had earlier had with the policeman in Santa Fe. A *homicide* investigation.

His first thought, of course, had been to fret that the inn itself was implicated, but he assured himself that it was not. And thus assured, he could revel in his possible role in the unfolding drama. Of course, his notion of such matters, such as what to expect from a visit by an FBI agent, had been formed mostly by watching television programs, and so he was nonplussed when the strange man in the blue windbreaker and curly hair showed up Sunday morning at the desk, asking for him. The agent now sat slumped in a chair in his office.

"So tell me about this guy Breeden," he said.

The manager leaned back in his chair behind the desk. He put a slip of paper on top of a neat pile of other slips of paper.

"He's been a guest of the inn for the last five, no six, years. He visits Tucson about once a year, usually in April or May. He makes his reservations—or I should say one of his people makes his reservations—about two months in advance. From Singapore. He generally stays for a week, two weeks. As, for instance, his last visit. He was here for two weeks until about ten days ago—a week ago this past Friday, to be exact."

The agent nodded.

"Then, last Wednesday, only five days after he left, he called to make another reservation, for last night and tonight, but those reservations were canceled."

"Any reason?"

"No. None offered."

"Okay, let me ask you this. How does this guy pay?"

"Typically, we receive a bank check from Singapore several weeks in advance, typically for the cost of the room plus about fifty percent. He settles any balance that's due in cash."

The agent nodded again.

"Does he come alone?"

"Alone? Well, yes. Except for a chauffeur."

"The chauffeur comes from Singapore?"

"I believe there is a man who meets Mr. Breeden here, works for him while he is in Tucson."

The agent brightened. "Got a name? Address?"

The manager opened a drawer before him and took out a white card, about four-by-six. "This is Mr. Breeden's latest registration card." He handed it to the agent.

"Chauffer or valet," the agent read. "Anthony Baca. No address. There must be a thousand Anthony Bacas."

"It is not that widespread a name in this area," the manager said.

"You know, this guy Breeden doesn't put an address down here for himself either. Do you have an address for him? In Singapore?"

"Yes, of course. In the files. We know him, of course, so naturally we don't require—we don't even expect him to put down his address every time he comes. I can get you the address."

"Classy place," the agent said as if to himself. "But you know something? You may think you know this guy Breeden, but you don't."

"I beg your pardon?"

"Well, look, he pays by a bank check and cash, so you got no credit card on him, nothing. He just shows up and then leaves. You've got an address, sure, but do you know if that's where he really lives? Do you know who he is, what he does?"

The manager was flustered. "I . . . I . . . we . . ."

"See what I mean?" the agent said with a grin. "This guy Breeden could be anyone. What do you know about him? What does he do when he's here?"

"In fact, as I told the officer in Santa Fe," the manager said, recovering slightly, "he is a sportsman. A hunter. He donated a collection of trophies to the International Museum of Wildlife. Last year, I believe. And, if memory serves me right, he is also a collector."

"A collector? Of what?"

"Art. Indian art. Mexican art. I believe that after most of his visits here, he stays in Mexico for a while."

"Why would he come here for Indian art? This ain't the center for that stuff. Santa Fe maybe. L.A."

The manager was miffed. Impatiently he said, "Perhaps he likes the accommodations."

"Yeah, yeah. And then there's that museum connection, with the trophies," said the agent, again as if to himself. "So tell me about this guy."

The manager looked quizzically across the desk.

"Description," the agent said.

"Oh. Yes. Well, he's a man in his early sixties, I'd say. Healthy-looking, as you'd expect with an outdoorsman. Tanned. He's about, what, five-six, slight, you might even think of him as small. White hair, a healthy head of white hair. Quiet-spoken."

"Where's he from?"

"What? Singapore."

"No, no. Is he American, British?"

"Oh, yes. He's American."

"What's the chauffeur, Baca, look like?"

"I've never seen the chauffeur."

The agent stood up. "Okay, thanks. You've been very helpful."

"Is there any—"

"I'm set," said the agent, and disappeared through the door. The manager felt cheated somehow.

T. Moore Bowdre sat on the front stoop of the house Connie's uncles had built, enjoying the feeling of the sun on his face, smelling the cedar smoke from the outdoor ovens. The screen door opened behind him and he heard the old man, Emory, step outside.

"Emory?"

"Yeah."

"I'm just sitting here enjoying the sun."

The old man shuffled up alongside and slowly sat down.

"No rain," he said, and Mo could tell that he hadn't put in his teeth this morning. The two sat in silence for a few moments, and then the old man resumed. "My brother's tellin me that the clouds came over his fields yesterday but they didn't rain. It's like that now. Dances don't work sometimes."

Mo was silent.

"You think that Eff Bee Eye man, Collins, gonna find them things?"

"He's sure trying."

"Hope so," said the old man. "Lot of trouble. The people all confused, you know, arguments, accusin each other. Troubles. Probably makes the prayers, what do you say? Thin."

"That's bad," Mo said.

"Maybe," the old man said, "maybe it's time."

"Time?"

"Time for some of those old ways to go. Some of those old ceremonies. Maybe things have got too, you know, complicated. That's what some people are sayin. They say we need to go back, back to simpler times, when the people were humble."

"I'm not sure I understand," said Mo.

"That's okay," said the old man. "We're just two blind men tryin to see."

"Hah—hah—hah."

The old man giggled and was silent.

"Anyway," he resumed, "there'll be troubles here till that Eff Bee Eye man gets those things, bring 'em back. Troubles follow 'em too."

"Follow them?"

The old man whistled tunelessly. "Them things are dangerous. People touch 'em, use 'em wrong, you know, bad luck . . . they say it was Darrel who took 'em, you know."

Mo recalled Collins's tale about the man in Phoenix driving

off the embankment in his brand new pickup. He wondered if there were a Hopi phrase, even a Hopi concept, that meant QED.

"Vengeance," Mo said.

"Something like that . . . maybe. I don't know. I'm a blind old man." Again Emory whistled tunelessly. "You goin back to Santa Fe today?"

"Tomorrow, I think. After Darrel's buried."

"Well, if you see that man, tell him to hurry up. We got to get this all over with, get it resolved. Lot of people here are forgettin . . . forgettin what's right."

Okay, it makes sense. Perfectly good sense.

Collins urged events to play into his hands. It was less a hunch than a prayer. Okay, this guy who uses the identity of Robert Breeden here in the USA has got to be the guy Meyers was going to sell those deities to. And Willie Blaine has got to be the guy who killed Meyers and then ran off with the deities. Somehow he gets the number or something for this Breeden character and is going to make the sale himself and heads off to L.A. Then he calls Breeden and the plans change, so he goes to Sedona, and the plans change again. Breeden *planned* to come here to Tucson, so probably Blaine came to Tucson. So where is he? Christ only knows. And where is Breeden? Shit. If I find Breeden, I'll find Blaine. And if I can find that no-good, I can get those . . . So there's only one place to look.

Routinely, he called in a description of Breeden to the Tucson field office, but he didn't expect anything to come of that. And a half hour later he pulled into the parking lot of the castlelike building west of town. The air temperature was pushing the mid-nineties and the sun was like a blast furnace when Collins stepped out of the air-conditioned car. Inside, it was dark and cool and Collins was relieved. He spotted a blond guy behind some kind of reception desk and went over to him.

"Can I help you?"

"Yeah, maybe. I'm looking for a Robert Breeden."

"Oh, are you here for the lunch?"

"The lunch?"

"There was going to be a lunch for Mr. Breeden. Obviously you're not here for that."

"Did you say 'was going to be'?" Collins asked.

The blond guy looked put off.

"Excuse me," he said, "but can I ask what—"

Collins flipped out his wallet and let it fall open about six inches in front of the guy's nose.

"Can you read those big red letters?"

"Yes."

"I'm trying to locate Mr. Robert Breeden. Talk to me, fella. What about this lunch? Start there."

"The museum had planned a small lunch for Mr. Breeden. He was going to be in town for a few days unexpectedly, and I guess it was all sort of hurried. But then, just an hour ago, he called to say that he couldn't make it. The people upstairs have tried to call all the guests, but some of them had already left, so they told me to explain things to them when they show up."

"So where *is* Breeden?"

"I have no idea."

"Does anyone upstairs have an idea?"

"You'd have to ask them."

"I will. Let me ask you this. Did you see a guy come here, medium height, medium build, short mousy-colored hair, a guy named Blaine? Did anyone like that come in here today?"

The man crossed his arms. "No. Not that I can remember."

A prissy little bastard. "And you'd remember, right?"

"Yes," he said, smiling. "We don't get many visitors here."

Collins reached out and picked up a small message pad that lay on the reception desk. He took a pen out of his pocket and said: "Okay, who do I talk to upstairs? This place have a director or something?"

The priss pronounced a name, and spelled it, while Collins scribbled on the message pad and tore off the paper.

"Thanks," he said, and headed for the elevator.

Once he had penetrated the gloom and spotlights—the old black-and-white photographs of sportsmen going back to a collection of toothy Teddy Roosevelt photos from Africa, apparently of an expedition mounted shortly after his presidency—and the rest of the upstairs decor of the museum, Collins came upon the museum's director, a round and good-humored woman of about sixty years. The woman was perfectly straightforward. Yes, she had met Robert Breeden once, a rather charming little man, soft-spoken. Yes, he had become a considerable benefactor of the museum by donating a collection of trophies of Asian wildlife and, importantly, a fund, the interest from which helped to cover the museum's overhead. No, she had never had occasion to contact Breeden directly in Singapore except, of course, by mail. No, come to think of it, he had never answered her few letters directly. He called up every now and then—it was as if he didn't read his mail. Yes, once she had heard he would be in town, she called a number of people, including three board members, to have a celebratory lunch. The others? Local sportsmen . . . and sportswomen, of which there were several. Yes, she was startled, to say the least, when he had called only an hour ago to say that he wouldn't be available for the lunch. After all, she had made these arrangements and . . . No, she had no idea where he was calling from, or in fact who had called. It could have been Mr. Breeden himself, yes, but . . . Yes, he was a bit of a mystery man, but very generous and no one, Mister, ah . . . Collins, who is trying to start a business like a private museum, is going to look a gift horse in the . . . Pencil? She had a pen. A pencil, an old-fashioned wooden pencil? No, she didn't have such a thing. Perhaps . . . well, she was sorry she hadn't been able to be more help . . . yes, of course, goodbye . . .

A half hour later Collins found a pencil—in a Circle K

store—and bought it, thinking that there was probably no hope for a world where it took a half hour to find as straightforward and basic a tool as a wooden pencil. Seated in his car, he rubbed it lightly across the sheet of paper he had taken from the museum's reception desk, and a telephone number, indented in the paper by the heavy-handed blond liar, emerged. Seven digits. Familiar. He checked his notebook. So, thought Collins. It's off to Patagonia. Me, Breeden, and Blaine. All on our way to Patagonia and the Institute of Sonoran Archeology, whatever the hell that is.

Stylishly discreet in a pair of gray slacks and a loose blouse of a quiet pattern, Marianna del Massimo made her way along the sidewalk through the clumps of tourists to the front of the Meyers Gallery. A formidable pair of dowagers stood at the door, looking at the sign that, without explanation, said CLOSED.

"It doesn't make any sense," one of the women said. "It's the height of the season. Closed?"

"How disappointing," the other said. "Eleanor told me that it had wonderful things. Well . . ."

Marianna waited until the two women had moved off, and opened the door of the gallery with three of the keys on her key ring. Inside, she took up a position under the archway between the anteroom and the gallery's main room and surveyed the domain that she had come to think of as hers. She noted with a tingle in her chest the satin patina of age on the curvilinear pottery nestled in the niches of the walls, the bizarre geometry of the kachina dolls pinned here and there between the niches, the plenitude of beads, the simple grace of a Cheyenne lance, feathered and multicolored, cheerful decorations of death—these morbid people, making so much of dying that they made light of it—the perky little umbilical fetishes mounted on the stucco walls, stubby little bags like lizards and turtles sewn with beads, the little saddle with a tiny man on it, his head made of a rawhide bag full of God knew what the old Arapahos thought was medicine, and on the mantel the simple sticks, nearly white, unfinished, lightly carved to suggest a head at the top, toys perhaps, or maybe something from some secret and unspoken ceremony at Acoma. An odd thought struck Marianna: they looked like dildos.

Moments passed. She stepped out of her low-heeled shoes and, barefoot, crossed to the shiny walnut stand that held the big Zuni kachina mask, slit eyes staring blankly at her, round beak nose thrust toward her, and lifted it up. Holding the mask at arm's length in both hands, she began to dance, swaying and turning, gyrating around the room, looking into the expressionless face, licking her lips with a darting tongue.

She stopped, holding the mask, and giggled. What am I doing? she thought. What *am* I doing? She put the mask back on its pedestal and padded across the cool tiles to the office. Behind the desk, she opened the door and looked for a time at the place on the floor where the police had drawn the outline of Meyers's corpse, where it had collapsed onto the floor. The chalk lines were now gone, erased. She wondered who it was who got stuck with such chores. The tiles were shiny and clean, as if nothing had happened. Nothing at all.

In the walnut-veneer filing cabinets, Marianna quickly found the telephone records and began her search. By the process of elimination, she arrived at three oddball numbers, two in Arizona, and one foreign. She noted that Meyers had called the foreign number every Tuesday for several weeks, then not for two weeks, and then one last time on Monday, the night he was killed. She noted also that during the two weeks when the foreign number had not been called, Meyers had called the strange numbers in Arizona. In fact, he had called each of the Arizona numbers several times, as if whoever was supposed to be there wasn't. But what struck Marianna as extraordinary was that all the calls to the foreign number had been made at eleven o'clock at night—long after Meyers was normally in bed. He had been, Marianna knew, fanatic about being in bed before ten, and so it was perfectly clear that whatever business Meyers had with whomever was at this foreign number, it was something of major importance.

Those sticks that the FBI agent had sketched.

Whatever they were.

Ugly, coarse. Like most ceremonial stuff—quickly made during some ceremony, not carefully crafted beforehand, something that was one of a kind. Something stolen. Something worth a lot of money. A *lot* of money.

It took Marianna no more than ten minutes to find Meyers's little cache of drawings, the ones he compulsively made of even the illegal artifacts.

Everything he owned, he had told her once, had a price, everything was for sale. If you have anything—any single thing—you won't sell for the right price, you are a sentimentalist and don't belong in the business. But, Marianna recalled, Meyers had a large and ferocious-looking Hopi ogre kachina doll with violent teeth and wild coarse hair that he kept on a mantel in his dining room. She had once overheard a visitor to Meyers's quarters exclaim about the ogre, wanting to buy it, and Meyers had said that it was, like everything else in his gallery and home and in the world, for sale. He had then, after what Marianna took to be a stream of ethnological double-talk, dropped on his visitor the price, which was about six times what Marianna had ever heard for any artifact of that sort. It was far too high for the buyer, and so she had assumed that Meyers was guilty of sentiment in at least one case. But of course there was no sentiment to it at all.

Marianna padded into the dining room and approached the ogre. She took it from the mantel and turned it slowly in her hands, and looked for a long time at the toothed beak, the bulbous black and white knobby eyes. She took the beak with one hand and wiggled it. Pop. The face came away, revealing a carefully chiseled-out cavity which held several neatly folded

pieces of paper. Most of these were drawings of especially stunning masks, unlike any Marianna had seen before. They were
labeled *Hopi*, and the most exquisite of them bore Meyers's
little notation 22500/95000. Nice little profit, there, Marianna
thought, and the most expensive Indian mask she had ever
heard of. The last piece of paper she unfolded showed four
pieces of what looked like gnarled sticks—cottonwood root,
maybe, like the junk wood that litters some of the old dry
washes out on the desert and along the Rio Grande. But by a
series of tiny dots made with pencil, Meyers had indicated a
crude, almost cartoonlike face carved—really just indented—
on the upper end of each stick. They were grotesque, even
tormented-looking sticks. They looked a lot like the FBI agent's
rude sketch. And in the lower left-hand corner of the paper was
Meyers's little record: Hopi, 45000/250000. No underlining.

He hadn't sold them.

A quarter of a million. Marianna's heart pounded in her
chest so hard she wondered if it could be heard in the street.

She folded up the drawings and put them back in the head
of the ogre. She popped the ogre's face back on and put it
back on the mantel. Her heart kept thudding against her ribs
and she felt giddy. She sat down on the floor, on a Ganado
Red Navajo rug worth twelve thousand dollars—peanuts, why
not put it on the floor?—and tried to catch her breath. All I
have to do, she told herself, is find those things, whatever they
are, and this whole place and everything in it is mine. The
whole . . . place.

No, there's more, she reminded herself. I have to find out
what the damned things are.

Ramirez. The quiet, sloe-eyed detective. He knew what they
were, working with that agent. She could find out from him.
The businesslike, quiet-spoken detective, full of police routine
and Hispanic courtesy and, Marianna smiled to herself, an
unmistakable hard-on for Marianna del Massimo.

Then, the buyer. This foreign number, the two numbers in

Arizona. She would see what she could find out about them
. . . but not from the gallery's phone. Maybe she'd get Nigel to
call them and find out who was at the other end. She was
elated. On her way out she scooped up her shoes, curtsied in
the direction of the Zuni mask, and walked barefoot out of the
gallery to her car. Forty-five minutes later, when Nigel Calderwood tapped on her door, she greeted him wearing a purple
and red silk kimono and nothing else.

"Take off your clothes, Nigel," she said as he stepped
through the door. "I've been feeling . . . carnal all afternoon."

When the greaseball blond had given Willie Blaine the bad
news, a strange feeling of calm took him, instead of the typical
adrenaline rush of fury and frustration. Willie himself was
amazed.

"Oh," Willie had heard himself saying. "He's been de-
tained. Nothing serious, I hope."

The geek shrugged. "He didn't say, apparently. But he did
leave word that you were to call this number." He tore a piece
of paper off a little pad and handed it to Willie.

"What's this?"

"It's a number somewhere in southern Arizona, but not local. You'll have to dial one."

So Willie had walked out of the museum, still feeling
strangely calm, got in his car and drove back toward Tucson,
looking for a pay phone. He found one in a gas station, and
it even had an intact telephone book hanging from a chain.
Willie hunted around in the front pages until he found a map
with the phone exchanges on it. So the number, he discovered,
was somewhere down around Sonoita and Patagonia, a couple
of little dots on the map halfway down to the Mexican border.

Hey, there you go, he thought to himself. Make the deal,
take the cash, and just drift over that border. Buy a hacienda
in some Mexican town, south, away from the fucking desert,
find one of those big-eyed Mexican girls, big tits, do anything

for you, "Si, Weellie, si," maybe get in the export business, start a little hotel for rich American tourists, what the hell . . . it sounded good.

In the phone booth, Willie called the number. After a few long seconds of silence, the phone buzzed, ringing. It rang ten times, then two more, and Willie hung up, thinking: shit, it's Sunday, maybe the place is closed. But what if it isn't a place, but a house, and there's nobody home—thinking he would try again in a half hour. It had all begun to seem fragile. This guy, Breeden, just a name on a piece of paper with a date and a phone number, L.A. area code, never there, always somebody giving him a message. Go there. Call this number. The guy always moving on. Was there a real guy, a real Robert Breeden? There had to be, Willie thought, there fuckin' had to be. Where else would Willie find this kind of high roller? He wasn't interested in any chickenshit five-figure deals, screwing around with greedy middlemen, pompous little cruds in galleries, nah. This was the big one.

The . . . big . . . one.

He had realized it once he'd heard what the guy in Phoenix got—thirty, forty large ones? And there was no way that criminal prick in Santa Fe wasn't going to quadruple it. Thinking back, Willie was outraged. He'd been had, screwed, robbed— but no more, no more. He didn't know what he'd do if this Breeden guy was a permanent no-show. He decided not to think about that possibility. He'd call the number in a while, keep trying, maybe drive down that way, spend the night in one of those little dots on the map in the middle of nowhere. He called the number three more times, with the same result, and headed south in his stolen car, thinking, I better get rid of this thing. He would not be disappointed. Maybe tomorrow he'd dump the car in one of these hick towns.

Glen Greene of Mesa, Arizona, was disappointed . . . and more. He had found that the congressional aide he was going all the way to Washington, D.C., to see was not, as planned, going to be in the city. So the hours in his firm's Washington office, preparing for the meeting, had been wasted, and the weather had been even muggier than Phoenix, and he couldn't just tell the managing partner in the D.C. office that he'd rather not stay over Saturday and have dinner at the partner's house in Potomac, so Glen Greene wasn't in much of a mood when he stepped off the plane Sunday afternoon in Phoenix, where it was a hundred ten degrees, and discovered that his car was not in the long-term lot where he had left it.

Within a half hour it had been established that Greene really did know where he had left his car, that it was no place else in the lot, that it had in fact been stolen. And it was only fifteen minutes later that an alert Phoenix cop had run the license of the beat-up Ford pickup, and the cops knew, and then the FBI knew, that it was Willie Blaine who had stolen Glen Greene's maroon Oldsmobile Cutlass. Police in all the mountain states and up the West Coast were routinely put on the alert for the car, but Willie pulled up in front of the only motel in Patagonia early that evening without having caught the attention of anyone at all. It was a place called the Wagon Wheel, and Willie said to himself, as he walked into the little room labeled OFFICE, Hey, wow, pioneers, maybe they got the Conestoga Lounge; but in fact it wasn't that sort of place at all. There was no lounge, and Willie, having put down two twenty-dollar bills and having received six dollars in change, got handed a key with a red piece of plastic on it that said 8. Inside his room, which had a double bed, a TV, a bathroom, and a weird painting/drawing/whatever of two guys with hatchetlike faces—sort of Indian but not really, signed "Pena," the two guys sitting on their asses, staring at pots they had evidently just found in their midst—Willie turned on the TV and Dan Rather was talking about some foreign bullshit, his eyes darting back and forth as if he had just been caught colluding in the problem. Something to do with international banks and

Arabs. It was always international banks and Arabs. Willie thought, Maybe, if this guy Breeden evaporates, I can find me a fuckin Ay-rab high roller to buy the stuff.

Next door, in Room 7, a man lay on his double bed watching Dan Rather's eyes flicker back and forth, thinking the whole world is going to hell and I'm not doing a thing to save it the way I was told I should, chasing this punk all around Arizona. It's a big world, Larry Collins thought, never mind all those goody-goody NASA photographs from the moon.

Eleven

A few minutes past six A.M., with the sun peering reddishly over the hills outside of town, Larry Collins opened the door of his motel room and stepped out on the concrete sidewalk to enjoy the coolest part of the day. He stretched luxuriously, and listened to the faint popping of his vertebrae. Then he said, "Jesus!"

Ten feet away, sitting next to his green Chevrolet, was a maroon Oldsmobile Cutlass, right there, the right year and—he darted out into the parking lot—yes, the right license plate. It was Blaine. Willie Blaine, probably sawing wood in the next goddamn room. Collins darted back into Room 7 and picked up the phone, dialing the office in Tucson. The graveyard shift answered, and Collins, speaking quietly but very distinctly, explained that he had located the car stolen by Willie Blaine from the Phoenix airport, and that everyone—*every*one—should be called off. He didn't want Blaine picked up, because he wanted to keep him under surveillance. Was all that clear? He hung up and stared at the phone for a moment, contemplating the odds that the message would get through to, say, some sleepy state trooper in southern Arizona cruising around before his shift ended.

In the parking lot, he opened up the hood of the Oldsmobile and removed the distributor cap, putting it in his pocket. He tapped his forehead, went to the Chevrolet and opened the window on the driver's side a few inches—enough for a man's arm—and locked the door. Smiling, he walked to the office and went in. The door jingled in the silence. Collins stepped up to the desk and hit the button on the old-fashioned service bell. More silence. He hit the bell again. "Excuse me?"

He heard a soft thump from somewhere down a hall behind the desk, and presently the swishing sound of slippered feet. The old proprietor appeared, looking startled, eyes drooping with sleep but bugged out, like a frog. He was wearing a worn bathrobe over pajamas, and he pushed a string of gray hair away from his face with a preternaturally large hand.

"Si?" he said.

"I'm Collins, Room Seven."

"What's the matter?"

Collins held out his wallet and let it fall open. "I'm with the FBI and—"

"I can't read that without my glasses," the old man said.

"It says FBI. . . ."

"I'll be back. Get my glasses."

Jeezus, thought Collins. Another one of these passive-aggressive back-country fed haters. In a moment the old man reappeared with a pair of trifocals on his nose. Collins held out his wallet, and the old man, his neck craned, peered at it.

"FBI," the old man mumbled.

"Like I said."

"So . . . ? It's awful early. . . ."

"I need to commandeer a vehicle. Federal business. What about that pickup out back, the Dodge?"

The old man blinked. "Commandeer? You can't do that.

What am I supposed— What's the matter with the car you came in?"

"It's going to be stolen."

"Huh?"

"Look, never mind all that. Give me the keys to that pickup out back, I assume it's yours. I'll leave you with wheels."

"Huh?"

"Get me the keys, now, please."

Two minutes later Larry Collins parked the big Dodge pickup across the street under a tree and wondered what he would do about the armed rebellion in his stomach. He'd eaten nothing but trash food for three days, and not very much of that. He craned his neck and looked back up the street at the little coffee shop. It was closed. He started the engine and slowly backed up until he could see the sign with the hours. Seven. Shit. More than a half hour. He could see the motel, the Oldsmobile, and his own car from where he sat, so he settled down in the pickup, grumbling to himself about what a special agent of the Federal Bureau of Investigation can, and cannot, commandeer.

By ten past seven Collins was in the truck parked under the tree, with coffee, toast, and a side order of bacon. At seven forty-five, Blaine's door opened and he emerged into the sun, squinting out at the road. He set out on foot for the coffee shop, crossing the highway behind Collins's truck. Moments later a state trooper's car appeared in Collins's rearview mirror, cruising down the highway through town like some big fish. It slowed in front of the motel, and Collins thought, Oh God, but it continued on through town. A long forty minutes later Collins watched his quarry recross the street and go back in his motel room. It was beginning to get hot in the street.

C'mon, c'mon, the agent said to himself. Get off your ass, Blaine, you schmuck.

At quarter to nine Willie sat down on the unmade bed and dialed the number on the little sheet of paper. It rang several times and a voice said, "Yes?" It was a man's voice, seemed oddly familiar. Be smooth, Willie thought.

"This is Blaine. Robert Breeden gave me this number."

"Yes?"

What d'you mean *yes?* Willie thought. "He asked me to call this number. We have business."

"Yes?"

Guy's some fucking machine or what? "So I'm calling this number Mr. Breeden gave me. Can you tell me who . . . what, uh, I've reached?"

"Yes, this is the Institute of Sonoran Archeology, Mister, ah . . ."

"Blaine. Willie Blaine. Is Robert Breeden there? We have a transaction to complete."

"Mr. Blaine, no, Mr. Breeden is not here at the moment, but he left word that you should come up."

Score, Willie said to himself. "Fine. I'll be right there. Uh, can you give me . . ." His chest was pounding.

"Yes. You're in Patagonia, I presume. South out of town two miles, left on the dirt road, you'll see it, it's just beyond a horse pasture. Follow the dirt road about five miles—it's quite steep in places—and you'll see us." He hung up.

Okay, okay, okay, Willie said to himself, easy now, we're almost home, almost at the end of the fucking rainbow. He stuffed his things in the duffel bag, patted his pocket with the locker key in it, and went outside. It was getting hot. He threw the duffel into the backseat, opened the hood, attached the wire, and got in the car. He applied the wire and nothing happened. Willie's forehead was wet with sweat. He tried again, and again nothing happened. What the fuck is *this?*

He scrambled out and looked at the mute engine, and it struck him like a blow to the head: some fucker had taken the distributor cap, some goddamned wise-ass local . . . He glared down at the office. I'll tell that—but then he thought better of it. Be smooth, Willie told himself again. He glanced around and saw that the parking lot, the whole town, was still: nobody around. He eyed the Chevrolet in the next space, calculated the odds, his needs. Fuck it, he said to himself, and reached in the Oldsmobile for his wire.

Two minutes later Willie Blaine backed out of the lot in the Chevrolet, spun the wheels and headed south out of town. He turned on the air-conditioning full blast. The guy comes out, Willie envisioned, sees his car gone, the manager, that old fart, comes out, they put it all together and figure that some guy named Glen Greene has stolen the guy's car. Now where's that fucking horse pasture?

Larry Collins stepped out of the commandeered Dodge truck, crossed the street and went in the motel office. The old man, now dressed in jeans and a cowboy shirt, looked up. Collins put the distributor cap on the counter.

"Here. If you need to go anywhere, you can put this back in that Oldsmobile. But if I were you, I'd sit tight. That's a stolen car."

"Huh?"

"Yeah, and you gotta hot-wire it too," said Collins cheerfully as he left the office. "No keys." He was in no rush. He knew just where Blaine was headed.

Dressed in a pair of white tennis shorts, Nigel Calderwood sat at the kitchen table, with a mug of coffee steaming beside the telephone which he had just hung up. Marianna, fresh out of the shower and wrapped in two towels, one around her torso and the other like a turban around her hair, stepped into the kitchen and sat down opposite Nigel with a smile.

"Well, what has the master sleuth found out?"

Nigel grinned, stared hungrily at her bare shoulders. "Aren't you hot in all that swaddling?" She smiled again. "Well, all right, not much, I'm afraid," Nigel continued. "One of these numbers in Arizona has been busy every time I've rung it. The other one is the International Wildlife Museum in Tucson. What would Meyers be doing calling up a wildlife museum, for God's sake? I found that it's a trophy hunter's museum— you know, what they call sportsmen."

"That's a puzzle," Marianna said. "What about the foreign one?"

"An enigma within a puzzle. I simply called it and it sounded like a restaurant."

"A restaurant?"

"Or a bar. There was all this clatter of what sounded like glasses or dishes. The person who answered didn't make any sense at all, some unintelligible language, sounded like Chinese. I kept saying who have I reached, who is this, and all that, and this Chinese madman kept ranting the way they do, very excitable people. I'm quite sure it was Chinese, because after I hung up, I called the phone company and asked them where this number was located. It's Singapore. I believe they speak Chinese there mostly."

"Interesting."

"Yes, but it doesn't get us very far, does it?"

"But it could," Marianna said.

"How?"

"You could call the wildlife place back, pretend you're something to do with Singapore, maybe the Chamber of Commerce, or I don't know, wildlife management or something, and see if they have some connection with Singapore."

"Well, I don't know. . . ."

"You'll think of something, Nigel." She smiled at him. "While you're sleuthing, I'll get dressed."

"Pity."

Willie turned onto the dirt road that wound through some grassy fields toward a tree-lined creek bed. A wooden bridge took him over the creek, and the road began to ascend. The unfamiliar Chevrolet bounced and slewed in the ruts, and he slowed down to a crawl. The road took him around behind a hill and up a series of switchbacks into the high country, mostly grasslands that looked oddly wild, untouched. Willie wondered if a herd of mastodons was going to appear over a hill. He saw a sign ahead and slowed down even more. It said INSTITUTE OF SONORAN ARCHEOLOGY, and he turned in the dirt drive that led through a copse of big trees. Then he saw it, a low building made of stone, little slabs of reddish stone, all designed to look something like one of those Anasazi ruins, Mesa Verde or Chaco Canyon, but huge. It seemed to go on for a half a mile. Willie took his right hand off the steering wheel and shook it limply.

"Classy," he said. "Class-*eee*." He wondered what kind of an outfit would spend the gross national product of fucking Venezuela to build this Anasazi replica here in the middle of absolute nowhere. To dick around in the dirt and gossip about dead people? No way. It had to be a front for something— weirdos, criminals. Willie was pleased with the thought. There was a super trade in all that pre-Colombian shit from Mexico. Maybe he was destined to join up with these guys, Breeden and his gang of supersophisticated smugglers. After all, he was about to make a deal that would make all that Mayan, Aztec crap look stupid. They'd be impressed with him, maybe ask him for some pointers about the craft, sort of talk around it for a while, but finally ask him if he'd like to join up with them.

Clad in such gaudy dreams, Willie pulled up in a spiffy little gravel parking lot with a sign that said VISITORS, and approached the entrance, a massive door made of wood that was silver with age. The door opened easily, silently, and Willie peered into a hallway. There was no one in sight. There had been no other cars in the lot, and he hadn't noticed any elsewhere on the grounds. It was utterly silent, and it gave Willie the creeps. The walls were hung with bright cloth hangings—

reds and oranges and purples—and at the far end of the hall was a table, with what looked like an open book on it. This didn't look like the kind of place where they would just let people—anybody at all—walk in. He looked around for cameras, like in banks, or electronic door-opening equipment. He had been expected, after all. But he saw nothing of the kind. He shrugged and walked down the hall to the table. The open book was a guest book, name, address, date, with a ballpoint pen lying on one of the open pages.

Willie scanned the dozen names, looking for Robert Breeden. No dice. The last visitor had come three days earlier, some broad from Winnetka, Illinois. He looked at the two preceding pages, but found no Robert Breeden. He wrote "William Barker" in the line below the Winnetka broad's, pondered the next blank space, wrote down a street address, Baltimore, Maryland, and the date.

Beyond the table two large wooden doors were open, leading into another hall. Willie went through them and found himself with a choice—go straight or go right into another hallway. He went right and walked into a large room lit with a skylight, an array of black-and-white photographs of Anasazi ruins lining the walls. They were all close-ups and weird angles and you couldn't really tell what you were looking at. But Willie didn't pause to look. Instead he walked on, through a maze of rooms and corridors, each with displays, mostly Indian or Mexican, mostly old. The turns and twists soon destroyed his sense of direction, and he doubted, in a minor panic, that he could find his way back. Finally he emerged in a long hall, and there, at the other end, was the entrance hall with the table and the guest book.

Jesus, he thought, there's nobody here. It's a trick. He walked quickly out to the table and looked at the book. William Barker of Baltimore was still last on the page.

"Hello!" he shouted. "Anyone here?"

Silence.

Willie decided to prowl the place again, see if maybe he had overlooked a door to the offices or wherever these dumb shits hung out. Beyond the room with the photographs was another, dimly lit, with six pieces of stone statuary that Willie had guessed were Mexican or something. When he entered that room now for the second time, he saw a figure leaning against one of the larger statues, a guy. He looked again.

It was the blond greaseball from the wildlife museum. He was standing with his arms crossed, smiling.

"What the—"

"Enjoy your tour, Willie Blaine?"

"What are *you* doing here?"

"What's more interesting is what you're doing here," said the geek.

"You're Breeden," Willie said.

"No." He laughed. He was one of those guys with a relatively low voice but a high-pitched laugh, which always aroused Willie's suspicions. A fag. Willie could take the offensive.

"Then what are you doing here?" Willie demanded. "How come you're turning up where I go? I'm cute but I'm not your type." The geek stiffened, and Willie guessed he had the bastard. "You got a name?"

"Yes, but you don't need to know it, Willie Blaine." It pissed Willie off, this calling him by both names.

"Look," Willie said. "I came here to see Robert Breeden. He wants to see me. We got business to do. So where is he? I want to see him." Willie said all this firmly, quietly, like a dude who means business. He was projecting danger, being smooth.

"I'm not so sure Mr. Breeden does want to see you, Willie Blaine."

"Whaddayou mean? Of course he wants to see me. I got something he needs real bad, something that's one of a kind. What, are you some kind of secretary for him?"

The blond geek smirked. "Mr. Breeden doesn't usually like to talk to people who have attracted the attention of the FBI."

"Oh bullshit," Willie said, covering a flash of panic. "Some asshole with a bunch of routine questions. Back in Winslow, last—last Tuesday. I've been gone since." And, Willie thought to himself, gave that fucker with the Noo Yawk accent the slip. "He doesn't know his ass from axle grease. That's old business, pal."

The guy was still smirking. "Not that old," he said. "An FBI agent was asking about you just yesterday, in Tucson. At the wildlife museum. I think he knows all about you."

Holy shit, Willie said to himself.

"It seems that you've left a trail behind you, you know, the way snails do."

Willie felt faint, like darkness was closing in on his vision. He stared at the geek and thought, I need to make a play here. Stay cool.

"Was he a guy with curly hair, sounds like Brooklyn?"

"That's him."

"What makes you think he's FBI?"

"He showed me his identification."

"The one with those big fucking letters on it, in red? He's a phony. That's not real FBI ID." How many guys, Willie figured, have ever seen FBI ID?

The geek looked uneasy.

"He's after me, yeah, but he's no fed, no agent. He's a nut, a weirdo, works as an unlicensed private dick, tries to help women find their husbands. My wife is looking for me, thinks I owe her money. So this guy is running around pretending to be a fed, gets people to answer questions better than just some guy walking in. You fell for it, huh?" Willie thought back to the card the agent had given his wife Cheryl. "Name he uses is Collins. Guy's a phony. And a criminal. Impersonation. Now when do I get to see Robert Breeden?"

"You won't. You'll deal with me."

"Who the fuck are you?"

"What difference does it make? As long as the transaction is made, what do you care?"

"I like to know who I'm doing business with. Most people do, you know?"

"I take care of Mr. Breeden's affairs in the United States. It's very much like the power of attorney. I can draw money from his accounts, if that's what's making you nervous."

"I'm not nervous. I'm impatient. If you're the guy, then let's get going with the deal. Sooner I get out of this mausoleum you got here, the better I'll feel. What kind of a place is this, anyway?"

"The mystery man from Singapore," Nigel Calderwood said with a theatrical pause, "is named Breeden. Robert Breeden."

Marianna del Massimo frowned.

"What? No ovation?" Nigel asked.

"I've never heard that name before. I wonder who—"

"He's an American sportsman, living in Singapore, comes to the U.S. once a year usually. Very wealthy."

Marianna stood with one hand on her hip, leaning on a kitchen chair. She shook her head. "How did you find out?" she asked, almost absently.

"You are talking to Nigel Calderwood, new travel editor of *Pacific Rim* magazine. Read by everyone who's anyone among the English-speaking community in the Far East, Hong Kong, Singapore, that sort of thing. That's all I had to say, and the director—directress?—was on the line. Mr. Breeden donated a collection of Asian trophies to the museum, along with what I take it is a pot of money. But he *is* something of a mystery man. The directress was a bit miffed with him. Apparently he pulled a no-show at the last minute, just yesterday."

"He was here?"

"He was supposed to be in Tucson. For a lunch at the museum. Called at the eleventh hour to cancel. The directress thought that was bloody rude, but of course she couldn't come right out and say so. Benefactor and all that."

Marianna frowned again.

"I said that of course I'd heard of Mr. Breeden. Everyone over there has. Then I asked where he was living these days, and she gave me an address. And there's the problem."

"What do you mean?"

"Well, I called information in Singapore to try to get his number. There's no such address. And no one living in Singapore by the name of Breeden."

"Shit," Marianna said, and Nigel's eyebrows rose. He hadn't ever heard her use the word, or any other vulgarism for that matter, not that she was the prudish type. "Obviously," she went on, "he's some kind of crook. False name. False address. Well, I guess that makes sense."

"May I ask what this is all about?" Nigel asked.

Marianna looked at him. "Don't you have rehearsal?"

He looked at his watch. "Oh, so I do." He went into the bedroom, emerging moments later having added a polo shirt and sandals. "I'll be done in a couple of hours. See you then?"

"Yes. I'll be here. We'll talk about this then." She rose up on her toes and gave him a peck on the cheek, and Nigel headed for the door, feeling uncomfortably like a messenger boy.

Idly, Sergeant Ramirez thumbed through the notes he had made the day before when Collins called him at home. Collins believed he would catch up with his man Willie Blaine soon, that Blaine had the stolen deities, and that Collins would have the whole thing wrapped up as soon as Blaine tried to make the sale. To whom? Whoever the guy is who pretends to be Robert Breeden, probably, and Collins could feel it—it would be anytime now. At the archaeological institute in Patagonia. That's where Collins would nail him, nail him for grand larceny, and murder, and probably the other guy—non-Breeden—plus recover the objects themselves.

Ramirez felt a bit wistful.

He looked at his notes and saw the name Anthony Baca. Collins had said that the hotel manager showed him a registration card with this name on it, the man who worked as chauffeur when "Breeden" was last in Tucson. Something had bothered Ramirez about this. What was it? Baca. A pattern: Baca was a very common name in New Mexico—there must be at least a hundred Anthony Bacas in the state. That was it. Baca was not a common name in Arizona. He stood up abruptly and went into the storeroom, returning with a telephone book that included Espanola. Ready for more dart throwing.

There were four Anthony Bacas in Espanola, three Antonio Bacas, and eleven A. Bacas.

"Damn," Sergeant Ramirez said, not at all surprised. He guessed he would have to run up to Ortega's in Espanola that night. See if an Anthony Baca hung out there, with a big light-colored truck.

"Two hundred thousand dollars! Two hundred? Hey, forget it, buddy, let's just forget the whole fucking thing, drop it, bag it, you're wasting my time." Willie Blaine stood up from the surprisingly uncomfortable chair that sat before an elaborate antique desk in a lavish but windowless office. Behind the desk sat the geek with his shit-eating prim little fag smile. "Three hundred," Will said. "Nothing less. These are gods, for chrissake, don't you understand? Deities! The Hopis don't just run down to the frigging kiva and crank these babies out. These are one of a kind. One . . . of . . . a . . . kind. They're hundreds of years old. There'll never be any more of these things. Three hundred or I walk."

The prim smile. "Willie, please sit down, so we can talk about this."

Willie shrugged the shrug of the tired, the bored. He sat down. "I think this is hopeless," he said. "I don't think you or this guy Breeden understand this stuff very well. What's he into, kachina masks or some shit like that? The difference here is like between Grandma Moses and Rembrandt."

A raised eyebrow. "Well, that's a bit overstated."

"Look, how many guys can own an actual god, an active *working* god? This is *four* fucking gods, a set, and there'll never be another one. Three hundred or I walk."

"Willie, I'm authorized to offer two hundred."

Willie stared at him. "So this power of attorney you were talking about? That was a bit overstated too, huh?"

"Touché."

"So call the guy up, whatever. You're not authorized enough to get these things. Tell the man he's got to think big if he's gonna be a real player."

"I am also authorized to, ah, make adjustments in the price."

"Three hundred, I told you."

"Two twenty-five."

"Two fifty," Willie countered.

"Two fifty it is," the geek said, and Willie almost died on the spot.

A quarter of a fuckin' million dollars. He could barely breathe.

The man stood up and stuck out his hand. It seemed oddly formal to Willie, who stood up and took the hand in his.

" 'Sa deal," Willie said.

They arranged to drive to Tucson in two cars, to retrieve the gods, and go together to the bank, where the man would present Willie with a bank check and they would go their separate ways.

T w e l v e

Gray-green sagebrush swept away from both sides of the highway to the familiar shapes of mesas lurking on the horizon, like old battleships in a frozen sea. Here and there dirt tracks wound through the sage, sometimes disappearing, sometimes leading to a lonely Navajo camp, a handful of sheds and buildings and, always, the octagonal hogan. Connie Barnes pondered again these strange people living so remotely from each other. There were some Hopi, one of her uncles included, who like to live off by themselves, looking after cattle in the desert, but Connie, like most Hopi, was a villager by upbringing and instinct. She was restless when alone for very long, irritable. Though, she had to admit, home life could get a bit claustrophobic—especially now, with all the trouble. Oppressive.

The truck sailed along through Navajoland, the world glaring in the white sunlight. Mo sat erect and silent on the seat, dozing. Connie realized that she was exhausted. Emotional wipeout. It was another two hours to Gallup, then three and a half to Santa Fe. She saw the highways linking the two places as if they were a string, and she was like a spider running back and forth on the string, a tenuous web. Maybe, instead, she was the fly in the web, pulled in both directions.

She thought of Darrel, her clan brother, driven, lost, now dead. Madness. The burial had been this morning after the traditional all-night wake. So many things at Hopi called for staying up all night. It didn't used to bother her, but now she was tired—physically tired as well. A vision of Darrel staggering around on the edge of the mesa came unbidden to her and she blinked her eyes rapidly, trying to claw the image out of mind.

"Mo?" she said softly. "You awake?"

"Yeah."

"I was thinking about Darrel."

"Yeah."

"It doesn't make sense."

"Nope."

"I mean, why did he come to Santa Fe?"

"He said he was looking for work," Mo said.

"Just before the dance?"

"Maybe he'd already decided not to take part."

"Then why," Connie asked, "did he come back?"

Mo cleared his throat. "How the hell should I know?"

Connie stared over at the big man. He was frowning. "What's the matter?" she asked. "You okay?"

"Damn throat's bothering me."

Like most people with a disability of any sort, Mo feared and detested any illness, Connie knew, and the slightest sign—like a sore throat—made him imagine that death was around the next corner.

"It's probably just a dose of Hopi dust," she said. "You'll be okay."

They drove on in silence, Mo confronting the grim reaper, and Connie trying to reconstruct her conversation with Darrel—when was it?—last Wednesday. Almost a week before. So much had happened. He had talked bravely about getting work, construction work, and trying to get into the Indian Art School in Santa Fe. They had talked about maybe Darrel meeting Dan Namingha, the Hopi artist who lived outside Santa Fe. He'd have some good advice. Darrel had been incoherent, jumping from subject to subject, feeling bad because people were blaming him for stealing "those things," making it hard on everybody in the family, and it wasn't their fault. He hadn't done it, he said, but he knew who had. He was "pretty sure" he knew, but he didn't know what to do about it. He couldn't just accuse anyone. He didn't know who to talk to, didn't want to talk to anyone about it, wanted to get away from it, get away from Hopi for a while. His dreams were bad. Making him sick. Poor Darrel. Poor alcoholic, hopeless, demon-ridden Darrel. And there wasn't much hope he'd find peace even now.

Connie shook her head, trying to get lost souls out of her mind. She thought about Mo, fretting for his life because of a sore throat. She smiled inwardly, reached over and patted him on the leg.

"When we get home, we can stop at Phyllis's place, get you something for your throat."

"Hah—hah. One of her herbal specials? Tea brewed from creosote bushes and desert weeds? I'd rather have surgery."

Sergeant Ramirez had given his daily report to Captain Ortiz and was crossing the anteroom in the SFPD when he saw Marianna del Massimo approach the building and begin to pull on the heavy doors. Quickly he stepped over to the entrance and pushed one of the doors open.

"I don't know why they made these doors so heavy," he said. "It's not very welcoming."

The woman smiled warmly at him. She was dressed in a pearl-gray suit, with small gold earrings, black high-heeled shoes. Her shining ebony hair was swept up onto her head.

Ramirez watched her mouth, even little white teeth. "Thank you," she said. "I've never thought about a police station being welcoming or not. This one certainly is."

Ramirez smiled. "What brings you here, Miz del Massimo? Is there something I can—"

"I wanted to check in with you, Sergeant, to see if it is all right if I reopen the gallery."

"Oh, okay. You want to come in and sit down?" He pointed toward the door to his little office. "Coffee?"

"No thanks." Once they were settled down in Ramirez's tiny office, she said, "The thing is that in this sort of business, you can lose a lot of momentum. It's a good season now, and—"

"The Santa Fe police have no problem with the gallery re-opening. There isn't anything we can do in there that isn't already done. The only consideration is, you know, what's proper, the right interval between . . ."

Marianna smiled. "Of course. Knowing Walt Meyers, I'm sure he'd wonder why we waited so long to get back in business."

Ramirez spread his hands in the manner of a blessing. He smiled at her. "You know," he said, "I've been thinking about the other night, those guys in the truck. Whoever they were, there's still a chance they might have been, you know, hired."

"For what, though?"

"I don't know. Anyway, probably I shouldn't discuss this with you—it's premature—but I have one lead. I'm going to try and find them, one of them anyway. If I can produce a guy, do you think you could identify him?"

"Well, Sergeant, I never really got a look at anybody, just the truck. . . ."

"Well, maybe I'll find the truck, too."

Marianna leaned forward slightly, put her chin on her fist and looked thoughtfully at Ramirez. "Can I be completely straightforward with you, Sergeant?"

"Yes, ma'am, I wish you would."

"The Meyers Gallery has operated under a certain cloud. I mean before poor Walt . . . There are stories, rumors, you know, about Walt dealing in illegal things, artifacts. I mean everybody simply assumed he was. Frankly, I never saw any sign of it. No sign of it at all. I couldn't have worked there if I had. One of the reasons why I wanted to open the gallery again as early as possible was to, well, get things back on track, try and make sure that the gallery's reputation isn't made even more cloudy. I'm not saying this very well. Do you know what I mean?"

Ramirez nodded. "I understand."

"But one thing has me puzzled," she said. "Worried."

"What's that?"

"Do you remember the other day when the FBI agent came into the gallery?" Ramirez nodded, and the woman continued. "He drew some figures, like sticks, on a piece of paper." Ramirez nodded again. "Well, as I said at the time, I've never seen anything like that. I don't even have any idea what they are. They looked like something Indian, but . . . but, Sergeant," she leaned forward, "is there some reason to think that Walt Meyers was involved somehow in . . . I'm just concerned about the gallery."

Ramirez thought briefly. "I'll tell you what I can. Those objects are part of a separate investigation, a federal investigation, and I'm not at liberty to discuss that. You know? All I can tell you is that there was some reason—suspicion, maybe—that they might have been linked at one time to Walter Meyers."

"Oh dear," the woman said. "I hope not."

"It's circumstantial. Just a possibility," Ramirez said sympathetically.

"I understand. Sergeant? I understand that you can't tell me much about all this, but perhaps I can say something. If these things are being investigated by the FBI, then I presume they were stolen. And valuable. And *if* Walt Meyers was involved in some way, God help us, then it would have been as a dealer. And so, if you think that someone ordered those people to harass me, it might be someone who thinks those objects might be ... that I ... It might be someone who wants them."

Ramirez looked at the woman. "That's very ... subjunctive," he said expressionlessly. "But it is one line of reasoning."

"Can you tell me what they are? Just so I'll know what I'm up against? Subjunctively." She smiled.

"They are from the Hopi," Ramirez explained. "They are like altar pieces, you know, in a ceremony. They are the only ones."

"My God, how awful."

A few moments later, after thanking Ramirez for his kindness, Marianna stood up to leave. Ramirez preceded her to the doors, which he opened for her, watching her slender figure move with liquid grace across the parking lot. Who knows? he thought. He knew about her loan request, knew her maiden name was Chavez. Maybe after all this was over ...

It was cool in the shade of the trees, and a breeze was stirring the greening grasslands on the slopes above the Institute of Sonoran Archaeology. Larry Collins had made himself comfortable, his back against the trunk of a tree, while he kept an eye on the building below. The commandeered Dodge pickup was parked about fifty feet away, out of sight. Down in the little gravel parking lot his Chevrolet baked in the sun, and he could see Willie's duffel bag in the backseat. There were no other vehicles in sight, though there could be a garage of some sort around the other side of the big red-stone building. It was an eerie place, up here in the middle of nowhere, not a sign of life. It seemed best simply to watch and wait. Collins was sure Blaine would not have taken the gods into the building with him. If he had them with him and not in safekeeping some other place, they were in the duffel. So he would have to come outside to complete the deal.

The front door of the institute opened and Blaine stepped out into the glare, squinting. He had a big smile on his face. Another man stepped outside. Breeden. No, this guy was fairly tall and blond, not white-haired and short. He looked familiar even at a hundred yards.

Then Collins recognized him—the guy at the wildlife museum. An entire new series of possibilities began to cascade in Collins's mind, but he put them aside and watched. Blaine paused beside the Chevrolet, and the blond man appeared to say something to him. Then he walked off around the corner of the building. Blaine got in the car, and after a few moments its engine erupted into life. The car eased forward a few feet and then stopped. Blaine craned his neck, looking back where the blond man had disappeared. In another few moments a black Jeep Cherokee swung around the corner of the building and followed Blaine down the driveway.

Collins took his time walking over to the pickup, and once on the dirt road, hung back to avoid getting into the line of sight of the two cars ahead. If they were going to collect the goods, they had to be going somewhere Blaine had been, and he hadn't been south of here. Probably they were headed back to Tucson. Probably Blaine had hidden the deities in a bus-station locker. Where else? Blaine wasn't the type to march into a bank and get a safe deposit box, even if you could fit those things in one. When Collins reached the highway, the dirt tracks leading out onto the tarmac turned left. South. Why south? He stepped on it, and about a mile later he saw up in front of him the black Cherokee and, just ahead of that, his Chevrolet with Willie Blaine in it, probably feeling better than he ever had in his entire life . . . the schmuck probably imagining himself on some island surrounded with bimbos. Collins hung back, keeping the black Cherokee on the horizon. Close enough.

T. Moore Bowdre contemplated his end, his disappearance from the plane of events, the imminent time when he would cease to be a part of the world, to love, to sense life, and he was lonely. Someone had once said that you are born alone, live alone, and die alone. Mo Bowdre knew for a fact that two-thirds of that maxim was patent nonsense. The umbilical cord is all the evidence needed for the first part: no one can be born alone. As for living alone, Mo supposed it was possible, but he never had. To the umbilicus, add laughter. But dying . . . a lonely proposition, especially since it was imminent.

For the burn in Bowdre's throat was clearly a sign of the end. Down deeper, he felt as if a bone were stuck in his throat, giving him an occasional jab. The symptoms metastasized throughout his entire neck, spasmodic pains like muscle pulls, the throbbing of esoteric glands, swarming with horrid insatiable cells: earnest people in green masks saying, "It's hopeless."

Mo shook his head and said, "Ohhhh."

"What?" asked Connie as the truck skimmed along Route 40.

"Nothing. Where are we?"

"Near Grants. You okay?"

Mo said nothing, and couldn't say anything out of the profundity of his sadness over ceasing to exist, over not being part of the world.

"Mo?"

"Yeah?"

"Before you give up the ghost, you owe me an eagle."

How is it possible, Mo thought, that this woman I've devoted myself to can be so callous? He knew that there was always a possibility that he was a hypochondriac, foolishly stirring his own entrails for omens, but he wanted comfort, not teasing.

"You can't make an eagle out of a rock," he declared.

"You can, Mo."

"Don't patronize me, dammit. I feel lousy."

"We'll be home soon, maybe two hours, two and a half. You're not dying yet."

"Of course I'm not. I'm fine. I just have a sore throat. I always get a sore throat or some damn thing when I go out there." He thought aimlessly for a time. "I'm sorry to be a grouch," he said.

"It's hard."

"What is?"

"Thinking about dying," Connie said. "People dying. Like Darrel. Things like that. Old ways. I hate to think about it. It's all so sad."

Mo felt stupid, oafish.

"They say," she went on, "that when I die, I'll be wrapped in my shroud, the one my uncles have woven, and I'll step on my wedding plaque and I'll soar out over the Grand Canyon and become a cloud. I'll come back and rain on my family's fields."

"That's lovely," Mo said. "I like that."

The truck hummed across the landscape.

"But," Connie said, "somehow, sometimes, that doesn't seem . . . enough."

"Maybe it'll seem enough when you're a cloud. Hah—hah."

Mo fell silent again. Even being a cloud wasn't in the cards he'd been dealt. It was hard to believe in something you didn't believe in. His throat twinged, a sense of constriction around the Adam's apple, and he lapsed into another eon of despair.

They skimmed through Albuquerque ahead of the rush hour, and fifty minutes later pulled up, miraculously, into a parking space on the street before one of the most peculiar establishments in all of Santa Fe, a place called the Natural Caduceus. Located on a side street north and west of the plaza, this shop was in fact the front two rooms of a small residence owned by Phyllis Lodge.

A long-limbed and loose-gaited woman whose strawberry-blonde hair swung down her back in a single long braid, she strode around Santa Fe in Levi's, bright shirts, and moccasins like she owned the place, and there wasn't a man who had laid eyes on her who wouldn't have given her the whole city if he could. She existed happily, almost joyously, on the near edge of poverty, unwilling to charge enough for her herbal remedies to cover all her costs, which included making strenuous trips into the field to collect the arcane plants involved. So practiced was she after several years studying informally with medicine men of various tribes, along with an old Hispanic *curandero*, that she held an unofficial adjunct professorship in ethnobotany at the state university's medical school, a small stipend from which kept her afloat.

More or less inadvertently, the three cultures met in Phyllis Lodge's shop, for her clientele, though relatively small, included Hispanics, Indians, and whites in about equal proportion. More often than not, visitors to the shop would also find themselves sudden enlistees in whatever issue Phyllis had thrown herself into with the same indefatigable gusto with which she tracked down esoteric roots and leaves in the deserts and mountains of the Southwest.

"Pumice!" she was saying in a good-natured sneer as Connie Barnes entered the shop. "Can you believe that, Pappy? Pumice! Those bastards want to tear up fifty acres of the Jemez National Forest to mine pumice. For what? You know what the chief use of this pumice will be? To make those phony stone-washed jeans for the lah-de-dah crowd in Los Angeles. The edge of the mine will be ten *feet* from a Jemez Indian shrine. Look, Pappy, sign this petition. It's to get our congressman off his flabby ass and vote to repeal the Federal Mining Act of 1873. Think of it, 1873! The same law for over a century. And that law—Pappy, get this—*that* law is almost identical to the rules the Spanish *king* issued so the conquistadors would feel good about digging up all the gold in the New World. So look, Pappy, just sign this . . . there, good, thanks

... and don't forget. You put two drops of that tincture in a tablespoon of warm water. Twice a day."

Pappy Pacheco, an elderly man who played piano at the La Fonda Hotel, smiled and hastened out of the shop, passing Mo Bowdre, who lumbered through the door emitting silent psychological lava.

Phyllis, in tight jeans and draped in a multicolored Peruvian shirt, beamed.

"Well, *hi* there, Connie," she said in her loud voice. "Hi. Where've you been? I haven't seen you guys for *months*." She gave Connie a bear hug. "You look wonderful. And, hey, look, you brought T. Moore Bowdre along. Hey, Mo, how're they hanging? Whoops. You don't look too happy there, Mo. What's the matter?" she said, taking his arm. "Is Big Sweetums in a grouch?"

"This place smells awful, Phyllis. Too goddamned many shamanistic plants. God, where do you find all this stuff? It's awful." He coughed twice, then once more.

"Aha!" Phyllis said. "Big Sweetums is sick."

"No, I'm not."

"He's got a sore throat," Connie said.

"Open up," Phyllis demanded.

"No, I will not," Mo said. "I won't put up with any of your odoriferous magic."

"Open up. I just want to look."

Sighing, Mo opened his mouth, and Phyllis stood on her toes and looked down his throat.

"It's terminal, Mo, terminal. There's nothing I can do for you."

"Good."

"Anyway, by law I'm not allowed to prescribe. Any feds in here? Are you secretly a fed, Mo, trying to set me up? Okay, good. You want something that'll really do the job, clear up all that abraded angry flesh and make it pink and sweet again?" She plucked a bottle off a nearby shelf, a little brown bottle like those that dispense nose drops. "This stuff is really great. Osha. Tincture of osha." She turned to Connie. "It's what you guys call bear root."

"Bear root?" said Mo. "The stuff to ward off—"

"*Ligusticum porteri*," Phyllis intoned. "Also called Colorado cough root. It grows above nine thousand feet. I get mine up near Taos. Wheeler Peak. There's a plant just like it that grows lower than that, up to about eight thousand feet. But that's called hemlock parsley, and you don't want that stuff, no, no. Highly toxic. But this stuff, man, I'm telling you—knock out a virus, stop a cough, bye-bye indigestion. It's the greatest! And of course it's perfect for sore throats. Very soothing. A lot of people here in town swear by it, a couple of radio announcers, singers, the speaker of the house when those birdbrains are in session, I kid you not."

Connie was leaning against the counter, grinning.

"Snake oil," Mo said.

"Mo, would I do you wrong? Me? Phyllis?" She poked him lightly in the stomach. "Trust me, Mo. Here, take it. On the house, try it. You got nothing to lose but your sore throat. And your lousy mood. Here, Connie, take it. Just follow the instructions on the label. So what have you guys been doing? Did you hear about those bastards with the pumice mine? Can you believe it . . . ?"

Never again, thought Willie Blaine, and it was an exhilarating thought. Never again. No more insults. No more scrambling. No more taking shit from *any*one. No more bluffing, pretending I've got the cards. This time I *have* the cards. It's showdown time, high noon. High fucking noon, and I, Willie Blaine, am Gary Cooper.

Such had been Willie's state of mind as the road hissed and thumped under the wheels of the stolen Chevrolet, and the overhead sun took all color out of the flat valleys and faded the sawtooth mountains on the horizons. Behind him, maintaining a steady distance, was the black Cherokee. The guy had blinked his headlights, and Willie had pulled over on the shoulder, walking back to the Cherokee. The greaseball had said they would stop in a few more miles at a Mexican joint north of Nogales and have an early lunch, which they did, eating at a roadside dump that served some dried meat that the guy went nuts about while Willie, in silence, dreamed of the time when no one, *no one*, would tell him when it was fucking lunchtime.

Back on the road, the main highway, Route 19, almost to Tucson. Brown land stretching stupidly away to the west, a few abject hovels, and some church looming out of the land like a huge white nun's hat, a beached sea gull. Spanish. Willie read the highway sign: SAN XAVIER DEL BAC. Some kind of historic Spanish mission. History was crap, Willie thought, his eye on the future, when he noticed in the rearview mirror the Cherokee's headlights blinking again.

"What is this shit?" Willie said out loud and pulled over. The greaseball thought it would be better if Willie went into the bus station himself and retrieved the goods, and they could go someplace that was "less public" to "verify" them. From there, they would go to the bank. Willie didn't want to go to some private place. He didn't want the guy to pull something, like killing him. The guy had professed himself shocked at the thought and had described a small public park located west of downtown Tucson, near the main highway, Route 10. A half hour later Willie had gone alone into the bus station, carrying his duffel bag. He was breathing fast, his chest constricting, telling himself to be cool as he opened the locker and stuffed the plastic-covered treasure into his duffel and left. And now he was nosing to a stop in the small parking lot where a sign said GARDEN OF GETHSEMANE. A couple of other vehicles were parked there, one an old pickup. The Cherokee slid up next to Willie, and the geek got out with a smile on his face. He gestured with his head toward a grassy area lined with trees, and Willie climbed out into the heat and followed, carrying the duffel. An old Hispanic couple was sitting on a bench under the trees, eating some stuff from a basket.

"What is this place?" Willie asked, feeling cool as he caught up.

"The life work of some old Hispanic World War One veteran. Almost died from a wound, so he offered his life to his Maker. Produced all the stuff you're about to see."

Willie thought, Christ, ask a question, you get a fucking guided tour. They stepped down into a large flagstoned area like a huge terrace with high walls on three sides. It was filled with enormous white plaster figures: first a giant, crude white cross with a huge white Jesus on it, and to the right a whole bunch of guys in robes sitting around—which Willie recognized as the Last Supper. Willie gawked. The apostles and old J.C. were all larger than life, maybe twice life-size, clumsy, dead-white, sad. The place gave Willie the creeps.

"After the veteran died, the city made all this a public shrine," said the tour guide, standing behind Willie. "Now, let's have a look."

Willie looked around the place again. A tiny old man was standing in front of something that looked like a tomb, maybe thirty feet away. Willie set the duffel down and unzipped it, his chest pounding. This was it. This was fucking it. Okay, you babies, okay, you gods, my fortune, my ticket . . .

He squatted down on his heels, the guy standing beside him, and pulled out the green plastic bag. He reached in and pulled out the wooden figures.

"What kind of crap is this?" the guy yelled, and Willie burst out, *"Jesus H. Fucking Christ!"*

The old man by the tomb scowled at them, and Larry Collins said, "Freeze!"

Seeing a man with a gun pointed at two others, the old man scuttled away. The blond head turned slowly and stared into the black hole of a gun muzzle. "What the . . . ?" he said.

Willie Blaine stared at the objects lying before him on the wrinkled green plastic bag, and the world around him shrank like he was fainting. He couldn't breathe. Four weathered, gnarled pieces of raw cottonwood. What had happened to the gods? Four sticks. Four worthless sticks he had hauled all over the countryside . . . a quarter of a fucking million dollars . . . Willie's entire world shattered like a mirror hit by a rock. He fell forward on his knees, held himself up from the pavement with his hands and gaped at the four stupid pieces of raw, uncarved, useless fucking wood. What had happened? What had *happened*? His stomach lurched and he thought he was going to throw up. Then he heard the agent say, "Get up, Blaine. And you, don't move."

"Hey, what is this?" the geek yelled. "What're you arresting me for? I haven't done anything. . . ."

"Those are stolen goods there, do I have to tell you more than that?" said the agent.

"Stolen goods? What're you talking about? The man has a bag of sticks. Just useless sticks."

"They're stolen gods, Indian artifacts. And you're—"

Willie moaned in agony, still kneeling on the ground.

"Look at the things, man," said the blond man. "They're sticks. Just sticks. I don't know what you've got on this turd, but you have nothing on me. I'm just standing here in the park next to a man with a bag of sticks."

Collins was mystified. He looked again. They weren't the gods. Just sticks. He grabbed Willie by the back of his collar and hauled him to his feet. "What *is* this, Blaine?"

Willie was speechless, gasping, thinking he'd throw up, his world gone, his mind limp. A siren sounded, a car screeching to a stop in the parking lot.

"I don't know what's going on here," said Collins, "but you two stay right where you are. I followed you all morning, and this schmuck here," he shook Willie by the collar, "is a criminal five ways from Sunday. So you're both coming with me."

Two cops in uniform leapt into the shrine with guns drawn. "Freeze!" they shouted.

"FBI," Collins barked.

"Drop it," one of the cops yelled.

"Goddamn it, I'm *FBI!*"

"Drop the weapon!" yelled the cop. "What's going on here?"

Collins slowly leaned over, his gun held in two fingers, and put it on the ground, all the while clutching Blaine by the collar. Standing up, he said, "I'm going to reach in my back pocket and get my ID." He slowly took out his wallet and let it flip open.

"Oh, hell," said the cop. "Sorry. But what's going on? We got a call from some old Hispanic guy—"

"It's okay. I'm glad you're here," Collins said. "These guys are under arrest for a half a million federal crimes."

"Not me," the blond guy whined. "Not me. You don't have—"

"Shut your mouth," Collins said. "You're coming with me. Would you boys like to read these clowns their rights?"

Willie Blaine gulped, heaved, and threw up his Mexican lunch and what was left of his spirit all over the four gnarled pieces of cottonwood and Special Agent Larry Collins's gun.

Handcuffed in the backseat of the squad car, Willie stared ahead of him, his eyes vacant. Beside him the geek had lapsed into silence after protesting yet again that he was guilty only of following a guy to a park. Collins was in the front seat with the cop who was driving.

"So what's going on?" the cop asked.

"It's complicated," Collins said. "Violation of the Federal Archeological Resources Act . . ."

Stirring, Willie said, "I didn't steal anything."

Collins turned around and gave Willie a carnivorous grin. "Blaine, shut your mouth. You *tried* to steal some federally protected artifacts. Then there's breaking and entering in the

Meyers Gallery. Then you did steal something, two cars, in fact. And one of them happens to be mine. FBI property. Stealing federal property is bad news, Blaine. Especially when it also causes obstruction of a federal officer in the pursuit of his duty. Then, oh yeah, there's suspicion of murder. You want me to go on?"

Willie shut his eyes. He felt as if he was going to throw up again.

T h i r t e e n

The sheet weighed heavily on his foot, and the ache in his toes made T. Moore Bowdre certain that he had been invaded by a microscopic horde of viruses, all weaseling in through the tender membranes of his important cells and reproducing there like rabbits, pumping out strands of ribonucleic acid, each with a strategy designed to reduce him to mush. Mo Bowdre hated these moments, knew they were temporary bouts and that he would recover, but sometimes he found it impossible simply to will them away. They had to play themselves out, conclude, like someone else's marionette show going on in his brain. He tried to think of something else, but each psychosomatic twinge in his mortal coil brought him lurching back to the brink of doom. Maybe, he thought, it's because the light never reaches my pineal gland. Maybe it's my biological clock, swerving and swaying. . . . He sighed. Damn. Probably, he thought, I'll never get to finish Connie's eagle. Finish it? Probably, I'll never get to start it, creative spirit simply packed up and gone, looking for another residence while I stand around dying and that shapeless lump of marble laughs at me, goddamn birds. Too fragile. Who needs an oafish hundred-pound eagle? And where the hell is that wren? Doesn't sing me into the work anymore. Gave up on me, the little son of a bitch. That's it, burnout. Kaput. Career's over. How long, he wondered, before Connie gives up on a blind sculptor who can't sculpt anymore? Big tub of decaying flesh, a real bargain . . .

Next to him, Connie's breathing was quiet, regular. He listened to it and then said, "Why aren't you asleep?"

"Why aren't you?" she said.

"I'm moping."

"Me too."

"Can I help?" Mo asked.

"No."

"You can't help me either."

Silence, but for the sound of slow breathing.

"You still dying?" Connie asked.

"Yeah."

"You'll stop. Those times always stop," she said. "Soon as that bear root clears up your throat."

"Snake oil."

"You could go to a doctor."

"Thieves."

Connie sighed, and the two lay in silence. "You know," she said, "sometimes I wish I wasn't Hopi."

Mo waited for her to say more, but she remained mute. She had had a white father, Mo thought to himself, but a Hopi mother. Therefore she was a Hopi. The matrilineal imperative. And if she and he had a kid, Mo thought, the kid would be a Hopi, even though it was three-quarters white. My God, imagine having a Hopi kid. Would she want to take it back to the reservation, raise it in the tradition? Or would she want to avoid that altogether? Or mostly? And what would he, Mo, want? And what difference did it make what he wanted? He'd be dead before the nine months were up, even if she was already pregnant. What if she *is*? Good God, what a thought.

No, I'll die without issue, just a bunch of metal and stone animals littering the landscape, junk I can't do anymore anyway.

He knew this would pass, but he was also convinced of his imminent demise, so he began the dreary inventory of his life, finding a series of pointless achievements, inanity. He had not been the brave scout about being blind that everyone thought: he had faced a life of darkness with terror. Only gradually had he learned to function, to put on a bravura act, to be defiant, to sculpt, to make animal shapes out of his memory, to hear acutely, to smell perceptively, oh yes, but what had he done? Nothing more than . . . He was little known outside of New Mexico, a third-world state. And when it all ended, he had no place to go, no house, no heavenly mansion awaiting him. No belief in a nice white existence. No cloud to become, to function in some useful way, still connected to the earth, to life.

It's tradition that's got her, Mo thought, religion, whatever the hell it is, those gods that got stolen. Now the whole damn tribe is on the brink. It's like they lost their gyroscope. What had Emory said? Without those gods, no more Hopi men can learn the divine law of the tribe.

Mo tried to imagine what that meant.

He thought of the old man, his eyes suddenly going and then . . . blind. He knew what that meant. He wondered what it would be like for a group of people to suddenly find themselves spiritually blinded. Was that it? Even Connie, half white, acculturated, at ease in the outside world, sophisticated in the ways of the "dominant culture," even Connie had lost . . . what? A kind of purpose?

What a nightmare, Mo Bowdre thought. What a nightmare. A nightmare without sleep.

Bastards, Mo said to himself. Why can't the bastards leave people alone, make their own gods?

Not for the first time, Mo felt contempt for his own tribe

rising, and an anger began to drive him, and he realized that the guy with the marionettes had left.

The headlights picked up a reflective green highway sign that said COCHITI, and the Chevy's cruise control read the rising angle of the road and revved the engine up a notch. Larry Collins, with nothing to do but steer, frowned. He was dog tired. He couldn't remember when he had spent so much time in a car. Another half hour to go.

"You know something, Blaine?" he said. He was talking more to keep himself alert than to get anything much out of his prisoner, who sat hunched down and miserable in handcuffs in the backseat. They had left Tucson seven hours ago, and Collins judged that they had made good time, but his tail end ached and his right leg felt like it would snap into a colossal cramp any minute. Blaine had said nothing since they had stopped at the little Rio Grande town of Hatch, New Mexico, to get a hamburger. "Hamburger," is all Blaine had said. He was like a balloon that had run out of helium, a sail with no wind. Collins wondered if he might have a whack at suicide once he was left alone. With an eye on Blaine, sitting like a bag of trash on the backseat of the car in the Dairy Queen parking lot, Collins had called ahead yet again to the Santa Fe P.D. and told them they'd have to keep an eye on Blaine once he was in the can. Have a man there around the clock, he had told them.

"What I can't figure out," said Collins over his shoulder, "is how you started out in a good job, coaching those kids, and wound up such a piece of crap. I looked it up, you know. You got canned there, Willie baby. A discreet little negotiated agreement. So what was it, huh? You get a little too touchy-feely with the athletes? What's the matter, your father run out on you? Your mother cat around while you were a wide-eyed little sneak? There's no excuse for people like you, Blaine."

In the rearview mirror Collins could see that Blaine was staring out the side window.

"I don't have to talk to you," Blaine said.

"No, don't bother. I know you people."

Impatient with the cruise-controlled straining of the engine, Collins pressed his foot down on the accelerator. He watched the speedometer hit seventy-five. In a few minutes the car crested the hill and began the descent toward the necklace of lights that lay before him. He flicked off his fuzzbuster when the television station set it blinking idiotically.

"There's another thing I can't figure out," Collins said. "Here you are driving all over the Southwest—for what, six, seven days?—stopping here, stopping there, and you never looked in the bag? You never wanted to *see* those things? Your meal ticket? You just took 'em out of the truck, put 'em in a car, put 'em in a locker, stuffed 'em in a duffel bag, and never opened up the bag and looked at them?"

The headlights of a semi toiling up the incline lit Willie Blaine's face, and Collins saw that he was looking down, his face slack.

"Huh, Blaine? I mean what kind of schmuck would have a quarter million dollars of stuff in a bag and never take a peek at it? Huh?"

"I don't have to talk to you," Blaine said again in a near whisper.

"Right, Blaine, right. You got the right to remain silent and all that, but you'll talk to me. You'll talk to me. I guarantee it. You'll tell me the whole story . . . which I already know anyway. The only part I can't figure out is what kind of a schmuck wouldn't look in the bag."

Willie remained silent while Collins pulled off Route 25 onto Cerillos Road, sped along through the array of motels, and pulled into the chain-link fenced yard at the police station. He said nothing when Collins came around to the door, yanked it open and tugged at him.

"Out, Blaine."

Clumsily, Blaine got out of the car and stood passively on

the pavement under the greenish glare of the streetlamps that lit the yard. Collins had to push him lightly on the back to get him walking toward the metal door of the station. Inside, he walked hesitantly, Collins prodding him toward the window where a gray-faced cop, licking the end of brushy white mustache, sat looking tired in the thin fluorescence from an overhead lamp.

"You're Collins?" the cop said.

"Right." Collins flipped open his wallet, and the cop nodded.

"I got all the paperwork done," the cop said. "You just got to sign these." Collins glanced down at the documents and scrawled his name on them, while the desk cop called out, "Hey, Gutierrez!" Then he looked incuriously at Willie Blaine for the first time. "Talkative, huh?"

"This guy?" Collins said. "Used to be full of piss and vinegar. But he sprung a leak. Didn't you, Blaine?" The gray metal door next to the window swung open and another cop, Gutierrez, stepped out, a large man of almost palpable gravity.

"I want to call a lawyer," Blaine said.

"Hey, you think the lawyers in Santa Fe sit around the office until eleven o'clock at night waiting to get a phone call? Tomorrow." Collins turned to the jailer. "Officer Gutierrez? Meet Willie Blaine. Have a nice night, Blaine."

Gutierrez took the prisoner by the elbow, turned him toward the doorway and pushed him through.

"Thanks," Collins said to the desk cop.

"Don't mention it."

"See you tomorrow."

"Not me. I'm off for two days. Soon as the sun comes up."

"Oh, okay. Is there a phone I can use?"

"Over there." The cop gestured with his head to a metal desk against the green wall, empty except for a push-button phone. "So this is the guy who did Meyers, huh?"

"You read the papers, didn't you? Suspicion. But sure, that's the guy." Collins went over to the desk and dialed the home number of Sergeant Tony Ramirez. He got the answering machine and left word for the policeman to call him at his motel.

Anthony Ramirez hadn't held out much hope that he would fool anyone, and one of the guys in a low-rider outside Ortega's had spotted him as a cop before he switched off the ignition. A routine computer check of the Department of Motor Vehicles had shown that of all the men in Espanola who could be "his" Anthony Baca, all but one had pickup trucks, and all but two of those were what could be taken as "light-colored." Still, it was worth a try, and he didn't have anything better to do that night.

Ortega's Bar lay on the road to Taos on the northern edge of Espanola amid a drive-in liquor store, a Laundromat, and an auto parts place. It was a long, low building modeled after the old territorial houses, adobe with portals, vegas, the whole thing. But no grandee of Nueva Mexico would have dreamed of setting foot in it. It was the kind of place that had even made Ramirez nervous when he was a young stud with a fair dose of macho, getting ready for college, the kind of place where some of his classmates assembled, trying to be big shots along with the twenty-year-olds and thirty-year-olds, driving up in their low-riders painted with the flames of hell after cruising the street in the endless quest to be noticed by some hot little chicita. Nothing had changed in the years that had passed, almost a decade and a half now, and places like this still gave Ramirez the creeps.

The sun had set a few minutes earlier, and the few small windows of Ortega's reflected a metallic-orange sky. He stepped out of the car onto the dirt parking lot, watched by the occupants of six vehicles, who grinned at him with a wolfish defiance. "Hey, where'd you get those hubs, mon?" a voice said. "Hey, where's your badge, huh?" said another. Laughter rippled among the faces, half seen in the vehicles. One of them, a shiny dark blue Chevy pickup, sat on wheels that had to be three and a half feet in diameter. It was so high off the ground that the other vehicles in the lot, standard low-riders squatting on the dirt, could have driven under it. *Cojones*, Ramirez thought. More balls in this lot than in a bullring. He saluted and went inside through an enormous oak door and heard the tinny blare of mariachi trumpets on tape.

The man behind the shadowy bar turned his head to the entrance and turned back to a pair of bikers on stools. He was a wide man with a thin gray line of a mustache and a spherical paunch thrusting proudly through the open flaps of a tooled leather vest. Ramirez took a stool three down from the bikers. The bartender looked at him, and Ramirez said, "Beer."

"What kind?"

Ramirez shrugged, and the bartender reached into an icy bin and produced a can of Miller Lite. Ramirez watched the steam rise from the open bin.

"Gringo beer for the police," the bartender said, and put the can down unopened on the bar in front of Ramirez. The two bikers turned their heads and stared. "Dollar and a half," the bartender said.

Ramirez put two dollars on the bar.

"So what're you looking for up here? Things too quiet in Santa Fe?" The bartender turned to the bikers. "I seen this guy around down there. Now you got to watch what you say. *Pez gordo.* Big-shot cop."

Ramirez half smiled. "No big deal. I'm looking for a guy named Tony Baca. Does he come here?"

"What'd this Baca do, you're looking for him?"

"Nothing. He may know a guy I want to talk to."

The bartender turned and stepped down to the other end of the bar and hoisted a case of Tecate beer from a stack on the floor.

"So what did that guy do?"

"It's personal," Ramirez said.

"Sure." The bartender set the case of beer down next to the bin and another rush of icy steam rose up. He methodically put the cans in the bin. "You're out of your jurisdiction up here."

"I said it was personal. So tell me, does Tony Baca come here?"

"Which one? There's three guys named Tony Baca come here, another guy I know in town named Tony Baca."

"He drives a big, light-colored pickup."

"Sorry," the bartender said, shaking his head. "I always want to help out the polizia. Sorry, muchacho. No Tony Baca with a light-colored pickup." He grinned at the bikers, who grinned back. Ramirez popped open his beer can and took a swallow. He looked down at the bikers, who were looking at him, and shrugged.

"There's money in it," Ramirez said, glancing at the bartender. "For this guy Baca."

"Too bad he don't come here," the bartender said. "Otherwise I could tell him."

So Sergeant Ramirez had headed back to Santa Fe, having wasted his time, as he had guessed he would. Some of the oncoming vehicles had their headlights on. In the gathering night a layer of clouds clung to the green peaks of the Sangre de Cristo Mountains up behind Santa Fe, a huge, milky down comforter that extended out over one valley between two peaks, as if someone were lifting up a corner, beckoning a lover in. Ramirez felt lonely.

How did the Anglos say it? Nothing ventured, nothing found. He could have just hung around the parking lot, but . . . what the hell. He was no undercover cop. No dart thrower either. Back to analysis, plodding, sifting, sorting. He wondered if Mr. Static, the FBI agent, had tracked down his man Blaine yet over in Arizona. Patagonia. He remembered visiting the archeological museum there years ago when he was a graduate student, off in the middle of nowhere.

When he opened the door to his apartment, he saw the little red light on his answering machine blinking. Without turning on the lights, he pressed the button, the tape whirred, clicked, whirred again, beeped, and Larry Collins's nasal voice said, "Tony, call me. I'm at the same motel as before. I'll be there by ten."

Ramirez turned on the lights, took a notebook out of the pocket of his jacket, which he'd left slung over a chair in the kitchen, and found the number.

"Collins," the agent said after the third buzz.

"It's Tony Ramirez."

"You won't believe this. This guy Blaine? I tracked him all over the goddamned state, he has his meet with a guy in this weird archeological place in Patagonia, you know, up in the hills, the middle of—"

"I was there once."

"Okay, anyway, the two go off in separate vehicles, back to Tucson, and Blaine goes in the bus station and comes out with the stuff. So they go off to this creepy little park, these ugly plaster statues around, and Blaine is going to give the gods to this guy right there, and bam! I hit 'em."

"Great, great," Ramirez said.

"But the dumb bastard didn't have them!" Collins shouted.

"What? I don't—"

"He had some old sticks. Old sticks. Not the gods. He'd been driving all over the goddamned place with this junk in the backseat, thinking—"

"What do you think happened?"

"Well, Christ, someone stole 'em from the dumb bastard. He's here in your jail. That big guy Gutierrez is watching him, see he doesn't commit suicide. Like the air going out of a balloon."

Ramirez shook his head, trying to get a grasp on the shattered world. "So where does that leave us?"

"Leave us? Leave us? It leaves us with Blaine in the can, suspicion of homicide, breaking and entering, all that. That's for right now, but it'll ratchet up tomorrow when we get to him, gotta wait until he gets a goddamned lawyer. Also theft of federal property, a big list of chickenshit, I'll tell you tomorrow." The agent paused. "And it leaves us without the gods, that's what it leaves us." He sighed. "So that's blown."

"Come on," Ramirez said. "You didn't—"

"That was my fucking assignment, man. You've got your killer now. I don't have shit. Look, I'll see you tomorrow. Seven-thirty?"

After Ramirez hung up the phone, he began to ask himself a long and familiar series of questions, along with some new ones. Notably, how to prove that Blaine had murdered Walter Meyers when there was no evidence now of any sort—not even anything solidly circumstantial—tying him to it. It wasn't enough simply to know it . . . even if they did know it. Ramirez stripped off his clothes and lay down on the bed, with a prayer to his santo for advice.

Connie had finally gone to sleep, Mo noted, as he lay in bed thinking about the Hopis, about Darrel's death, the funeral, sitting up all night in the little room, about Emory, the old patriarch of the Eagle clan, the watchers, the guardians, the blind old man who shared responsibility for keeping the gods safe, to be ceremoniously fetched from time to time to dispense the divine law of the Hopis . . . Things were obviously going to hell without them. Hadn't Collins said that some guy in Phoenix had had them for a while . . . dead. Meyers? Dead. Darrel? Had he been involved? Anyway, dead. *Jesus.*

His throat felt better. No more chicken-bone stabs in the larynx, no more cramping around the Adam's apple. That stinking bear root . . . Maybe there's something to it after all. How would he confess to that crazy *curandera*, Phyllis Lodge? He listened again to the regular breaths of the woman next to him, and fell asleep.

Fourteen

"I've had a vision," Mo said as he walked into the kitchen and sat down at the round wooden table. "Hah—hah—hah. And it has restored my faith in the staying power of the human brain, even one as old and abused as this one."

"You stopped dying," Connie said. "I'm real glad. What do you want for breakfast?"

"I had it just now, when I was waking up. The scientists've got some damned tin-eared word for it. Hypnogogy or something. Anyway, it's that period when you're half asleep, half awake, and stuff comes to you. Visions. Out-of-body experiences. All those journeys the fruit-loops are always taking, zooming off to nirvana. They say there's a good reason for it, something about the way neurons work between sleep and waking, I forget. Anyway, I had a vision. Just now."

"Is that why you forgot to get dressed?"

"You're right." Mo pulled his chair closer to the table. "Naked as a pig. Hah—hah. Well, I'd better get dressed. You want to hear my vision?"

"Yes."

"Maybe I better get dressed first. The telling of a vision is an event of dignity, gravity, right?"

"If you feel that way. What should I cook while you're putting on your dignity?"

"Do we have any of those lamb chops left?" Mo said, standing up.

"Yes."

"And eggs? Like mainlining cholesterol?"

"Coming up."

Minutes later Mo reappeared in a pair of old blue jeans and a flowing black silk shirt that would have looked effeminate on most men but gave Mo something of the appearance of a retired kung fu warrior.

"It's bear root," he said.

"That gave you your vision?"

"No, no. That *was* the vision. It was an olfactory vision. Smell. My long suit. Something had been bothering me, like a chigger bite you can't quite scratch. These last few days. Then, this morning, while I was lying there wondering why you had hauled your lissome body out of the bed, leaving me utterly bereft and . . . Well, hah, it came to me. Bear root."

Connie put a plate in front of him and he sniffed deeply. "This is of heaven. *This* is nirvana."

"You realized that the bear root had fixed your throat? That's not much of a vision, Mo."

"Well, I suppose it has. What if Phyllis finds out? God, how she'll crow. See, I told you so. Nyaah, nyaah. Oh well. Just another humiliation. No, look, this is serious. I realized there that I had been smelling bear root for several days now. Before you whipped it out at your mother's house. By the way, how come I didn't get any? Never mind." He cut off a piece of lamb chop, stuck it into the fried egg, and then into his mouth, and sat chewing for a moment.

"As a matter of fact, if I'm right, then this is all bad news. The worst kind of news. When I went into Meyers's gallery the day after he was killed . . . Remember? You were there with that del Massimo woman, and I was talking to Tony Ramirez."

"Yes, of course I remember."

"Well, I asked where it had happened, and Tony took me back to that little anteroom, and I was sniffing around. And there was a lot of stuff there, including that woman's Opium perfume, but there was something else, a trace of a pungent, oily smell that I didn't know. Didn't even really register at the time, you know? It just sort of laid back there, buried somewhere in my brain." He took another bite.

"Aren't you eating?" he asked.

"I already did," Connie said from across the kitchen. "So?"

"So there must have been bear root in there sometime not too long before we got there in the morning, or otherwise it would have dissipated."

"And?"

"And that's all we really know about that. Now, the next time I smelled it was when Darrel was here, you know, that morning I found him in the hammock, and God, did he stink of last night's booze, and then of course he threw up, and I never did smell such vomit, could have killed a rattlesnake at forty yards. But, and again I didn't really register it at the time, there was this undertone, overtone, whatever, of something else. Bear root. Now I know it was bear root."

Connie was silent.

"And even when the smell of it filled up your mother's house—do you notice when you use it how penetrating a smell it is? But even then, I didn't register it. Only this morning. It all came together in one of those . . . olfactory memories."

Dishes clattered in the sink. "So," Connie said icily, "what you're saying is that Darrel was in the gallery before we got there. You think he killed Meyers and took those deities. You want coffee?"

"Yeah, sure. No. I mean yes, coffee, no, I'm not saying Darrel did all that."

"But that's what it looks like."

"All I'm saying is that that looks like a possibility. Now, don't get angry."

"Oh, Mo," Connie said. "Mo. Angry? Of course I'm angry." A pot clattered, and Connie crossed the kitchen and sat down. "But not at you." She poured coffee in his cup.

The big man put his hand out, feeling for her forearm, and held it. It was like warm velvet. "It's just something that happened, this bear root smell," he said. "It's got to mean something."

"What are you going to do?"

"Well, I suppose I got to tell Tony Ramirez."

She sighed. "I suppose." She fell silent. Mo sipped his coffee. "Mo? Darrel didn't do it. He didn't kill Meyers. He couldn't."

"Okay," Mo said, thinking about the limp rag doll of a man he had plucked out of the hammock and held off the ground by the neck. Not much to him. On the other hand, Meyers was a little shrimp too.

"He was a mess," Connie said. "A mess. He was a good kid, a good little boy. He took things seriously. He wasn't like some of these kids now, they think some of the old ways are too hard, too . . . I don't know. Some of them think they don't make any sense today, the old beliefs. It's hard. But Darrel . . . Darrel, he'd been taught *properly*. He knew what was right. I remember my grandfather and Darrel's father once, they were talking about Darrel, about getting him a godfather that would, you know, bring him along till one day he'd be in one of the religious societies. They had Darrel picked already to be a priest one day. He wasn't even ten years old. But they saw things, those old men."

Connie stood up and crossed the room. More dishes clattered.

"But it went wrong. One time when Darrel was little, maybe six, some of his friends found a nest of birds. And they got the little birds, you know, featherless, out of the nest and were playing with them. Darrel got real upset, he knew the little birds were going to die, so he told a bahana, a white woman who was there for one of the dances, he told her he would give her the birds if she would take care of them. He didn't want to tell on his friends, so he just got the birds when they weren't looking and gave them to the woman." She paused and Mo sat silently.

"Darrel was always like that. He couldn't kill anything. He wouldn't even go out on rabbit hunts when the men were trying to feed the eagles on the roof. He was a misfit that way. People, other kids, made fun of him. They would say maybe he was really a girl. He never could have been a priest. But there's no way . . . he couldn't have killed Meyers. He didn't have it in him."

"But he was an alcoholic," Mo said.

"Sure. Yes, he was. And that's why he stole those things in the first place."

"He did?"

"Yes."

"Did he tell you that?"

"Not in so many words," Connie said. "But that day, after you found him, he was talking. He was ranting and raving, jumping from one thing to another. He was blaming another guy. But he kept saying he was alone, all alone. No place, no people. He was talking about how bad he was, how he hated himself, all that, how he was lost because of what he had done, and he never said it was alcohol or what, but I think he took those things in the first place, to get money for drink, and then he was trying to get them back. If he was at the gallery that night, that's what he was doing there. Trying to get those things back."

Mo cleared his throat. "Well, we don't even know that he *was* there."

"I'm sure he was," Connie said. "Doing what I said."

"Damn."

"So I'm angry, Mo. Real angry. I'm angry at a world that gets a good little boy given to it and turns him into a kind of monster and then makes him do what other people want, steal things, wreck things, ruin lives . . ."

"And turn a good thing to shit," said Mo Bowdre.

"Well, what can we do about *that*? That's *my* world that's turned to shit, Mo, my people, my *world*." Connie's voice rose for the first time Mo could remember. "What the *hell* are we going to do about that?"

When Nigel Calderwood, clean-shaven, his cheeks tingling from a few pats of a new men's cologne, emerged from Marianna del Massimo's bedroom, she was seated in a white easy chair in the living room wearing a brief, lacy black chemise, something she had gotten from the people at Victoria's Secret. Nigel had spotted the catalog while poking around the apartment one day and had been pleased to find himself able to tick off, in its soft and languorous photographs, all of Marianna's underthings.

Marianna had the receiver of the phone cradled in her neck, and he went around behind her and let his hands drift down her shoulders. She brushed him off, shaking her head, and pointed at the phone receiver. Nigel, like all truly egotistical men, was especially sensitive to rebuff, and his antennae went up. He sat down in the white chair opposite her and watched her drum her fingers impatiently on the chair's arm, frowning. He looked at her chest, the black lace so perfectly revelatory of the merest hint of nipples, and noticed for what he guessed was the first time that Marianna's breastbones, or whatever they were called, were quite pronounced. He hadn't thought of her as having a bony chest between those . . .

Suddenly she smiled and leaned forward—a lovely glimpse, that, Nigel thought—and held the phone to her ear, her other arm wrapped around her waist.

"Sergeant," she said, her voice low and soft. "Thank you so much. I hope I'm not disturbing you . . . Oh, good. I'm glad. Yes . . . Well, Sergeant, perhaps you can. The other day you mentioned that there might be someone who knew who it was . . . Yes, yes, that's right . . . Last night? Don't you ever rest? I was just curious, you know, because of . . . Yes, the gallery." She smiled winningly and crooned into the phone. Nigel wondered if the cop had creamed his shorts yet. She leaned back in the chair and crossed her legs.

"Oh." Her face fell. "Oh. Yes, of course. I understand. Time, yes. Yes, well, of course. Sergeant, I think you're . . . heroic . . . to keep . . . Yes, thank you. I know you are. Thank you."

She hung up.

"Shit!"

"Bad news," Nigel said.

"He's trying. He's *trying*, he says. He sure as hell is." Marianna stood up. "Damn!"

"Well, you're certainly giving him an incentive to keep on trying," Nigel said with a smile. "I wouldn't have been surprised to see him ooze through the telephone and into the lap he pants for."

"Listen, Nigel, I need information, and how I go about getting it is none of your goddamned business. In fact—"

Nigel held up his hands. "I think it's just marvelous the way you play that lonely little Spanish guitar of a copper, don't get me wrong. That was a compliment, intended and delivered. Now, tell me . . ."

Marianna sat down in the chair and crossed her arms. "Nothing. He was very coy, very cautious the other day, telling me that there might be a lead to this man Breeden. He doesn't know I know the man's name, won't tell me what it is. He's that coy about all this. And he was going to look into the lead. Someone up north of here, probably one of those hoods who chased me around the plaza. Anyway, he didn't find him, dammit. How are we going to find Breeden, Nigel? We haven't got forever. And whoever Breeden is, he's got what we need. What time is it?"

"It's twenty past eight."

"I've got to go."

"Too bad. I was thinking about a little preprandial—"

"Nigel," she said, getting up and standing beside his chair. "Don't you think of anything else but—"

"Not when you wear things like that. XB-13, is it? Fragile little thing, isn't it?"

"Nigel, we need to find this man Breeden. Get your mind out of my lingerie and think. I'm not kidding."

"No thinkee, no, ah, nookie?" Nigel said.

"Yeah, like that." The bedroom door closed behind him and Nigel's eyebrows rose a half inch on his forehead.

"They really should give an important detective like you a bigger office," Mo Bowdre said. "How can you possibly think in this airless box?"

"You're the taxpayer," Ramirez said. "Write the mayor."

"It wouldn't do any good. The mayor and I don't get along."

"How come?"

"Hah—hah. Neither of us suffers fools lightly."

Ramirez smiled at his big friend, sitting opposite him in one of the two idiotically small metal chairs. Not for the first time he wondered if, in losing his sight, Mo Bowdre had also been lifted beyond certain other mundane restraints. Or maybe he had always been that way. Bowdre, the self-deprecating egoist, bombastic to a fault, was the only Anglo, in fact one of the few people anywhere, with whom Ramirez felt completely at ease. An odd thing, thought the policeman, and not explainable. He looked around the familiar confines of his airless box.

It was a crappy office, he thought. Maybe he should have stayed in archeology. Professor Ramirez, specialist in settlement patterns among the pre-Mimbres cave dwellers of southwestern New Mexico.

"May I ask why you are interfering with the work schedule of a public servant?"

"You mean your investigation of the Meyers murder?" Mo asked.

"That's not the only fish on my plate," the policeman said.

"Tony, you just butchered not one, but two Anglo clichés. In fact, I am here to help your investigation," Mo said. "An essential clue has come to light. I want you to be the first to know."

"We've got that guy Blaine in here. Collins brought him in last night. Suspicion of murder, breaking and entering, a big list of charges. We've got him. The killer."

Mo leaned forward. "Tony, you sound a bit, ah, hesitant. Suspicion? Mere suspicion? Where are the gods, by the way? Wouldn't that make matters certain?"

Ramirez sighed. "Okay, the problem is this. Collins arrested Blaine when he was making the deal, handing over the gods. In some park in Tucson. But he didn't have them."

"What?"

"Blaine didn't have them. He had a bunch of sticks, not the gods. Somehow someone must have pulled a switch. Without Blaine knowing it."

"Aha," Mo said.

"Aha? What do you mean, aha?"

"Where's Collins?"

"He's due any minute."

"This is going to be interesting."

"What is? What, are you trying to play some kind of Nero Wolfe? What's up? What's this *clue*?"

Mo touched his nose. "You remember the morning after the murder, we were—"

"Hey, Tony," Larry Collins said from the doorway. "Blaine got a lawyer yet? When can we— Oh. Bowdre. What're you doing here?"

"He has a clue." Ramirez said. "He is bringing us a clue, like a cat brings you a bird. He is very proud of himself. Sit down."

The agent flopped into the other metal chair. "Great," he said noncommitally. "Let's hear it."

And so Mo Bowdre explained to the two lawmen what he had explained to Connie earlier that morning—the scent of bear root at the scene of the crime the next day, the scent of bear root on the breath of Darrel the day after that, the Hopi use of bear root as a protection. He did not explain Connie's belief that Darrel was incapable of killing a man. When he was finished, Larry Collins said, "Your nose that good, huh?"

"You're a skeptic?" Mo said, turning his face toward the agent.

"It ain't exactly what we in the trade call hard evidence."

"Mine's harder than yours . . . hah—hah. From what I understand, that is."

Ramirez, for the second time, wondered if the two bulls were going to back off or— "Let's think about it," he said. "So this Hopi kid was in there that night too. Wasn't this guy Blaine a coach out there? Maybe the two of them . . . see?" Ramirez said, getting wound up. "It's the classic pattern. Blaine worked on the reservation, uses kids like this guy, what's his name, Darrel, to steal stuff, masks, all that stuff. I've heard these guys like Blaine, they get these kids in some border-town bar, just open up their wallets and let 'em look at the cash, tell 'em what they want, the kid needs the dough for his habit, booze, whatever. Maybe Darrel was one of Blaine's students, who knows? Anyway, the kid steals these gods, they go to Blaine, then to the guy in Phoenix, then maybe to Meyers. Yeah, to Meyers. Okay? Then Blaine realizes he got ripped off or something, they're more valuable than he thought, he learns that somewhere. So maybe he and the kid decide to get them back, steal them back. So they go break in the place and kill Meyers and the kid is chewing on his bear root for protection—I guess killing a guy is a specially bad crime among these Hopis—and they run off with the stuff. But then the kid pulls a switch and Blaine is running around all over looking for a buyer and all he's got are these sticks, so it all goes to hell when Collins here jumps him in the park when he's making his deal."

There was silence.

"What d'you think of that?" Ramirez said.

"Nah," Collins said. "Blaine was working on his own. He's a selfish, greedy bastard. Christ, he even dropped his wife and kid, just took off, left them in a campground in Sedona. The guy's a real prick. A sociopath. Why would he let the kid back in on the deal? He didn't need the kid. Maybe, some kind of coincidence, Jesus, the kid shows up around the same time, sees what's going on, pulls a switch. But Blaine's our killer. It's got to be."

Mo cleared his throat. "Not very satisfying," he said.

"What d'you mean, not satisfying?" Collins snapped.

"Well, you don't seem to have much evidence—*hard* evidence—on Blaine. Just that he was running around under what we think is the illusion that he had something valuable. Can you convict someone for thinking he had something he didn't? And, of course, Darrel is dead. There's nothing you can do about him. I'm sure you're right, Blaine was on his own. But I don't like the coincidence of Darrel showing up at the same time as—"

"We'll get Blaine to talk," Collins said. "His ass is so far up the creek, stolen cars, you name it, he'll talk."

"And you'll simply take his word for it," Mo said. "There's something unesthetic about all this."

Collins snorted. "Life isn't art, pal, let me tell you."

"Hah—hah—hah. Sometimes *art* isn't art, let me tell you. But this is a mess."

The phone rang on Ramirez's desk. He picked up the receiver and said, "Yeah, Ramirez. Oh, bueno. Good. Put 'em in number 3. Yeah. Me and Collins." He hung up. "Okay, Blaine and his lawyer, they'll be in the interrogation room. Two minutes about. He's your collar, you lead, right?"

"Yeah," Collins said. He stood up. "Okay, let's go. See you around, Bowdre." He stuck out a hand, realized Bowdre couldn't see it, and said, "Thanks."

Mo stood up with a grunt. "Does that room have one of those mirrors? I'd like to listen."

"What the hell for?" Collins asked. "This is police business."

"Oh, esthetic reasons. Okay, Tony?"

"It's pretty unusual."

"Okay, never mind," Mo said.

"But it's okay with me, if it's okay with you."

"I don't really give a damn one way or the other," Collins said. "It's your police station out here in the Wild West. Just have a cop there with him. So we can tell the lawyer that people from the station are watching."

Interrogation Room number 3 was designed for maximum discomfort. An overhead fluorescent light hummed quirkily like an insect. The chairs on either side of the scarred wooden table were the metal folding type, unyielding, like sullen, silent witnesses. Otherwise, the room was empty, just gray walls, oppressively close, with the big mirror on one wall. The air-conditioning didn't work—in fact, it had been cut off. When Larry Collins entered the room, followed by Ramirez, Willie Blaine looked up, then down. His lawyer also looked up, but kept his eyes on the agent.

"Special Agent Collins? I'm Griego, Public Defender's Office. Sergeant Ramirez."

The two lawmen sat down on the other side of the table. Ramirez had seen Griego around the jail many times. What a lousy job, Ramirez thought, being sent in to sweep up the trash. Over and over, sweeping up one or another pile of trash. Griego was a small man with a large head and a sad-eyed expression. He looked about fifty years old, but Ramirez knew he was in his early forties. A lousy job. Blaine, on the other hand, looked young, almost boyish, vulnerable—like a lost orphan. A nondescript orphan too. Ramirez would have had a difficult time describing him in a way that would have made him recognizable. Average size, build. Brownish hair. Eyes a kind of murky hazel. Unremarkable features. A nobody.

"So?" Collins said.

"I've discussed the charges with my client here," the lawyer began.

"All of 'em?" Collins said.

Griego stared at Collins. "All of them. Of course. And my client is aware of their gravity, of the penalties they bear if they were to be proved in court. He is also aware of the highly circumstantial nature of the evidence against him. . . ."

Collins thumped the table with a stiff middle finger. "There's nothing circumstantial about car theft, theft of government property, obstructing a federal officer—"

"I'm aware of that, Mr. Collins, and so is my client. I am referring chiefly to the charges of suspicion of murder, breaking and entering, attempted theft of federally protected archeological artifacts—those charges for which he was brought to this jurisdiction. Now, my client wants to be reasonable—"

"Reasonable?" The word hung in the air. The fluorescent bulb flickered and buzzed. Blaine glanced up, then down again. "Your client had better confess his ass, that's what's reasonable, counselor."

"That is precisely his intent. He is aware that he has engaged in a cascading series of criminal acts and is going to spend a good deal of time in the federal penitentiary. He wishes to confess to those crimes, but he will not confess to murder because he is not guilty of that charge."

"Shee—"

"You will listen?"

"Sure, we'll listen. Take it all down. Let him sign it. But we don't have to believe it. Right, Ramirez? Let's get someone in here to take it down."

"Surely this is all being taped, listened to from behind that mirror."

"Yeah. Okay. Let's hear it, Blaine."

"All right, Willie, tell these gentlemen the whole story."

Willie looked up, his eyes flickering back and forth between the lawmen. Ramirez thought this orphan might burst into tears. He looked down and began talking in a monotone.

"About two weeks ago, no, three—"

"Hold it," Collins said. "You're William Blaine? Formerly of Winslow, Arizona?"

"Yeah."

"That's correct?"

"Yeah."

"Go ahead."

"So it was three weeks ago, I found out how valuable those things, those deities were, and I decided I'd been screwed. So I decided to get them back, sell them myself."

"Wait a minute. Tell us how you got 'em in the first place."

"Guy from Phoenix, Jenkins, Karl Jenkins, came to me a few months ago, like February I think, described these things, said they were altar pieces. Said they were worth seven grand to him. He had a vague idea where they were, some shrine in the cliffs below Oraibi. So I got a Hopi kid, Darrel Quanemptewa, to go get 'em."

"How?"

Blaine looked up at the agent. "I waited till Darrel came in the bar in Winslow, you know the place, and told him I'd give him seven hundred bucks if he got them. Kid was always lookin' for fast money. Drank like a fish."

"You ever use any other Hopi kids for this kind of thing?"

"Yeah, a couple."

"Who?"

The lawyer cleared his throat. "My client wants to cooperate fully, and he's prepared to give you the names of everyone he's dealt with in this, ah, trade. But perhaps we should get on with this basic—"

"Okay, good."

"So a couple weeks later, Darrel turns up at the bar, says he's got these things in his truck. So we go out, look at the stuff, and I give him seven hundred bucks and he took off. He was broke again in a month. So I call this guy Jenkins in Phoenix and tell him that these things are hard to get, it's real dangerous to try and get 'em from this cave they're in, and my expenses are double what I thought. So Jenkins says he'll make it eight thousand, and two weeks later I go to Phoenix and give him the stuff and collect my money."

"And two months later, *you're* broke, huh?"

Willie Blaine shrugged.

"Habit?"

"I had to pay off some guys I owed."

Collins's elbows splayed out on the table and he lowered his head. "Okay, go on."

"So then three weeks ago, I was in the Sunset Gallery in Winslow, you know, looking around at the stuff he's got there, a lot of Navajo jewelry, a lot of it shit but some good things, and I saw this newsletter. You know, a dealer's newsletter, I forget what it's called. The McSomething letter, I don't know. On the back page it had these things, you know, the Hopi gods I'd sold to Jenkins. It said they'd been stolen and it said what they were, so I figured I'd been screwed. I figured they were worth at least two hundred thousand, and I'd gotten this lousy eight thousand, so I decided to get 'em back."

"How did you know where to find them?"

"I didn't. I guessed. I figured Meyers was in on it, he's one of the big-time guys, I mean everyone knows . . . So I went to Santa Fe and checked out Meyers's place. Like last week, when was it, a week ago yesterday. Monday. I went in and looked around for a while in the afternoon, you know, looking at the place. Then I went back later that night. I thought I'd check it out again, see what kind of problems I'd have when I went in some night."

"What time was this?"

"Oh, I don't know. About eleven, eleven-fifteen. I parked in the alley a couple of doors down and went around the back, you know, to his apartment or whatever, where he lives. I was looking around at the windows, and so I gave one a push, and it opened. I mean it just opened, like it wasn't locked or anything. So I said: hey, why not? And I went in. I looked around some of the rooms back there, there wasn't anyone there, and then I figured I'd go see if anyone was in the gallery. So I'm going through a door into this little anteroom, and then I see him. He was lying on the floor all crumpled up, blood all over the place. . . ."

"You expect us to believe that?"

"Yeah, yeah, I swear that's what happened. I come in the anteroom and here's this dead guy on the floor, in the light from my flashlight. Christ, I'll never forget it, this dead guy all crumpled up. . . ."

Collins nibbled the back of his thumb. "So?"

"So I was scared outta my fucking mind. I just stood there in the dark for a few minutes thinking. Then I figured I'd better see if there was anyone in the house, so I looked around, you know, the gallery and then back into the apartment. I was opening doors and I opened up one in the bedroom and it was a closet. All these clothes, sports jackets, slacks, hundreds of them, and shoes, Christ, the guy must've had some kind of fetish." Willie looked up at the agent, who was staring at him as if he were a bug.

"And then I saw this garbage bag rolled up on the floor, right there, in the middle of all those shoes, and I figure it doesn't look right, this garbage bag, you know, crap of some sort, right in the middle of this guy's stuff he has all neatly arranged. So I open it up and there they are. The altar pieces, those gods. Right there on the *floor*. In a fucking garbage bag! It was all so easy, I thought maybe I had been set up. So I look around some more, you know the office, and there's a piece of notepaper on the desk, with a name and number on it. L.A. area code. Name of Robert Breeden. I figure maybe this guy's a client, so I take the paper. Then I took the gods out to the truck and stuck 'em under the sand.''

"Sand. In the truck.''

"Yeah, I was going to build a cement wall. At the house . . . in Winslow.''

"So then you left.''

"Yeah. Well, no. I went back to the apartment. See, I was so excited, I went out through the window with the stuff and forgot to close it. So I went back and closed the window and rubbed it, fingerprints, and then I left.''

"And you never looked in the bag again, huh?''

"No.''

"Until I caught you in the park.''

Willie hung his head. "Yeah.''

"Sergeant Ramirez, you got any questions?''

"I'd like to go over the whole thing again,'' said Ramirez. "Okay, so this guy Jenkins . . .''

Sitting on an uncomfortable chair in the little room opening via the mirror to Interrogation Room number 3, Mo Bowdre stretched contentedly, stood up and let himself out, leaving a man in uniform to listen to the rehash. Outside in the hall, he stood uncertainly. A woman's voice said, "Can I help you, sir?''

"You work here?'' Mo said.

"Officer Maria Martinez.''

"Well, you could do me a favor. If Tony Ramirez gets done

in there, tell him I'll buy him lunch at Tiny's. Collins too, the FBI agent."

"I'll tell him."

"Thank you, Officer Martinez. And maybe one more favor?"

"Certainly."

"I don't know how to get out of here. Hah—hah—hah."

He felt a hand on his elbow, smelled perfume and a hint of coffee, and allowed her to guide him.

Fifteen

It took a second or two for Samantha Burgess to turn the unexpected cameo before her into anything meaningful. A tiny, Hispanic policewoman like a trimly uniformed tugboat was leading a huge blond-bearded man toward the door. Mo Bowdre, the sculptor. What was he doing in the police station? She watched the little policewoman take him out through the big heavy doors and then return. On an impulse, Samantha took off and found Bowdre standing on the curb, sniffing the air.

"Mr. Bowdre?" she called.

The big man turned his face toward Samantha.

"Mr. Bowdre," she said again, coming up to him. "It's Samantha Burgess, you remember? I interviewed you for—"

"Oh, sure, I remember. How are you? Ever wrestle all that baloney into an article? Hah—hah—hah." Bowdre was standing on the edge of the curb, and traffic rushed past him only a foot or two away. Without thinking, Samantha reached for his elbow and tugged him back a few steps.

"Oh yeah. It came out pretty well, I think. I handed it in

last week. I saw you in the police station, so I thought I'd come out and say hello."

"That's very nice," Mo said. "But satisfy my curiosity. What sort of art story were you looking for in the police station?"

"Oh, I got a new job, I mean I got a job. With the *New Mexican*. I'm a reporter, I guess you'd call it. Assistant to Jim Billings, you know, the paper's investigative reporter. He heard that the cops had arrested someone in the Meyers murder case so he sent me down here to find out about it."

"Congratulations. I'd say that covering murderers and thieves is a definite step up from interviewing sculptors. And what did you find out?"

A semi rumbled by just as Samantha was about to answer. She paused, then said, "Can I take you somewhere? This isn't the best place . . ." She looked around, saw nothing.

"Let's live dangerously and cross the street," Mo said. "We can get a cup of coffee in the doughnut shop." Samantha guided the blind man across Cerillos Road and into the shop. In a few minutes they were seated in a plastic booth near the window looking out onto the street. Samantha was nearly exploding with the thrill of the chase, with the excitement of having put two and two together in a creative burst of insight into the criminal world, and she found herself telling T. Moore Bowdre what she had found.

"They have a man named William Blaine in jail on suspicion of murder of Walter Meyers. Okay, he used to be a coach or something with the Bureau of Indian Affairs, on the Hopi reservation. For seven years he's lived in Winslow. Now that fits the classic description of one of those guys who prey on Indian people, you know, stealing artifacts for the trade. And of course Meyers had a reputation. So, a falling out among thieves. Don't you think?"

"It certainly sounds plausible," Mo said, sipping his coffee, which had now cooled down enough.

"But there's more."

"More?"

"I think I know what it was all about. There's this newsletter to dealers in Indian artifacts, comes out six times a year. The *McFarland Report*. It had a story last issue about some weird objects from the Hopis that got stolen. They're really important. One of a kind. Deities, they said they were. Stolen last winter from one of the villages. My guess is it would take something pretty valuable to instigate a murder, so I figure it's them."

"My guess," Mo said, "is that Jim Billings had better keep an eye to his backside, hah—hah—hah."

A few minutes later they recrossed Cerillos Road. Samantha steered Mo to her old Toyota in the public lot at the police station and dropped him off at Tiny's Restaurant. As she pulled out into the traffic, her eyes rolled up, and out loud she said, "Damn!"

Some kind of great investigative reporter, she thought scornfully. In all of what she realized was self-congratulatory excitement, she had forgotten to ask the man what *he* was doing in the police station.

"You may be interested to know that there's a young reporter who's already linked Meyers and Blaine and the Hopi gods. At least she's linked them in her mind." Bowdre threw this out as a mild challenge, and pursed his lips expectantly. When his gauntlet was not taken, he added, "Her name is Samantha Burgess. She's a rookie on the newspaper."

"She's right," Collins said. "They are linked. Blaine killed Meyers to get the gods back. That's how it was. Who else could've done it?"

"Darrel?" Ramirez said.

"Why would Darrel go kill Meyers," Collins said, getting impatient, "then leave the gallery and wait around outside— for what? Then, hey, miracle, Blaine shows up, comes out of the gallery with the gods, goes back *into* the gallery, so Darrel swipes them. C'mon. Blaine is a wheedling, lying bastard, and I don't care what shit he serves up, he did it. I don't see why you guys want to talk, talk, talk."

"I thought people from New York liked to talk—hah—hah." Collins grinned and, looking over at Ramirez, shrugged.

"You know," Mo went on. "Indian people, Navajos in particular, believe that speech—talking, singing—actually creates the world. Or re-creates it. Makes it harmonious and whole when it's gone to hell. You think until you know how it should be, then you put that into speech, and that is what the world becomes. It's a very artistic view of the world, almost romantic."

"And you take a romantic view of the world," Collins said.

"Of course. Otherwise why bother? Now, what about Marianna del Massimo? She has something to gain from all this."

"No good," said Ramirez. "Her whereabouts are accounted for. Solid alibi. And I don't think she knew about those gods. She's been asking me about them, she seems real curious, but I'd bet she had never heard of them a week ago."

Mo leaned forward. "Doesn't she have a boyfriend? That tenor at the opera? Didn't you tell me that, Tony? What about him?"

"Yeah, Nigel Calderwood," Ramirez said. "He was at the opera, as a matter of fact. They were having dress rehearsals, or something, and they ran on well past midnight. He's out. Is there anything in the Breeden thing, that guy who—"

"I don't think there is a Robert Breeden," Collins said. "There's a creep who was with Blaine in the park, he was gonna get the gods, supposedly acting for this Breeden character, but who knows? He's got a sheet, arrested, not convicted on a couple of narcotics charges, spent two years in the pen for smuggling pre-Colombian statues or something. There's a little guy with white hair who poses as Robert Breeden every so often in Tucson, but who knows who *he* is?" Collins shrugged. "If there *is* a Robert Breeden, he's like a ghost, drifting around at some third, fourth remove. No one'll ever see him. Forget him."

"And," Ramirez said, "I guess we'll never know which Anthony Baca got the call in Espanola."

"And maybe," Mo said cheerfully, "none of that makes any difference."

Connie knew.

Even before Mo had announced his "vision" that morning at breakfast—yet another reason to believe that her clan brother had been at the Meyers Gallery, had been the original thief, and had brought shame down on her people—Connie knew that she had to turn around. It was like a distant and barely heard insect clangor, insistent, sad, coming from beyond the horizon, coming nearer, louder. Part was the memory of her mother's eyes, fearful, suddenly aged by an increment too great to be accounted for by the mere passage of time. Part was her grandfather's eyes, now utterly blind in a matter of months. How odd, she thought, that the two most important men in her life were blind. Sardonically, she wondered if white doctors had identified a Seeing Eye dog complex among certain kinds of women. She felt as if she had passed into an especially strong flux of gravity, immobilized, enveloped.

She stared out the kitchen window, across the emerald grass, idly contemplating the old stone mill house where Mo worked. . . . But not for how many days? Where there had been a great profusion of aromatic lilac flowers festooning the great bush outside his studio, there was now a tattered array of weedy brown corpses littering its greenery. So things wind down, every year, their end written in their beginnings, like the seed of a corn plant that produces its stalk, its ears of corn, and then the stalk is finished. It is pushed over, stepped on, allowed to rest, like an old woman or an old man bending over farther and farther till forehead touches ground and a life is gone. . . . In this flux of gravity she felt her grandfather's exhaustion, the sorry burden clogging the heart of an old man who had only tried to do what his uncles had taught him, had sought to live an exemplary life for his people, and now was blinded and bent. She turned away from the window with a shudder and went to the bedroom, where, without thought, she began taking clothes from the bureau drawers, working in what felt like slow motion, underwater.

Once packed, she carried the suitcase into the living room and set it down before a gleaming array of electronic equipment, a CD player, tape recording devices—Mo's "sound studio." She pressed a small green button and a tape started.

"Well, Mo," she said. "I know this isn't a good time, it's never a good time. But I've got to go back home. I'm scared about Grandpa. So I got to be there. *You* know." She sighed. "I don't know how long. Maybe till this is all over. I called the Wheelwright and the others, so they won't be pestering you. Anyway . . . I'm sorry, real sorry."

She pressed the little green button and the tape shut off with a click. She toted the suitcase outside, put it in the pickup, and went back into the house. Again the little green button.

"Mo, I really feel bad about this. I'll call you. Tomorrow. I . . . I love you."

Click.

On her way back to the truck, she thought: how strange. In all these years—four? almost—I've never told him that out loud. It's the Hopi way.

The wooden gate in the wall creaked open and Connie looked up to see Mo duck under the adobe arch over the gate and emerge into the backyard. She stood silently and watched as he methodically closed the gate, jiggled the broken latch into place, and began taking his measured steps across the grass. She thought of her grandfather picking his way through his familiar territory, a skinny old man all bent and blind, and then this big man with the blond beard, head up, back erect, big forearms swinging with an odd precision, like a dancer's. How much vaster, more complex, a map of the physical world he had to keep in his mind.

"Mo," she said softly.

He turned with a smile growing, opaque glasses facing her directly.

"Connie."

"Mo, I put a message on . . . I think I better, you know, for a while . . ."

The big man sighed. "Back to Hopi." He began walking in her direction.

"It's Grandpa, you know?"

"Sure." He stood in front of her, lifted a big hand and took her arm.

"It's since those things were taken. He feels like, well, responsible, sort of. That's why he went blind so fast."

"Connie, there could be a medical reason for that, you know," Mo said gently.

"There is probably, but there's a reason for the medical reason. That's what we think."

Mo turned his head away and sniffed the air. "That's what I think too. You know, you Hopis aren't the only people who know this kind of stuff. God*damn*, I'm sorry all this has happened. I'm sorry you have to go. But I suppose you do. You could call me . . . if you can get that damn pay phone to work. Well, damn, I'm going to miss you." He wrapped his arms around her. "A man gets used to having his Indian princess around the place, you know? I love you."

"Oh, Mo—"

"Don't say it," Mo said. "It's against tribal custom."

He stood by while Connie got in the truck and started the engine, then turned and went into the house. Connie backed out into Canyon Road and let the truck drift down around the curve.

"Well I'll be damned," Mo said, and pressed the replay button. He listened to the tape again, both messages, and again said, "I'll be damned."

She probably never *would* say such a thing to his face, he thought. Hopis. Strangest people on the whole damn globe. Pleased, doubly pleased, he went to the phone and punched 411, asking for two local telephone numbers which he committed to short-term memory.

The first one rang six times before Phyllis Lodge answered.

"Phyllis Lodge," she said.

"Phyllis, this is a totally humbled and penitent Mo Bowdre."

"Aha! It worked."

"Yeah, it did. Wonderful stuff. I swear by it. Bear root. Say, Phyllis, I'd like to ask you a few questions about that stuff."

"Questions?"

"Yeah. I'm so taken with it that I've decided to make a bit of a study of it. . . ."

"Mo, don't bullshit me. What're you up to?"

"Hah—hah—hah. Well, let me explain that to you . . ."

"New Mexican."

"Yes, I believe you have a new employee there. In the editorial department. Samantha Burgess?"

"Hold on."

The line hummed.

"Burgess."

"You sound pretty hard-boiled there."

"This is Samantha Burgess."

"The star reporter?"

"Who is this?"

"It's Mo Bowdre."

"Oh, hi! What . . . uh . . . ?"

"I need some information. Of course, I'm willing to trade. I know how you investigative types work."

"Uh, like what?"

"Well, I know that you're into murder and rapine, but it's only been a week, right? So maybe you haven't forgotten everything you learned about the greater cultural scene of Santa Fe."

Samantha giggled. "What's the trade?"

"Let me explain to you about that . . ."

S i x t e e n

Flames licked at a tangle of piñon logs lying in the shallow pit, and glinted from Mo Bowdre's glasses. He put a paper plate of chicken bones down beside him on the flagstone floor and wiped his mouth and beard with a luxuriant pass of his beefy forearm.

"I'm going to tell you boys a story," he said.

The three sated men sat in canvas director's chairs around the open pit, with its pungent smoke rising to be swept away by a cool breeze into the night. The mill house across the lawn was barely visible from the fire's glow. A sliver of new moon had just risen above the eave of Mo's house, and it hung in the obsidian sky like a golden smile.

Ramirez leaned back, smiling himself, a half-full bottle of brown Dos Equis beer in his hand. Collins fidgeted in the chair, crossing, uncrossing, and recrossing his legs.

"A story?" the agent said.

"Yeah, like men of old. Hunters. Puzzled by the day's events, unexplainable things that have happened during the day. A river run dry maybe, or a familiar landmark altered. The sudden disappearance of game long before it's time for migration."

"Jesus."

"He wasn't invented yet. No, see, these old guys, they'd sit around the fire and wonder, and try to think up a plausible answer. They'd tell stories to each other, see which one was the best. And that would be the story, *the* story, the way things were. Come on, Collins, give it a try."

"What the hell," Collins said good-naturedly. "But I like my story."

"Your story depends, among other things," Mo said, "on that little man in Tony Ramirez's jail giving up *his* story and going along with yours. It might not happen. And your story leaves a number of things unexplained, mysterious, bothersome, the same kind of fearsome unknowns that haunted our forebears, sitting in the gloom of their caves wondering why the earth beneath their feet had quivered and lurched . . . what gods had—"

"Okay, okay," Collins said with an odd, donkeylike laugh. "I get the picture." He crossed his legs. "Shoot."

Mo sat erect in his director's chair, forearms resting on the armrests, big hands dangling. He pursed his lips as if he were about to utter a complicated French vowel sound.

"The scientists have a rule they invoke every now and then," he began. "Especially when it's convenient—hah—hah. It's called Occam's razor. It says that of all the various explanations for a set of facts, you take the simplest one and that's probably correct. In this case, there aren't very many facts, but the explanation that explains them all—the *only* explanation that explains them all—is wildly implausible, so full of coincidence as to make you think it's impossible. But history is full of coincidence—history *is* coincidence. . . ."

"This is a story?" Collins said.

"All right," Mo said. "Let's take Darrel first, the Hopi kid. Shows up here Tuesday night, unbeknownst to anyone, drunk as only an Indian can be, tormented by his guilt. Slept in that hammock over there. He was the guy who stole the gods, of course, passed them on to Blaine, just like Blaine says. His own people got after him in their old, indirect ways, letting everyone know that the Hopis have ways of taking care of such foul acts. How? Well, we might call it the kangaroo treatment, banishment, loss of one's society, loss of identity, the ultimate isolation. Others, like the Hopi, would consider it a matter of supernatural retribution of some sort. Anyway, we have Darrel, covered with shame and fear, trying to do penance, to *repent*, brothers, and the only way to do that is to get the gods back. He arrives in Santa Fe sometime Monday, guessing that the gods would be at the Meyers Gallery. Probably he buys a little courage through the grape, and sometime after eleven o'clock he arrives, emboldened but not yet sodden, outside the gallery."

Mo paused and sniffed the night air.

"We can imagine that he was scared shitless, wine or no, probably hung around in the shadows on the street for a few minutes, trying to get it up to snoop around. Then he hears, maybe sees, something moving. He stops, his heart in his teeth." Mo's voice dropped to a whisper. "A shape emerges from around the side of the gallery. He ducks. He watches. My *God*, it's Blaine! He watches Blaine—carrying some kind of bundle—walking up the street, and he sees him put the bundle in the back of a truck. Darrel hasn't any idea what's going on, or maybe he wonders if Blaine has stolen the gods from the gallery. What to do? Anyway, he waits in the shadows by his own truck and sees Blaine go *back* and disappear around the side of the gallery. On an impulse, he runs over to Blaine's truck, sees nothing but a pile of sand in the light from the streetlamp that's about twenty feet down the sidewalk. I checked that on my way home this afternoon.

"Where's the bundle? he wonders in a kind of panic. He digs around, finds it, peers into it—it's them! He grabs them and runs back to his truck, thinks, takes some cottonwood roots out of his truck—that's what the Hopis make kachina dolls out of, cottonwood roots—and he races back and sticks them in the bag and buries it under the sand. Then back to his truck and he ducks behind it. Blaine comes out and drives off. Probably filled to the eyeballs with adrenaline, Darrel gets in his truck and off he goes, for a celebratory injection of Thunderbird's finest, which is like piss, in case you haven't tried it."

Mo stood up.

"I'll be right back," he said, and went over to the wall of his house, returning with two piñon logs. He dropped them into the pit and a violent cloud of red sparks leapt up. Collins and Ramirez lurched back in their chairs.

"You could burn the house down that way," said Collins.

"I've been told that before," Mo said, sitting down. "So Darrel has the gods," he resumed, "and goes off to get drunk and rattles around Santa Fe in a state of complete, sodden indecision, and turns up here at my place the next night. Somewhere along the way, he has stashed the gods. Now this fits perfectly with Willie Blaine's story, the one he confessed. You simply have to believe the remarkable coincidence, that they both turned up at almost the same time, with the same thing on their minds."

"But it also fits my story," said Collins. "Blaine got there, killed Meyers, took the gods, and Darrel swiped 'em."

"Remember Occam's razor," Mo said.

"I don't see—"

"The bear root. The smell of bear root in the gallery."

"Okay," Collins said, becoming impatient. "So the Hopi kid is chewing this crap, goes in the gallery, sees that Blaine is there, goes out, waits—"

"Messy. Clumsy," Mo said. "It's a far simpler story if we imagine Darrel not going into the gallery."

"So what about the bear root?" Ramirez asked.

"You're awake, Tony. Good. Thought you might've dozed off there. Let's assume—and it's the only reasonable assumption we can make—that your captive, Blaine, is not a habitual bear root chewer. He may have worked at Hopi for a while, but he hardly absorbed their, ah, value system. Hah—hah. This leads us to a conclusion that seems preposterous." He paused. "It is this: there was not one coincidence that night, but two. There were not two people—against what odds? imagine—that showed up at the Meyers Gallery that night. Even greater odds. There were three."

Mo waited. His head turned from side to side, as if he were looking at the other two men, but they remained silent.

"No guffaws?" Mo asked. "No snorts of derision? Well, then. See, there were three utterly unconnected crimes committed there that night. The third, in time, was Darrel swiping the gods from Blaine. Second, Blaine swiping the gods from the gallery. The first crime was the murder of Walt Meyers, and it had nothing whatsoever to do with the gods. It happened before—maybe only minutes before—Blaine got there."

"So who—" Collins said.

"Someone who uses bear root," Mo said, beaming, his teeth shining in the firelight. "Tony, you know Phyllis Lodge?"

"The herbalist? Over on—"

"Right. A character. She sells all kinds of remedies, Indian, Hispanic, very knowledgeable. Now bear root is also called osha, it's from a plant up in the mountains. The Hopis use it for protection, you know, warding off evil. But it's also touted as a remedy for sore throats. In fact, I can attest to it. I just got rid of a sore throat using the stuff. Tastes awful. But it works. Anyway, it's good for throats. My point here is that a lot of people use it, including people who overwork their throats . . ." Mo leaned forward, "including, that is, a number of singers in the Santa Fe Opera." He leaned back, grinning. "And one of the singers that buys osha regularly from Phyllis Lodge," he continued, "is Nigel Calderwood."

"Del Massimo's boyfriend," Collins said.

"But he was *at* the opera that night," Ramirez protested. "Rehearsals. Until past midnight."

"So it seemed to everyone there," Mo said. "But these artists—hah—hah—a dress rehearsal is as nervous-making almost as a performance, and they're all thinking about themselves, they wouldn't notice if someone else wasn't there."

"But the rehearsals," Ramirez said. "They went on continuously. No breaks. That's what everybody said. The whole opera company can't be in cahoots."

"But Tony," Mo said, "they were rehearsing *Coronado*. It's a new opera about the Spanish conquest, and of course the Indians all hate it, but then, how many Indians go to the opera? Anyway, in that opera, from the middle of the second act until the middle of the third, the second tenor is not onstage. That's an hour's time, an interval of one hour, plenty of time to drive to the gallery, bludgeon Meyers to death, and drive back. Meanwhile chewing bear root to get ready for the finale. Who among all those self-centered singers would notice where the hell Calderwood was? Okay. Why would he do it? My sources say that he's almost washed up, losing his voice, in spite of all the bear root he pours down his gullet. So he's desperate. He hooks himself up to Marianna del Massimo, a kind of sinecure, and they plot the thing, plan the killing of Meyers so Marianna can get her hands on the gallery and the two of them can . . . Get the picture? See, she says, you murder the old creep and your future is assured. So is mine. Our future. A perfectly straight deal. A mutual service agreement.

"And it had nothing to do with the gods. She didn't know anything about them. Otherwise, why, Tony, would she have been trying to find out from you what they are? Anyway, sometime a little bit after eleven o'clock, Calderwood slips into the gallery, probably from the back, through a window, doesn't find the little twit in bed where he usually is at that hour, notes that he's in the office, waits a bit in the anteroom, then blam!

And back to the opera. And of course Marianna nips off to that restaurant—Café des Artistes—with some fanfare and then sits around all night with the owners, happens to be carrying a bottle of scotch to try out on them. The memorable detail. Right? I'll bet she even remembered the brand."

"She said Old Sheep Dip," Ramirez said, and laughed.

"And who could forget that? In retrospect, it's too perfect. And as a matter of fact, I wouldn't be surprised if Calderwood found himself bumped off before too long, some kind of accident. If I was that snake of a woman, that's what I'd do. So tell me, boys, what do you think of *my* story?"

"Smooth," Collins said. "Maybe even true."

Mo leaned back in his chair and sniffed. "More wood," he said, and stood up.

"I'll get it," said Ramirez, returning a moment later with one log, which he placed gently in the pit.

"Of course," Mo said, still standing, "it's all supposition. A story. Just a tale we spun in front of a fire. A myth. Very subjunctive. Can't prove a bit of it, can you? But it's the *only* story that fits our few pathetic facts."

The fire hissed and glowed.

Ramirez sat down, his elbows on his knees, head down. "Well, yeah. It does fit the facts we know. And I have an elaboration. The day before the murder, that afternoon, Marianna del Massimo sits down at the computer on Meyers's desk before she leaves, and does something—I don't know what. Some kind of override to the electronic security system. So it looks like it's on when it's not. So it's easy for Calderwood to get in—and also Blaine, by coincidence. Then in the morning, when she shows up at the gallery, she goes over to the computer and cancels the override. It would look like part of the job, you know, pulling up the inventory records, that stuff. Maybe there's some trace memory in the machine of the override. I don't know. But—"

"But what good is this whole story? Is that what you mean?"

"Yeah."

"You got a good story, you make it come true. Do what I do," Mo said.

"Yeah? What?"

"What I have to do as a sculptor is take an idea, a mental image—a story, you might call it—and turn it into something concrete." He grinned.

"I don't get it," Ramirez said.

"Well, let me explain that to you—hah—hah—but first I'm getting another beer. You guys want one?"

Through a curtain of dreams filled with unfamiliar colors, colors with no name, and the tops of trees growing down, not up, like shoots from seeds sinking into the earth, the phone rang, and Mo Bowdre became aware that he was asleep. The phone rang again, and Mo waited for Connie to pick it up. Again it rang, and he remembered that he was alone. On the fourth ring he rolled over, stretched across the bed and picked up the receiver.

"Yeah, hello."

"Mo?"

"Yeah."

"Did I wake you up? It's Connie."

"I know. I'm awake."

She laughed. "Barely."

He rolled onto his back and sighed. "Miss you."

"How are you? Everything okay?"

"Sure, I'm fine, just fine. Lying here in this huge empty bed. You know how I like my privacy. What time is it?"

"Around seven. Eight your time. Listen, Mo. I found something."

"What's that?"

"Darrel. You know, we buried most of his things with him, his clothes, tools, you know, that stuff. But he had some old books and things, and I was looking at them. He had a year-

book, well, sort of, from school here. A mimeographed year-
book. Guess who his baseball coach was in the eighth grade."

"Don't tell me. Let me think."

"William Blaine."

"You didn't let me guess."

"Well . . . but isn't that interesting?"

"Yeah, it is. Perfect. Fits like a glove. Listen, this is all working. You know you said you could come back once this thing
was all over?"

"Uh . . ."

"Tomorrow morning. Can you be here tomorrow morning?"

"What do you mean?"

"I mean tomorrow morning. Bring Emory."

"But—"

"Trust me, okay?"

"Around eleven tomorrow?" Connie said.

"Sold. 'Bye."

" 'Bye, Mo. Hey, did you get my message?"

"Yeah, I did. You sold out your cultural heritage."

" 'Bye, Mo."

Mo spent most of the day in his studio, the dank, cool mill
house, tinkering, reacquainting himself with the block of marble. He didn't have much of anything else to do until later that
night. And he began to imagine that he would turn that cold,
inert block into an eagle, one way or another.

At two o'clock in the afternoon the phone rang in the Meyers
Gallery. Marianna del Massimo said "Excuse me" to a Texas
couple who were admiring the artifacts. The man, a lean, soft-
spoken octogenarian, had an elaborately inlaid bolo around his
neck—turquoise and coral mostly, with a few bits of lapis, and
in terrible taste, Marianna thought. The old guy smiled and
bowed awkwardly.

Thinking that she would have to get some help soon, at least
some nitwit to answer the damned telephone, Marianna strode

through the main room, past her former dancing partner—the Zuni kachina mask—and, leaning across Meyers's desk—her desk—picked it up.

"Meyers Gallery," she said.

"May I speak with Mrs. del Massimo?" said a man's voice.

"This is she."

"Mrs. del Massimo, this is Robert Breeden."

She felt the rush of blood draining out of her face. She leaned heavily on her hand, turned and sat on the edge of the desk.

"Yes?" she said. The voice sounded . . . what? Foreign? Breeden! God.

"I am a sometime client of the gallery. As you may know."

"Yes, Mr. Breeden."

"And I had some business with Walter Meyers at the time of his death. Unfinished business."

"Yes, I know." Her heart was pounding.

"I would like to conclude it," Breeden said. "As soon as possible."

"That's . . . I think that would be highly satisfactory, Mr. Breeden."

There was a pause on the phone.

"Yes, good. The material is . . ."

"Of course, Mr. Breeden. And the agreement on . . . ?"

"Yes, as Walter and I discussed. A shame about Walter. When was it, a week ago or so? I suppose things have, uh, settled down now at the gallery?"

"They have. The evenings are totally quiet."

"Tonight, then? Say, nine-fifteen?"

"Good," Marianna said, and the line went dead. She stared into the distance, heart still pounding in her chest, her throat almost constricted. God, she thought. God almighty! A quarter of a million dollars. It was hers, the gallery, everything.

She stood up and headed for the anteroom, finding the Texas

couple gone. The hell with them. Peanuts. She went back into the office and dialed her own number, listening as the phone rang seven, eight, nine times. She slammed it down. Where the hell *is* that son of a bitch?

Seventeen

A few minutes before nine o'clock Mo Bowdre walked in the entrance of Café des Artistes and stood with a smile on his face, rather like a large and indecisive dog in an unfamiliar house. He sniffed a phantasmagoria of aromas—sauces, at least seven, five of them French.

A woman's voice said, "Yes sir, can I help you?"

"Well, yes, you can," Mo said. "Unless I'm too late for dinner?"

"Not at all. Can I show you to a table? For one?"

"Thank you. As you can tell, perhaps . . ."

"Oh, yes, of course," said the woman. "May I guide you?"

"Thank you. I've heard good things about this place. From Marianna del Massimo. I take it she's a regular." The woman guided Mo by the elbow through a series of right angles.

"Yes. In fact, she's here tonight."

"Perhaps," Mo said, "I could say hello."

Another right angle and a slight pressure on his elbow to stop.

"Miz del Massimo?" Mo turned to his guide and bowed

slightly. "Thank you." Turning back, he said, "I'm Mo Bowdre. Glad to have a chance to meet you."

"Well, I'm glad to meet you, Mr. Bowdre. I've admired your work. Well, much of it."

"Hah—hah—hah—let me guess. My Franciscan. You didn't like my friar. Nobody liked that poor old friar. Damned shame."

Mo heard her laugh. "Won't you join me?" she said. "I'm eating alone."

"Well, I don't want to intrude or anything, you know, privacy and all that. But I'd like to, very much. Hate eating alone myself." He pulled out a chair that his fingers had found and sat down. "What do you recommend here?" he asked. "It's a shame about Walt Meyers. I didn't get a chance to say anything to you last week when I was—"

"Oh yes," Marianna said. "When you were in the gallery."

"Yeah. I was accompanying Connie."

"How nice," she said. "Tell me, Mo . . . is that all right? What are you working on now? Some new surprise for the Santa Fe art world?"

"Yeah, I'm trying something new. For me anyway. It may blow up in my face, but then you can get in a rut if you don't force yourself to do something a little dangerous. Don't you agree?"

Nigel Calderwood sat at the desk in the Meyers Gallery, just beyond a pool of light about a yard in diameter cast on the desk's polished surface by a snake-necked lamp. Otherwise, the gallery was black and, but for Calderwood's somewhat elevated heart rate which only he could hear, silent. One last chore before he sailed safely into haven. He put his hand in the pool of light, turned his wrist and looked at his watch. Nine-thirteen. He hoped the mysterious Breeden would be prompt. This waiting was intolerable.

He heard the front door of the gallery open and close, felt

his muscles tense, and breathed deeply and silently through his mouth. Tentative footfalls, starting, stopping. A shadow passed in front of the big Zuni mask on its pedestal in the main gallery.

"Mr. Breeden," Nigel said.

Silence. Then a voice said, "I was expecting Mrs. del Massimo. I don't like surprises."

"My name is Calderwood. Nigel Calderwood. I'm her partner in this matter."

"How do I know that?" the voice said.

"I know that you arranged with Walter Meyers to buy four Hopi gods, and I know that you agreed on a price."

"Which was?" the voice said.

Here they were guessing, Nigel knew, and he found himself sweating slightly. "A quarter of a million dollars."

The shadow moved across the Zuni mask again and loomed in the doorway. "Okay, let's get on with it," the figure said. Nigel made out a man of medium height, broad in the shoulder, wearing a sport coat, probably navy-blue, a light-colored shirt. The lamp's light picked up the silver rim of a bolo tie. He was carrying a large briefcase.

"Well, come in then, Mr. Breeden," Nigel said, standing up. "I'll show you the gods."

The figure stepped into the office and paused a few feet inside the door, still well beyond the direct light from the lamp. Nigel went around to the other side of the desk, picking up a bundle wrapped in a small but exquisitely woven Navajo rug, one with the rich yellows of the Crystal weavers. A generous grace note, Nigel had thought. He pulled the edges of the rug back and revealed four gnarled pieces of wood, strangely curved, tormented almost, each one with a lightly carved tip. "There," he said, and Breeden stepped forward, bent slightly to examine the replicas hastily crafted that afternoon from Meyers's drawing.

From the shadows beside the desk, Nigel plucked a four-foot crowbar and swung it in a vicious horizontal arc at Breeden's head. Breeden's hand shot up and the crowbar slammed into his wrist.

"Shit," he screamed, and Nigel raised the crowbar again.

"FBI. You're under arrest," shouted the figure that had been Robert Breeden, and stuck his other hand inside his jacket. Nigel swung again, but the agent ducked and grappled awkwardly in his jacket, his other arm hanging limply. Nigel bolted past the man and out of the office.

In the archway between the main room and the anteroom, he turned and hurled the crowbar at the pursuing figure. Its straight end plunged into the Zuni mask, which crashed to the floor, impaled on the iron bar. Nigel reached out and snatched a long, feathered lance from the wall and lunged at the archway and what seemed in the shadows to be the man.

Crashes, shouts, chaos, the gallery was suddenly bathed in bright light and, blinking, Nigel spun around, holding the lance in two hands before him. Two policemen were standing inside the entrance, two pistols pointed at his head. Two more cops entered, one of them in plain clothes. The lance bounced and clattered on the shiny tile floor, and Nigel's head drooped, watching it. Its gay feathers of death danced around the shiny point which, after what seemed an eon, came to rest between Nigel's feet.

"Just in time," Larry Collins said, stepping over to take Calderwood by the arm. "Son of a bitch was going to skewer me like a pig. Here. He's all yours." Collins pushed the Englishman at the cops. "You don't have to read him his rights. He hasn't got any. He's a fucking alien. Well, maybe just to be polite."

"You okay?" said Ramirez. "What's with your arm?"

"That's when he tried to kill me with a crowbar. Over

there." He pointed at the Zuni mask staring blankly up at the ceiling. "He killed a mask instead." He was breathing heavily. "So, you got your man, huh, Tony?"

Mo Bowdre put his last sweetbread in his mouth and put down his fork. He wiped his mouth with the linen napkin and said, "Exquisite."

"They are very good, aren't they?"

"The lemon grass," Mo said. "Out of this world. What execution. Do you have the time, by the way?"

"Yes," Marianna said. "It's nine-forty."

"A civilized hour to be finishing dinner," Mo said. "And so much the nicer for having had your company." He reached out and put his big hand on her forearm. "And your friend Sergeant Ramirez will be finished now as well."

"Sergeant Ramirez?" Marianna said. She pulled her arm back, but Mo's hand clamped tighter around it.

"Yup. He and his officers will have your gigolo quivering in a jail cell by now. They'll be along for you any minute. Would you like a cup of espresso while we wait? Of course, it's on me. Hah—hah—hah."

"What are you talking about?" Marianna said through her teeth. "I don't—"

"We figured it out. The whole thing. There's no point in tugging like that. You might just as well be still. Tonight you were true to type. Patterns, is what Tony Ramirez calls it. Shipped old Nigel off to do the dirty work while you lolligag here in everybody's sight. A pattern, Ramirez said. We counted on that. You know, for our little sting. Hah—hah."

"Goddamn you."

"Oh, no, I think it will be you who feels the hellfires and brimstone, the anguish of the doomed."

"I don't know what you're talking about. You can't link me to . . . anything."

"We don't have to. Nigel will. The police will scare him to death, explain that he is without rights in this foreign country, break him down, explain how abruptly aliens are executed, you know. The only way he can escape having his failing throat throttled by the noose is to confess your conspiracy."

"You bastards. He has rights just like anyone else."

"Yes, he does, but he probably doesn't know that for sure. Oh, do I hear . . . yes, that must be Sergeant Ramirez now. Thank you for a very pleasant dinner. I'm told that you are quite attractive."

"What's this all about? More Bowdre theatrics?" Larry Collins sat slumped in a director's chair on Mo's flagstone patio. His left arm was in a sling, the wrist in a cast. Sergeant Ramirez, seated opposite, leaning back with his legs stretched out before him, yawned. It had been a long night at the station, but highly satisfactory.

"I don't know. Probably," Ramirez said. "We'll find out."

"Yeah, I suppose." Collins looked around at the yard. "Nice place. But, you know, all these walls you guys put up around your yards, they're sort of claustrophobic."

The restless agent of the FBI, Ramirez thought, as Mo Bowdre appeared on the patio.

"They should be here any minute," said the big man. He had on a gaudy flowered shirt, mostly shades of bright orange, and a narrow-brimmed black cowboy hat about two sizes too small sat on his head. "You boys want some coffee?"

Outside the gate an engine revved, the gate opened, and a thin, brown old man ambled in. He had a red bandanna around his head. Mo's truck eased through the gate, and the old man closed it and waited. Connie jumped out of the truck and fetched him.

"Hi, Mo," she said. "Here we are."

Mo introduced the two men to old Emory, pointing out that he was the patriarch of the Eagle clan. "So I'm supposed to be making an eagle out of a piece of rock, and here's *the* eagle man of our times standing in my backyard," Mo said. "Well, let's get on with it."

"Another story?" Collins asked.

"Yeah, something like that. Maybe more of a brief play— hah—hah. I need an actor. Collins. You be my actor."

"Look—"

"It's simple, don't worry. You see that big lilac bush over there by my studio? I need my actor to crawl under the bush." Silence.

"Give it a chance, give it a chance." Mo said. "Go ahead."

Collins walked over to the studio, followed by the others, and looked skeptically at the tangled mass of branches. "Jesus," he said. He got down on his knees and, with his good hand, pushed indecisively at the branches.

"Can you get in there?" Mo asked.

"Yeah." Collins gingerly crawled into the bush.

"Anything in there?" Mo asked.

"No, just a lot of . . . yeah. A birdhouse, on the ground."

"Any loose dirt?"

"Uh . . . yeah."

"Dig."

"Huh?"·

"Dig," Mo said. In a loud voice he said, "See, that house belonged to my muse, a little wren that used to sing there every morning in that bush. Then a few days ago he stopped. Really messed me up, couldn't get on with my work. Of course, I had some other things on my mind. We all did. You find anything yet?"

"No."

"Keep digging around. Then a couple of days ago I figured out what happened to the wren. Darrel was running around town for almost a day with the deities in his truck. Panicked, confused. So he got here late Tuesday night, mind all messed up, didn't know what he was going to do with them, so he buried them under the bush. Went in there and knocked the wren's house down. Find anything yet?"

"Yeah," Collins said. "I found something." The bush's lower branches swayed as if hit by a wind, and Collins crawled out with a green plastic garbage bag, covered with clods of dirt. On his knees, he set it down and with one hand dusted it off and slowly unwrapped it. He peered in.

"It's them," he said, his face knit into a frown. Suddenly he grinned. "It's them!"

Ramirez saw Connie put her arm around the frail old man and heard Mo's staccato laugh. "Hah—hah—hah." Collins pushed himself up on his feet and picked up the bag.

"If you knew about this a couple of days ago," Collins said, "then why didn't you say something?"

"Well, let me explain to you about that. See, because I had to have you and this old man here at the same time. I mean, isn't that what you wanted? To find those stolen gods and return them to the Hopi? Well, this is the man."

Collins stood still, staring at the plastic bag. Ramirez watched the agent step over to the Hopi, who was still propped up on Connie's arm. He thrust the bag gently into the old man's chest. "Here, Emory. We may need these later. Evidence. But probably not. Here."

The old man cradled the package in his arms, staring down at it with unseeing eyes. He opened the bag, and Ramirez caught a glimpse of weathered wood. With one hand the old man reached in a pouch that hung by his belt and sprinkled some coarse white powder into the bag. His mouth moved silently for a few seconds, and Ramirez guessed that he was praying. Then the old face burst into a smile, every seam and furrow of it, and drops of water trickled down the canyons of his cheeks.

Ramirez leaned over close to Mo's ear. "You should see the smile on that man's face," he whispered.

"Hah—hah. Yeah, well, I think it's time for a beer, don't you? Dos Equis okay?"

Mo Bowdre pulled his too-small hat over his forehead at a jaunty angle and with measured steps crossed the emerald lawn to his house.

About the Author

Jake Page has been a ranch hand, a hard rock miner, an editor at *Natural History* and *Smithsonian* magazines, and a book publisher. The author of hundreds of magazine articles and columns, he has written many books, including *Hopi* (in collaboration with his wife, Susanne, a photographer). Mr. Page lives in Corrales, New Mexico.